"I loved this book. I loved it, I loved it, I loved it. A beautiful story, built around characters that take up residence in your heart. Robert Elmer has become one of my favorite authors."

> —PATRICIA H. RUSHFORD, author of The Angel Delaney Mysteries and
> The McAllister Files

"Robert Elmer invades the secret places of his characters' public lives. He turns them inside out enough for us to find our own longings, questions, anger— selves—among the pages. And in doing so, he makes one thing blissfully clear in *The Celebrity:* We can try to run away from our circumstances, but we cannot run away from a God who loves us. It is God's desire to make us whole."

> —CHARLENE ANN BAUMBICH, author of the Dearest Dorothy series

"As charming and delightful as a beloved black-and-white movie, *The Celebrity* will make you yearn for simpler times and quieter days, and for those small towns that still hold true to the values so many of us adore. A lovely romantic story with a fun premise!"

> —RENE GUTTERIDGE, author of *The Splitting Storm, BOO*, and *BOO WHO*

"*The Celebrity* is a tale of two lost souls who find connection and meaning in a small town. It is a story of hope, of looking beyond yourself for purpose. Here cynicism melts in the face of kindness. Anger fades in the act of giving. A worthy read. I highly recommend it."

> —TRACI DEPREE, best-selling author of *A Can of Peas* and
> *Dandelions in a Jelly Jar*

"Robert Elmer gives us what we love—a story with small town flavor, brimming with characters we cheer for and a plot that doesn't quit. Readers of *The Celebrity* will have just one thing to say: 'More, please!'"

> —LOIS RICHER, author of *Forgotten Justice*

"Robert Elmer's new book, *The Celebrity,* reminds us of the important things: that life isn't always fair, that even Christians struggle, that God is in the second-chance business, and above all, that grace comes from unexpected places. This is one sweetheart of a story. Way to go, Bob."

—THOM LEMMONS, author of *Jabez: A Novel, Sunday Clothes,* and *King's Ransom* (with Jan Beazely)

"Prepare to burn the midnight oil! *The Celebrity* has it all—characters so real I laughed, cried, and rejoiced with them; a storyline so honest it could have been taken straight out of today's headlines; a small town so charming I want to move there. Anne and Jamie will live on in your heart long after the last page is turned."

—DIANE NOBLE, author of *The Last Storyteller* and *Phoebe*

"Bob Elmer's *The Celebrity* tackles difficult questions: What is success? How does one find it? Is it worth the trouble? Jamie becomes Everyman as he seeks the answers. But watch out for the twist at the end!"

—LYN COTE, author of The Women of Ivy Manor Series

"Robert Elmer hits a home run with *The Celebrity*. Like *The Duet,* this is a close-the-cover-give-a-contented-sigh-and-think-about-the-characters-for-the-rest-of-the-day kind of book. I loved it!"

—DEBORAH RANEY, author of *A Nest of Sparrows* and *Playing by Heart*

"I jumped on this book, knowing Robert Elmer had never disappointed me with any of his previous work. The unusual heroine invaded my heart from the start. I rooted for *The Celebrity* living incognito as he deals with his mother's death. Add the monks who make fruitcake and the delightful quotes at the beginning of each chapter, and you have another winner from a gifted storyteller."

—DONITA K. PAUL, award-winning author of *Dragonspell*

"Robert Elmer has penned an enthralling tale of two people struggling to be 'normal.' One is fighting her way back from devastating personal loss, and the other simply wants to reclaim himself from the demands of fame and publicity. Elmer mixes in a monastery, a thief, and a donut-making machine to create a world you'll hate to leave."

—JANELLE CLARE SCHNEIDER, author

the Celebrity

the Celebrity

A Novel

ROBERT ELMER

WATERBROOK
PRESS

THE CELEBRITY
PUBLISHED BY WATERBROOK PRESS
2375 Telstar Drive, Suite 160
Colorado Springs, Colorado 80920
A division of Random House, Inc.

The characters and events in this book are fictional, and any resemblance to actual
persons or events is coincidental.

ISBN 0-7394-5254-1

Published in association with the literary agency of Alive Communications, Inc.,
7680 Goddard Street, Suite 200, Colorado Springs, CO 80920.

Printed in the United States of America

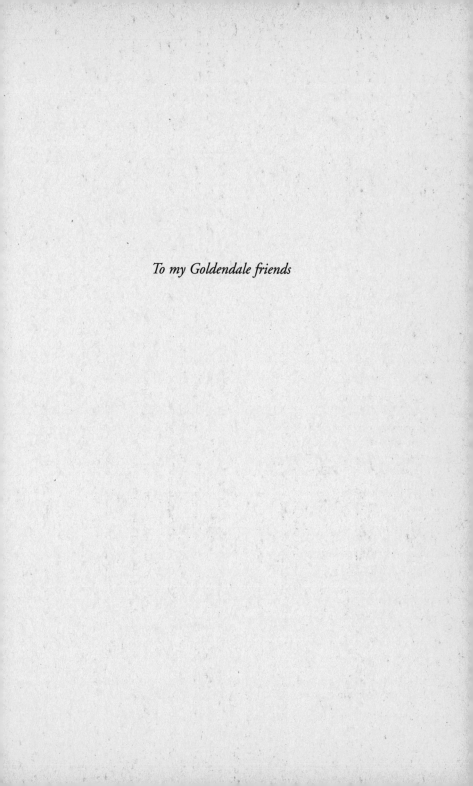

To my Goldendale friends

Fame lost its appeal for me when I went into a public restroom and an autograph seeker handed me a pen and paper under the stall door.

—MARLO THOMAS

F ive minutes, Jamie." The stage manager hurried through the set with his clipboard, brushing the red-velvet curtain as he flew by. Jamie took his place and let the sound tech adjust his headset-style wireless mike as once more he mentally ran through the words of their opening number: a jazzier updated version of an old choral favorite.

I will not cease from mental fight, nor shall my sword sleep in my hand, till we have built Jerusalem in England's green and pleasant land.

Okay, got it. They wanted British; he could do British. Around him members of the London Symphony Orchestra adjusted their instruments, while 103 red-and-white-robed kids from the Oxford Boys' Choir fidgeted on special risers set up behind him.

Ready? The choir director glanced his way and adjusted his headset as Jamie returned the nod. They'd been promised a larger than usual audience for this special summer coproduction with the BBC and one of the big East Coast public broadcasting stations, WNET, New York. *We'll see.* But even Nick had told him over and over how the crowd would eat it up.

Maybe agents were supposed to say that kind of thing. But Mom would have loved it, a few years back. Now they might wheel her in front of the TV set and tell her that her boy was singing, again. In England, no less. Live from London on the Fourth of July. Look, they're going to sing a special arrangement of "God Save the Queen," combined with him singing the American song "My Country, 'Tis of Thee," which of course shared the same tune. And his mother would stare blankly at the wooden man on the screen who had long ago lost the thrill but had become very good at faking it. She would not see the puppet strings that made Jamie's arms wave and his jaw move up and down while they lifted the corners of his mouth in a Pinocchio smile.

"Four minutes. Choir ready?"

Jamie took his place and tried to breathe in the excitement the way he once did. Only now it was like trying to suck oxygen at the top of Mount Everest. And as he gasped for life before the curtain went up, he tried not to remind himself of everything he'd left behind.

It had been Mom's idea to enter him in the North Angeles Young Talent Show fifteen years ago. At age seventeen he'd come on like a young, blond Frank Sinatra, blowing away the judges with his clear-as-a-bell, soulful delivery. And right from the start he knew his mother had been right, that he'd been given The Gift: an amazing set of pipes that did everything he asked them to do, and more.

"I told you so! I told you so!" Back then Mom had fallen apart in front of everybody when he'd collected the grand prize, a five-hundred-dollar U.S. Savings Bond he'd had framed. It still hung on the living room wall of his Santa Barbara beach home, a reminder of the ambitious single mother who had first recognized The Gift and despite all odds just wanted the best for her son.

The best for her son. He could say that now. Back then he'd only felt her two hands on his back, pushing him through a maze of singing contests, interviews, and performances. Back then she worked all day as a hotel maid and got home late to make a hot dog or mac-and-cheese dinner for the two of them in their little West Covina apartment. (He never told anybody about the mac-and-cheese details though. Sounded too much like a rags-to-riches cliché in a made-for-TV movie.)

But Mom didn't know anything about clichés. Back then she'd been too busy saving her nickels, dimes, and tips to pay publicists and managers and voice coaches—people who eventually demanded all of Jamie's after-school time. People who became his life and eventually convinced him he had no other.

"Three minutes, Mr. Lane. How's your mike?"

Mom used to giggle at how her son used more makeup than she did. She teased him about the hairdressers and the handlers. Now she had her own, even if she hardly knew it. Now the fifty-four-year-old skeleton just sat in her wheelchair at the Belle-Aire Convalescent Center and fantasized about the place where she had grown up—this little nothing town in Washington State Jamie had never been to and had no intention of ever visiting.

Riverdale. Sounded like something out of a comic book, a name from the distant past. And that seemed strangely appropriate, seeing as Jamie's mother over the last year had successfully retreated into her own past. She called her nurses imaginary names such as Jasper and Maryanne and wondered why Virge was late delivering the milk. She worried who would feed her chickens, until the nurses assured her it was all taken care of as well. Even worse—if there could be worse—they all knew that as early-onset Alzheimer's robbed her of her mind, emphysema would strip away whatever was left.

And yet Jamie watched from a distance, knowing that no amount of money could change a thing about his mother's condition. He could pay the thirty-five hundred dollars a month for her care at the Belle-Aire, but in her mind she would still be living in their five-hundred-a-month apartment back in West Covina, with the harvest gold linoleum and the lime shag carpet and the olive green refrigerator that never kept things cool. Of course she hadn't lived there in years, but she seemed to prefer the memory—even over the nice condo he'd bought her before they'd had to move her into the Belle-Aire. Some things didn't change, couldn't change.

So Mom coughed a lot, and they didn't know how much longer she would live. Through the summer, maybe not that long. Meanwhile Jamie could only keep writing the checks for the most expensive nursing care in the San Fernando Valley.

As if that would make up for what he'd never said. He did forgive her for pushing him into the spotlight that had sucked away his life. Even so, he had to hate the crippling disease that had sucked away hers. And he couldn't help resenting her just a little for checking out too early, far too early.

"In thirty seconds, please." If nothing else, the British stage crew seemed to have their act together, so while Jamie daydreamed, he let them be as efficient as they wanted to be. But the note they'd brought him just before rehearsal only reminded him of everything he'd never said to Mom, so he crumpled it into a tight little ball, tighter and tighter.

"Are you quite all right, Mr. Lane?"

Jamie shook the cobwebs from his mind, tried to focus on the now, tried to forget the words of the e-mail from the nursing home supervisor.

"I'm ready." He wasn't sure he'd convinced anyone. Still, the picture of his mother staring at the big-screen TV would not leave him. He thought he saw her reflection in the lens of a boom camera swinging into place. Seconds later he noticed her face in the front row of the theater audience, so he closed his eyes until the lights hit, the music came up, and the applause began.

"Live, from the historic Prince Albert Hall in London…" A timpani roll backed up the very British announcer. "It's a Hands-Across-the-Atlantic Patriotic Extravaganza, featuring the American mezzo-soprano Jolene DuBois…"

Jamie let the intro fade away to background until the little green light on the camera told him he was on and his mother was watching from the Belle-Aire. Normally she didn't miss it; he'd made sure his publicity people had faxed the home a local schedule with airtimes and channels. So normally, yes, she would be watching—if one could be allowed a rather loose definition of the word. At least she would be facing the television, and it would be tuned to the right channel. Only this time…

"…and the incomparable Jamie D. Lane!"

This time he reacted on pure instinct, singing through the applause and the cheering the opening numbers with the choir and orchestra. And of course he added his signature blend: a little bit of pop, a little bit of opera, the way Mom had taught him. Last month one of the nurses at the rest home told him Mom had clapped after watching him perform "This Is the Moment" for a *Good Morning America* concert in New York City. So he sang to her after the introductions and the orchestral interludes with the big finishes. And he remembered the time she had stood in the kitchen, back when he was fifteen or sixteen, listening quietly to him practice over and over.

"You're singing from here." She had stepped up and pointed to his lips. "Sing from here, instead." With that she had rested her gentle hand on his heart—her own pledge of allegiance.

That was a long time ago, but how could he forget? So, for the first time in years, he poured what remained of his heart into the songs, one after the next, until he had no heart left, only his hand to cover the spot where it had once beaten.

That's it, Mom. I sure hope you were watching, 'cause that's all I've got.

By then Jolene DuBois arrived to revive the program. But the "Hands Across the Waters" duet slipped through his fingers when he missed one of his cues, and then he didn't remember actually singing "God Save the Queen" with his singing partner. As far as Jamie was concerned, God could save her or not, and it didn't really matter either way.

All he really remembered was apologizing silently and holding Jolene's hand afterward as they bowed together and smiled. How could the audience not like it? Or rather, *her*. His performance had quickly slipped into amateur night at the karaoke bar.

Mercifully, only two songs remained after Jolene left the stage. So when at last he stood alone in the spotlight, he knew the orchestra strings were due back in four beats, just as they had rehearsed. He also knew he should have let it happen, just like everything else up to that point in the program.

But the tears streaming down his face wouldn't let him, and even Nick had told him a little emotion was good. A strategic tear or two would be fine once in a while, if he could manage it. Emotion sells records, kid. Connect with the audience. Listen to your manager.

But this? Jamie willed himself not to look backstage, where Nick had surely dropped his jaw on the floor. The orchestra played gamely on even as the conductor glared at Jamie over and again. Shall we try this once more, please? Jamie took another breath, but whatever had stopped him still held his lips in check and his voice in a vise grip.

And for the first time he could remember, he looked out into a deathly quiet sea of faces...and envied them.

That older couple, there in the front row: They would return home after the show, without the permission of their agent, perhaps with the young girl seated beside them. A granddaughter? He stared at them through the white glare and wondered if they might not agree to trade places with him for just a couple of days. In fact, for a moment he seriously thought about walking over to them and making them an offer. You come deal with Nick and the firestorm of critics sure to consume him after this performance from purgatory. I'll take the Underground train home to your comfortable little flat in a comfortable little London suburb, where the dog will be waiting with his tail wagging, ready for a quiet walk in the rain before bed.

A fair swap? Instead, he closed his eyes for a moment, took a deep breath, and unplugged his microphone headset. The crowd gasped as he shuffled across the stage, over to where the orchestra conductor stood staring, his arms now at his sides. Jamie took up a smaller mike perched on a stand by the wind section. He took another deep breath and looked straight at the older couple.

"I'm sorry," he whispered. "I guess I…"

He sighed and rubbed his eyes with a free hand. In the sudden stillness of the ornate Prince Albert, he might not have needed amplification. Someone coughed from several rows back. And he knew of course that he would not be going home to the comfortable, anonymous flat in South Kensington. So he glanced at the unblinking camera once again, wishing he had a signal or something that would get through to his mother. A tug on the ear, a wink, anything. "Hey, Mom, I made it. You okay?" He might have shouted at her if it would have done any good. Instead, he turned from the stage and simply stepped out of the light, his footsteps echoing in the shocked silence.

So this is what burnout feels like. Utter, poof-I'm-done burnout. He might have stumbled in the darkness had Nick not grabbed him by the arm and hissed in his ear.

"What are you, sick or something?" Sick as in *ill,* or sick as in *crazy?* Jamie could guess which one his manager meant. And Nick didn't let go of him. "You can't just walk out of the show like that! You're not done yet!"

Jamie looked back over his shoulder at the pool of light still bathing the orchestra conductor. And really he could not have cared less if no one applauded. Not this time. In fact, it sounded kind of nice, this silence. He'd never heard it like that before. Quiet as a cathedral and just as empty, and he imagined that was quiet enough.

But as he stood watching and Nick stood grousing…there! The first lonely clapping started out with a brave trickle, then a few more joined before it ultimately exploded into thunder. Nick paused long enough to realize what was happening.

"I can't believe it." He shook his head and mumbled, barely loud enough to hear over the thunder. "I can't believe it."

Granted, this applause probably came more out of sympathy and surprise than appreciation. But it continued on, demanding more, an encore, something Jamie could not give even if he'd had it. Nick even tried to lead him back out, but he dug in his heels.

"No." Jamie shook his head and broke free, checking again for the crumpled note in his pocket. He knew the way to the back door, back to the hotel. If he left right away, he might be able to get back to the Belle-Aire in time.

2

I seldom think of my limitations, and they never make me sad.

—HELEN KELLER

And heavenly Father..."

Anne tried to pray quietly as she adjusted her stride to the up-slope of Simcoe Hill and approached the old one-lane bridge over the Little Klickitat River. She had given up halfway through her mental list of Baptist General Conference foreign missionaries and was about to mention Mrs. what's-her-name's unsaved sister to the Lord when her right foot scooted sideways.

Whoa. Even with a brand-new pair of mail-order Adidas cross-trainers, she'd have to be careful not to slip on the loose gravel. She waved an arm, caught her balance, and continued over the little bridge.

Slicker 'n snot, as Scotty Richardson would have said, but the memory made her shake her head in wonder. Like a bad dream about being late to class, where had that come from, after more than ten years? And why was it only the old stuff she could remember anymore?

Unfortunately, she already knew the answer to that question.

"Excuse me," she whispered to God, as she was not accustomed to using that kind of language in the middle of her running prayers. *Snot,* that is. "I didn't mean to be rude."

No one else would hear, of course, besides the Lord. And no one else would see her if she *did* slip, though she'd done that plenty of times before, on other back roads and lumber trails that laced these wooded Eastern Washington hills overlooking the town of Riverdale (population 2,138, not counting Suze Daley's new baby girl, which would make it 2,139). This time of year, the midsummer runoff gurgled more slowly down the southern slope of the pine-flecked mountains, but sweet water still fed the creeks and watered their wheat-carpet plateau before cascading to the Columbia River Gorge. Beautiful? Anne often wondered why more people didn't move here, and why more people who were born here didn't stay. Though she'd grown up on the scenery, it still struck her as near-perfect, and she often told God as much. Nothing like San Francisco, where she'd chased her dreams after leaving home, before she'd been robbed of—

No! She wasn't going there again. Just up the hill, steeper and through the oak woods that crowned Observatory Hill. But as the road climbed past Huntington's five-acre Appaloosa ranch, she felt her entire body tense at the ugly memory. Her fists clenched once more at the thought of months spent in the hospital, then in rehab, before she'd come running back home to Riverdale. And if she remembered nothing else in her life, she could still smell the nose-tingling mixture of medication and dirty laundry that assaulted her every morning she woke up at Kaiser General Hospital. The scent seemed to mock her, challenging her to forget.

"Forget, forget…" Instead, she wrestled with her memory to bring back the words she had once stared at for hours, taped to the railing of her hospital bed.

"Forget…" She pulled out the limp three-by-five card she'd carried with her all these years, still edged with tape. At least she could still read (much better now). And jog (slowly). And drive (though they'd made her retake all her driving tests).

"Forget the former things." She checked the card again as she read aloud: "Do not dwell on the past. See, I am doing a new thing! Now it springs up; do you not perceive it? I am making a way in the desert and streams in the wasteland."

There. Isaiah 43:18-19. But even the verse in her hand couldn't seem to drive back her worst memories and the tears they dragged along. Tears she had rarely known before the crash. And she appreciated that no one was there to see her break down once again. Only Drake Huntington's horse noticed, leaning out over the barbed-wire fence and staring at her as she labored past the field and on up the hill, step by step.

Keep running. At this time of the morning, she might again startle the quail family out of its nest in the meadow just past Huntington's. Yesterday she'd discovered the mama and six chicks, jogging along behind as if being pulled on a toy string. Anne could use a little pulling too just now...

"Forget the former things," she told herself once again. And so she settled once more into a pattern of breathing and climbing, putting one foot in front of the other. The quail didn't show, but Anne still knew the way. After all, she had jogged this road hundreds of times before, ever since she and Melissa Bainbury used to race all the way up to the Observatory and back just to impress Scotty and the other boys in their class.

The two-girl Riverdale High School girls' cross-country team!

Today Anne would be happy enough to tag the Huntington's mailbox and head back down the hill to town. So she did, still thinking of Melissa, wondering how many kids she had by now. The girl had only wanted to get married and have babies and escape Riverdale, not necessarily in that order, but as soon as humanly possible. Impressing the right boy had been her ticket out.

It hadn't taken much to impress the thirty-five boys who made up their graduating class, though. Thirty-five boys and twenty-six girls. But Anne hadn't seen Scotty and Melissa Richardson since graduation, not since she'd missed the Riverdale High School ten-year reunion.

Forget the former things...

So maybe they would have a fifteen-year reunion. It might be fun to see everyone again. In the meantime, Anne would keep jogging. It gave her a small measure of confidence, she supposed, to call it that. Better than hobbling, or limping, or staggering. It might not look so pretty, but she would get there. And as she neared the bridge, this time headed downhill, she could once again smell the cottonwoods that lined the river.

From the cottonwoods, her usual route would take her through town, past her father's bakery (Andy's Do-Nut Barn) on Main Street, then back around past the wooded city park to the end of Grant Street and her wonderful little converted train-caboose cabin behind her parents' home. And only a few folks would notice her running by; usually the only humans awake at this time of the morning were Do-Nut Barn regulars having a glazed doughnut and a cup of her mother's strong coffee. She smiled at the small-town cliché, but by 6:15, they'd be on their third cup.

"Oh." The stab of pain in her temples made her stop to grip the bridge railing. She was glad no one saw her bend over and grimace in pain. Time to rest.

She gasped for breath and peered into the shadows beneath the sagging bridge. The date chiseled into a concrete pillar told her it had been built in 1937 by a WPA crew, but it did not mention the fact that the crew had included Jack P. Stewart, her own grandfather. He'd come from Seattle and had never left.

Her sudden headache wasn't leaving either.

Maybe she should keep running, the way Principal Watson had always told her to. Besides taking them out in the driver's-ed car donated by Pete Stauffer Chevrolet, the former Riverdale High principal had also served as cross-country coach. She remembered that, even if she forgot what day it was.

"Don't stop!" he always yelled at them through that megaphone with the big gold R on the side. "You're never going to win standing still!"

And so she did her best to keep her legs moving in place before she hugged the bridge railing and fell to one knee.

Just a little headache, she lied to herself, as tears streamed off her cheek and dropped to the cold flowing waters below. It occurred to her that if she wasn't careful, she might follow.

Only where was Coach now, when she needed him? Maybe buttering a piece of morning toast, pouring his wife, Margaret, a cup of coffee. Though he'd retired a few years back, he still lived in town, in a little yellow house on Maryhill Drive.

"Coach?" she whispered, and her strength had run away to hide like the little quail family. Her other knee dropped to the slippery-as-snot gravel, and it poked her through the knees of her gray sweatpants, and she hurt like she never had before—so much that she lost her grip on her little Bible verse card, and it fluttered down to the water.

Oh! What if she really passed out here on the bridge and slipped into the Little Klickitat too? She wondered for a moment if she might drift all the way down the Columbia River, just like her card, just like the river barges loaded with local wheat, all the way to Portland.

Still she hung on, tried not to pass out, tried to pretend her head didn't hurt…like…blazes. And she heard the squeal of brakes behind her, the slam of a car door.

"Annie!" Maybe Coach Watson had finished his coffee and had finally caught up with her. Or maybe it was another farmer on his way to the bakery. "Annie Stewart! Girl, are you all right?"

3

If I get big laughs, I'm a comedian. If I get little laughs, I'm a humorist. If I get no laughs, I'm a singer.

—GEORGE BURNS

onight's guest is Jamie D. Lane, the performer who has dominated North American pop charts for the past five years with his passionate blend of classical and contemporary. If velvet could sing, it would sound like Jamie D. Lane…"

Jamie smiled politely as the gravel-voiced host of *Barry Rice Live!* repeated the line that had followed Jamie around the world, the "velvet" silliness. He looked at his watch once more as the bespectacled host leaned into the microphone for his first line of questions. Nick had promised him it would be quick, less than an hour, in and out, and their plane needed to stop over in New York anyway. They could still get back to California at the same time. So okay.

But Nick had also promised him the questions might be a little sharper this time. Don't expect any softballs after that sick performance in London. Like the first caller.

"Millie from Cleveland, you're on the air." Barry adjusted his hairpiece. "Do you have a question for Jamie Lane?"

"Uh, yes, Mr. Lane." Millie from Cleveland sounded like someone's grandmother as her voice filled the studio. "You sing a lot of religious songs. But tell me, young man, are you saved?"

Jamie saw the color drain from Barry's face, and he knew the call screener would probably be out of a job, but he gave the host a little wink. As in, *no problem.* Actually, a rabid fan had once lobbed the same word grenade at him from the middle of a crowd after a concert in Philadelphia. So Jamie was usually prepared to give his standard "You have your religion, I have mine, so let's just keep it that way, shall we?" response.

But not this time. He pasted on his best stage smile and leaned into the question.

"Absolutely, Millie. Hallelujah!"

Which sounded pretty good for starters, so he added a line he'd heard on one of those comical late-night religious shows: "And I've been rinsed in the blood, praise God! Washed. Whatever."

That ought to take care of Millie. He heard her sputtering before they finally cut her off and rerouted the show to Barry's own questions.

"Okay…" Barry was quick to recover. "We'll leave it at that."

Jamie guessed they might not be taking any more calls from the audience this time.

"But let me ask you about London." Barry ran his fingers through his thinning hair as he got to the point. "What were you thinking when you bailed out of that show? Brilliant performance until your duet with Jolene DuBois, and then, well… Rumors are you had food poisoning. Were you well?"

So all right. Nick had prepared him a plausible answer about a touch of flu, about how all traveling performers get sick now and then, how he'd wanted to be fair to his fans, all that. He looked at the veteran interviewer and wondered if he could pull it off. Or if he wanted to. He took a deep breath.

"I don't have any excuses. I'm guess I'm just a little worn out."

Just off camera, Nick tossed a script in the air and stalked away. So be it. Rice arched his eyebrows, and Jamie pulled his beard. Camera 2 was ready for the reaction.

"Okay, a *lot* worn out," Jamie continued. "We were at the end of a three-week European tour. Just did a big TV concert in Athens with the Three Tenors that took a lot out of me. Finished recording our third live album in Dublin, then this patriotic show in London, when I got an e-mail from…"

His voice trailed off as he realized what he was about to say: *An e-mail from Mom's nurse, telling me to get home if I wanted to see her again alive. So what am I doing here?*

Barry's eyes seemed to rope him in closer. As in, "Just between you and me, kid."

You and me and one-point-two million of our closest friends.

"An e-mail?" Rice didn't let it drop.

"No." Jamie back-pedaled hard. "I was just worn out. No excuses. Tell you the truth, though, I wouldn't wish this kind of schedule on anyone."

"Okay." The host sat back with a grin and scratched his chin. "But let me just read something that appeared in this morning's *Times* of London. Apparently you must have said something to this fellow after your concert there."

Jamie rubbed his forehead, trying to remember. As usual, a pack of reporters and photographers had hounded him at the airport. Had he said anything dumb this time?

"This is David Mayberry's column, as I said, in this morning's *Times.*" Barry scooted the glasses up his considerable nose as he read the clipping. "Pity poor Jamie D. Lane. After an inspired start to an inspired performance, the hapless American performer apparently ran out of petrol, to borrow an American turn of phrase, and, like a spoiled child, stormed off the set of his live BBC concert—several songs before the end."

"Two." Jamie corrected him. "And I didn't storm."

"Pardon?"

"I said two." Jamie wished he hadn't said anything. "Not several. We only had two numbers left. And I walked. Walking isn't the same thing as storming."

Did it matter? Rice nodded over his glasses. "Sure, Jamie. I think your American audience understands what a tough life you're leading. That's why I'm sure any one of them would trade places with you in a heartbeat."

"Maybe so." Jamie wished. Rice turned back to reading the column, in which the *Times* reporter skewered the cheeky American for leaving before his time was up. Apparently, that was not cricket, not at all proper.

"We should all be so lucky," Rice finished the column, "lucky to be able to leave our jobs when a poor day or a spot of fatigue comes crashing in on us, and we can simply announce to our employers that we are done. In fact, dear readers, Jamie D. Lane has inspired me. I believe I've had enough of writing for today, and you'll have to—"

Barry Rice laughed and held up the column, which, when the camera panned in, ended in midsentence and showed the second half blank, all the way to the bottom of the page. Blank, as in no printing, nothing. Jamie could only smile his publicity smile.

"I like Mayberry," he finally admitted. "He's clever even when he's wrong."

Which got enough of a laugh to end on a positive note from Barry Rice and supplied a good transition to the commercial break.

"Always a pleasure to have you on the show." Rice extended his hand, off the air. "Sorry about that caller."

"Not a problem. It's always a pleasure to be here," Jamie lied as he ran a hand through his own thick hair, shook Rice's hand, and stood. Rice wasn't actually such a bad guy.

"Say, I hear your mother's ill." The famous eyebrow went up in a question mark, and Jamie nodded. "Sorry to hear it. We'll be hoping the best for her recovery."

Jamie thanked him as he left for the backstage hallway where he knew Nick was probably waiting for him. And sure enough…

"Jamie, Jamie, Jamie!"

Jamie didn't slow down as Nick came alongside.

"I can't help you, Jamie, if you don't stick to the script. Don't you get it? I'm just trying to protect you. But I can't keep you from jumping over the edge, which is what you're doing here."

"I get it, Nick. I just don't think—"

"That's exactly it, my friend. You don't. So that's why you pay me the big bucks, isn't that right?" He held up his hand. "Correction! That's why you pay the C. J. Patterson Agency, C. J. gets the big bucks, and I'm left with…with *baby-sitting*."

The words seemed to echo backstage as Jamie looked for the exit. The quicker the better.

Jamie shrugged. "We should go, Nick. When's our flight?"

Nick answered his chirruping cell phone and told the caller he'd get right back to him, okay? Then he turned back to Jamie with the look of doom on his face.

"Look, Jamie, I didn't mean that. Everybody's on edge here, right? You just have to keep your head on."

"It's on, Nick. Believe me."

"I'd like to, but honestly? You're scaring me, kid." He studied the number on his cell phone display and sighed. "All right. Maybe I've been too hard on you lately. So let's schedule you a nice vacation sometime in the next couple months, after we tape the next couple of shows. What do you think? Have Erica meet you in Maui or something, huh?"

"Erin." Jamie sighed, and Nick only gave him a puzzled look. "Her name is Erin."

"Right. But don't worry about a thing. I'll make the arrangements. Hey, and did I ever tell you about Erin's friend? Incredible. She was on the set of the *New Dating Game,* and…"

Jamie nodded as he tuned out the story he'd heard before. And he knew what the Maui "vacation" would be like with his staff of bodyguards and various "assistants" trying without success to scare off the paparazzi hiding in the hibiscus bushes. He didn't want to hear what kind of ridiculous pose they'd snapped and sent for publication in the tabloids. Add a *Dating Game* trophy date, and the photographers would be going wild. Jamie rubbed his temples, not realizing he had stopped short of the dressing-room door.

"What's wrong, bud?" Nick held the door open. "Maui's not good for you? No problem. We'll find someplace else. The Med's pretty nice this time of year. Or—"

But Jamie just shook his head and held up his hands.

"No, Nick. You don't get it. I'm not talking about a vacation that you arrange. I'm tired of all this celebrity garbage, this never-ending schedule, this—"

"See, that's what I mean about you scaring me." Nick just looked at him and snickered. "You sound like an old man, like you did back there with Barry Rice."

"Maybe that's because I mean it."

"You don't know what you're saying. You're a born performer, Jamie, and that's all you'll ever be. You can't look me in the eye and tell me you don't belong in the spotlight."

"I don't know." Jamie sighed and rubbed his forehead. "It's just…I live in a bubble. I want a life, Nick."

"Like the fairy tales you sing about?"

"Something like that. It's just that…before I even knew who I was, everybody knew my name."

Nick put his head back and laughed.

"That's really cute, but let me tell you something." Nick leaned in closer, much closer. "I hope you're not forgetting who brought you all this. Not C. J. Not anybody else back at the agency."

Jamie brought his hands up in surrender.

"I'm not forgetting, Nick. And I appreciate—"

"No kidding you do. Here I've been working my tail off to get you to where you are, and does anybody recognize what I've had to sacrifice to lift you up this high?"

Jamie had a pretty good idea. But Nick's drinking, the girls, the divorce…whose fault was that? He had no answer.

"…and I am not about to let you throw it all away because you're having a bad day or jet lag is getting to you."

"I'm not sure what this is," Jamie answered, "but it's not jet lag."

"Okay, depression, whatever." Nick pulled out his PDA and began punching buttons. "I'll schedule a doctor to come give you something for it."

"See? That's exactly what I'm talking about! It's your schedule, it's your…barbed wire you've strung all around me. I'm dying here, and you don't even know it."

"Man." Nick leaned closer and put a hand on Jamie's forehead. "You really do need—"

"I only need two things right now." Jamie jerked his head away. "One, I need to be on a plane to L.A., A.S.A.P. And two, I need a real life."

"Fine, but let me understand this *real life* you keep talking about. Are we talking about a *real life*, like the ghetto you came from in West Covina?

With the bill collectors and the dope dealers on the corner? 'Cause you know where to find all that, back in your beautiful hometown."

"That's not what I'm talking about."

"Okay, so then are we talking about the *real life,* like in one of those Thomas Kinkade paintings with the cottages and the heart-shaped windows and the cup of tea simmering on the stove? 'Cause if that's the kind of real life you're looking for, you're worse off than I thought. Nothing a little therapy or a trip to Disneyland couldn't help, though."

"You don't get it, Nick." Jamie tried to get by Nick to the dressing room.

"That's the problem. I *do* get it."

When Jamie didn't answer, his manager grabbed him by the shoulders. "Jamie, look at me."

Jamie rolled his eyeballs up slowly enough to make a point, while Nick took a deep breath and went on with his sermon.

"Listen, you've had a rough week. We've all had a rough week. So as your manager and as your…your *friend,* I just need you to relax now. Let me take care of things. Got it? Stick with the script. Don't go weird on me. Have some faith."

"In what?"

"What are you, kidding?" He gave Jamie a *Godfather* pat on the cheek. "Take your pick. In me. In your music. In the universe. Like you told that caller, hallelujah, right? That was kind of bizarre, by the way. Now lighten up, would you?"

Jamie started to say something, changed his mind, and shook his head. No, Nick still didn't get it. And maybe Jamie didn't either. But for the first time in his life, Jamie knew what he had to do.

Now he just had to find out how to do it.

4

A small town is a place where there is little to see
or do, but what you hear makes up for it.

—IVERN BALL

I t was just a little headache, Daddy."

"Little headache, my foot." Daddy looked up from the cash register later that day, tipped his narrow face, and squinted at her in the blue-green hue from the bakery's overhead fluorescent lights. His head sort of glimmered from beneath the Marine buzz cut he had worn for the past thirty years. "A little more than a headache, the way Marty tells it."

"The way Marty tells it, I practically died there on the bridge and he saved my life."

"Did he?"

Anne sighed as she gave the glass entry door a shot of Windex. "I told you the whole story, Daddy. And I wish you hadn't put it on the prayer chain so soon. I mean, I appreciate it and everything, but…"

But it was too late. If a deacon from Riverdale Community Baptist Church called up the prayer chain, every Baptist in town knew your problem within twelve minutes, thirty-seven seconds. Pastor Ray had timed it once, even posted the PRT (prayer response time) in the bulletin. Oh well.

It didn't take long for word to get around to everyone else, too. That included members of Riverdale United Methodist Church, Shepherd of the Hills Lutheran (Missouri Synod), and Immaculate Heart Catholic, especially if they were part of the bakery crowd. And Don McNair from the paper spent most of his mornings at the Do-Nut Barn too, so if it was especially interesting news (like this), it would more than likely make front-page news in next Wednesday's *Sentinel.*

Anne's saving graces: One, she didn't pass out. And two, by the time Marty Matthews stopped that morning on the bridge to check up on her, she had caught her breath just enough to tell him she was okay, but thanks anyway for stopping. And by the time he drove her into town in his rust-bucket Ford pickup, she had explained once more that she was thankful for his help, but if he could let her off at her place at the end of Grant Street, that would be perfect, and thanks again for the ride.

Marty had just sort of looked over at her, pushed his red and black Case Tractor cap back from his wrinkled forehead, and frowned. Probably he was disappointed he didn't get to ride along in the Riverdale volunteer aid car this time, all the way down the river to the general hospital in The Dalles.

Anne's dad cleared his throat. "Still think you ought to at least call the neurologist when he's in town next week," he added. "Wouldn't hurt."

"He'll just tell me the same thing he told me last time he was here." She frowned. " 'Take it easy, stay in touch, and we'll see what happens. Brain injuries are strange things.' "

"You think you ought to explain to Lance what happened, so he hears the straight story?"

That would be Lance Howell, Riverdale Christian School's principal.

"Dad. I'm sure he already knows. And what am I supposed to tell him anyway? I had another headache, and I don't think I can handle the teaching job after all? School starts in—"

"I know, I know." But her dad wouldn't let it drop that easily. "I just worry about you."

"You're sweet, Daddy." She tried to smile and didn't let the twinge of pain in her head slow her down the way it had on the bridge. She was used to it after all. It used to be much worse. And hadn't those San Francisco doctors told her after the crash that she would probably never even be able to walk? She could handle a few headaches, now and then. But, suddenly blank, she looked at the rag in her hand, trying to remember what she had been doing, what she needed to do next.

"Here's your list." Her dad handed her a piece of note paper. "Only a couple more things to do. You need to be getting ready for classes, not working in your old man's bakery."

"I don't mind, really."

"I know you don't mind. I just want you to have a normal..."

His voice trailed off, and she felt an onslaught of tears rising once more, so she grabbed the list and limped out to the sidewalk before she started leaking from the eyes. The Tuesday afternoon Greyhound bus rolled into town a couple minutes late, stopping on its way to Yakima, and a few of the passengers stared out their windows as if they'd never seen an honest-to-goodness small town before.

"On your left we have the town cripple," she could imagine the bus driver saying as she turned away. "Thought she would change the world, once, but now after her accident, she came running home to Mommy and Daddy."

Well, even if he didn't say it, he could have.

"The folks at the local Christian school felt sorry for her, so they offered her a part-time teaching job nobody else wanted and that didn't pay beans. Of course, most people think she can't handle it, since she can hardly remember her own name after coming back from the big city."

Anne threw her cleaning rag in a sidewalk planter and ran around the corner, away from the prying eyes of the bus passengers, away from Daddy's concern, away. Look at her! These days greeting-card commercials on television sent her searching for the Kleenex. Trouble was, anywhere she went in Riverdale, people knew her. She'd always thought that was a big part of the reason she'd returned. Now it was the curse, as Mrs. Wiggin waved out at her from the window of Wiggie's Hair Salon. Anne waved back but didn't wait for Mrs. Wiggin to open the front door of her salon.

"You all right, dear?" Mrs. Wiggin called out after her, but Anne didn't stop until she was safely into the alley. She thought she heard music from somewhere, a man singing. Or maybe not. She sighed and rested her head against the aged brick back wall, next to the faded green door of the American Legion Club service entry. Maybe she would get to bed early that night. She'd been staying up too late, putting together lesson plans for the coming year.

Sure she'd taught before, but just thinking of seventh- and eighth-grade English at Riverdale Christian School made her sweat more than the prospect of confiscating knives and drugs from street kids back in south San Francisco. But that was before. Here she just had to remember what to do each day. And as the doctors had told her, you couldn't predict what would happen with a head injury.

Beep-beep!

The cheery horn of a brown UPS delivery van jolted her from her daydreaming. Anne moved to the side when a twenty-something young woman stepped around the corner of her vehicle with an armload of boxes for the American Legion Club.

"Hi there." The driver seemed friendly but charged right through.

And she left her music blaring, a male pop singer with a showy voice, singing something smooth and classical sounding. Never mind that; for one crazy moment Anne thought of slipping into the back of the truck just to get away, to find a place where no one would know what she was supposed to be like. Portland maybe. Wasn't that where the truck came from? A place where the limping, forgetful, emotional Anne would be the only Anne people had ever met. Where they would not think it odd if she laughed a little too loudly or cried for no reason at all. Where they might even understand her moments of red-faced anger at the man who had done this to her.

The driver greeted her with another smile as she returned, then jumped back into the cab and jotted something on her clipboard. Her pop-singer music was still going strong. But before starting up the engine, she looked out the open side door at Anne.

"Can I help you with anything?"

"No, no…"

Why did Anne just stand there? Her hand went instinctively to cover the scar across her forehead, the one makeup could not quite cover. And she quickly tried to come up with something…conversational.

"I was just…uh…that singer…who is it?"

"You're kidding. You don't recognize Jamie D. Lane?"

"Heard the name, sure." Anne shrugged. "Guess I've never paid much attention."

"He's only the best baritone in the world. You know, like that Groban guy, only better? Every female in Portland *loves* him. Everywhere else, too."

"Oh." Anne finally thought of stepping back out of the way.

"Besides being the most eligible bachelor."

"Not around here, I don't think." Not that the fellow wasn't good, just not her style. His silky baritone seemed a little overdone maybe. Borderline schmaltzy.

"Oh, that's right. I forget where I am." The driver put her van in gear. "If it ain't country…right?"

Oh, right. A joke. Anne returned the smile, wondering why she had brought it up in the first place. And she stood there waving, waiting for the driver to disappear down the potholed cobblestone alley, unwilling to display her wobbly gait to yet another stranger.

Oh, and she still held her to-do list crumpled in her fist. It reminded her she still had counters to wipe down before quitting time, plus the doughnut fryer needed cleaning before her mother came in for the night shift. And a ton more lesson plans to prepare. Meanwhile the last bits of Jamie D. Lane's song drifted down the alley:

"You'll never walk alone!"

5

A celebrity is a person who works hard all of their
life to become well known, and then wears dark
glasses to avoid being recognized.

—FRED A. ALLEN

Nothing against staying at the Omni on Chicago's Magnificent Mile. The penthouse suite was one of the nicest in the country, no question about it. Oprah's guests stayed here, too, in some of the floors lower down. But just then, a stay in Chicago wasn't quite what Jamie had in mind. Not after the note from his mother's nurse.

"Look, I'm sorry about the plane, all right?" Nick faced Jamie with his hands-free headset on, which put him in the "speak to me!" mode. But when he was wired up that way, one could never really tell whom he was talking to.

"No, not you." He touched the microphone dangling off his ear, toggling over to the phone conversation. "I was talking to Mr. Lane. Actually, you're the one who should be telling *me* you're sorry."

(A pause for groveling.)

"Okay, we'll see." Nick held up his "just one second" finger as he paced across the suite and continued browbeating the unfortunate person from the charter jet company. "It's just that when we charter a *direct* flight from New York to L.A., we don't like to have to put down halfway, right? Mr. Lane has an urgent family emergency he needs to attend to, and…"

(Another pause.)

"That's right. It had *better* be free of charge. And that plane had better be waiting at Midway when we get there first thing in the morning."

First thing in the morning? Jamie groaned at the apparent delay as Nick touched his phone again. At this rate...

"Perfect timing, honey." Nick's voice went from vinegar to saccharine. Now he was talking to...well, definitely not the Learjet person.

"No, we're not doing anything." Nick paced around the suite. "Just stuck here in Chicago for a few hours while the Learjet people switch planes for us. Jamie's on the couch, watching one of those old black-and-white movies he likes. You know Jamie."

He nodded and smiled, looking over at where Jamie had propped himself up with a pile of pillows. On the television, Audrey Hepburn was just getting to the part where she told her lady-in-waiting how much she hated being a princess.

"No, no, we're doing fine," Nick continued. "If you're going to be stuck, you want to be stuck in one of these rooms, if you know what I mean."

Jamie wasn't so sure he agreed, but what could he do about it? Meanwhile, Hepburn looked out her window and caught a glimpse of how everyone else lived their normal lives. Her chaperone brought her warm milk and crackers at bedtime and proceeded to tell her all about the next day's schedule: the press conferences, the receptions, the affairs of state. Knowing the next line by heart, Jamie punched the volume on the DVD remote to high.

"Stop!" yelled Hepburn, as Jamie lip-synched.

Nick looked over at him and frowned. "Do you mind, Your Highness? How many times have you seen *Roman Holiday* anyway?"

Seven times—no, eight—but who was counting? Jamie turned the volume back down but returned to Rome as a doctor was called to give the princess a sedative.

"I'll be calm and relaxed," she told them, but they wouldn't listen. *"I-I'll bow and I'll smile and improve trade relations, and I'll..."*

Nick paced around the sitting room as he spoke, still on the phone.

"You saw the concert on PBS, eh?" he asked the person on the other end of the line as Jamie glanced over at him. "Yeah, I don't know. He started strong, but the poor kid just kind of ran out of gas. Not his fault. But I tell you, we're going to fix that, and I think you're going to like it. Here, I'll let you talk to him. He'll tell you all about it."

Nick pulled his phone from a pocket, unplugged the earphone, and held it out across the room, while Jamie waved his hands and shook his head no. Nick ignored him.

Jamie finally took the Nokia with an uncertain frown. "Hello?"

"Jamie?" Erin sounded as if she was calling from a cell phone from across the country, probably because she was calling from a cell phone from across the country. "You didn't call me today."

He didn't answer; she went on.

"So I started to get worried."

"Nick told you about the plane, right?" He didn't mean to sound as rude as he probably did. But even from this distance, he could feel this woman's hooks, and he squirmed to loosen them.

"Oh yeah, he told me." She paused. "But what was he talking about? I mean, what am I going to like?"

Jamie paused as Nick turned his back. Anyone could still hear everything from the far side of the suite, though. Jamie cleared his throat and held the phone out a few more inches, then twirled it by the stubby antenna for effect.

"Can you repeat that, Erin?" He lowered his voice. "I think the signal's cutting out."

Jamie caught a couple of her words. "I said" and "for me," but not much else.

"Hello? Hello?" Jamie covered the mouthpiece with his hand as he spoke and then grinned as he punched the red Off button and tossed the phone across the room at Nick.

"Hey!" Nick nearly dropped it.

"So *you* talk to her next time. She likes you better anyway."

"You're crazy, you know that? Certifiably, absolutely crazy. She's drop-dead gorgeous, and you don't even want to talk to her."

"I'll call her when I get back to L.A. Right now I just can't put up with the groupie scene."

"You're not being fair to the girl. I don't know why I knock myself out for you if you're going to be this way."

"I know." Jamie held up a finger to his lips and turned back to the movie. "This is the part where Gregory Peck has her wear his pajamas after she…"

Nick sidled around to see, while Jamie had to explain.

"Actually, it's not like that at all. 'Course, if the film was made today instead of in 1953, it'd probably be pretty different."

"Pity. But about this vacation you're *going* to take…"

Jamie paused the movie and sighed.

"All right, Nick, I give up. Let's figure something out if it makes you happy."

"We're not talking about *me* being happy, Jamie. It's all about *you.*"

"Right." Jamie stared at the freeze-frame image of Gregory Peck standing in his Rome apartment, frozen in time.

"Good." Nick pulled out his notebook. "We're making progress. So let me write this down. Forget Maui. We're talking St. Bart's, okay? Didn't you say the Caribbean?"

"No. But even if I *did* agree, it would have to be totally private."

"Totally anonymous. I understand. You want three days? Four?"

"I wouldn't even want the *resort* to know who's coming. They always tip off the press."

"No problem. I just give 'em another name. So you'll be Mr...."

Jamie had already hit Play once more. Gregory Peck's newspaper reporter character, Joe Bradley, headed in to see his boss after he rescued the princess during her escape from the bondage of royal life.

"Where's Joe Bradley when you need him?" he wondered aloud, only dimly aware that Nick had asked him a question.

"B-r-a-d..." Nick scribbled the name down on a pad. "Whatever you say. Hey, you want something to eat? I'll order room service for you, too."

While Nick disappeared into his own bedroom on the other side of the suite, Jamie watched his movie for a while longer, the part where Gregory Peck—make that Joe Bradley—and the princess wander the streets of Rome together for the first time. The markets, the vendors, the—

"Room service." Someone rapped on the door, and Jamie paused to pull it open, but not before he had an idea.

A crazy, wild, unlikely idea.

"Put it down over there." He pointed to a coffee table in the middle of the room, then fished a couple of bills from his wallet. He held one of the bills out as a tip but did not let it go.

"I need you to help me with something."

The bellhop recognized the face on the bill and grinned. "Say the word."

"I want you to show me a way out of here that doesn't take us through the lobby, or any other place where people might be waiting for a snapshot."

"Don't you think it would be easier to bring her here? I could help you with that, too."

"Her? What? Oh, uh-uh." Jamie shook his head no. "It's not like that.

All I want to do is get out of here for a while and not have the whole world tagging along."

"For this kind of money, you want my uniform, too?"

"No, no. Just show me that way. You have a staff elevator or something, right?"

"It's all yours."

The raised voice from the adjoining room told them Nick still wasn't happy about something. Probably the charter jet people again. And for a moment Jamie thought of leaving a note. But no. He turned to his new accomplice, who nodded like 007 after he checked up and down the hall. All clear.

"Follow me, sir."

Behind them the movie continued, and the princess turned to Joe Bradley.

"I'm a good liar, too, aren't I, Mr. Bradley?" she asked him.

"Best I ever met."

Jamie let the door click shut behind him and followed the bellhop.

"You sure you don't want anybody to come with you, Mr. Lane?" The bellhop held open the service elevator. Going down. "You know, like to run interference? People are going to recognize you out on the street."

Jamie let the elevator hit bottom before he finally answered.

"I'll take my chances. Now, look. There's another tip in it for you." He held out the hundred before stuffing it back in his front pants pocket. "All you need to do is meet me here at the back door in a couple of hours." He checked his watch. "Say, 1:00 a.m.?"

"Not a problem for me, man." The kid looked up and down the alley and shook his head. "But for you, I dunno. Here, take this hat, at least. And are you sure—"

"I'm good." Jamie yanked the bellhop's navy blue watch cap over his head and started off down the alley. A minute later he hit a dead end and did a quick about-face as if he'd planned it that way. He looked straight ahead on his way back out.

"My exercise program," he told himself. "Bored to death with those fitness room stairsteppers anyway."

Which was true, in a way. He also picked up the pace before he changed his mind and detoured around an aromatic Dumpster. He was out of there, paparazzi or no paparazzi.

At least Michigan Avenue still brimmed with people, a good thing for someone wanting to blend in. And at first no one gave him a second glance. Maybe the bellhop's watch cap helped after all. Only, what next?

Nick's going to go ballistic, he told himself. But with all the food smells hitting his nose, well, he would deal with Nick later. Giordano's pizza. Dao Thai Noodle Palace. BBQueen. His head spun, along with the rest of him.

"Room service was never like this." He stopped to look at a bright blinking ad for a Chicago-style hot dog stand and laughed at the thought of being out on the street, after eleven, all on his own. But he must have stopped in somebody's way; a guy bumped into him—hard—and walked off complaining.

"Excuse me!" Jamie held up his hands, but the guy had already continued on down the sidewalk toward Chicago Avenue. But his empty stomach still rumbled, so he pushed his way into a well-lit Burger King just around the corner of a side street. The cap was a little itchy, so without thinking he pulled it off before ordering.

"I used to go to this kind of place all the time, when I was a kid." He couldn't wipe the grin off his face as he faced the round teenager behind the counter. "You still have the two all-beef patties special sauce lettuce cheese pickles onions on a sesame-seed bun?"

There. He could still say it, fast. Not bad. But the kid behind the counter didn't look impressed.

"I have no idea what you're talking about, sir."

"Oh." Maybe they changed ad campaigns. So he studied the sign, then decided on a Whopper and fries with a chocolate shake. He thought he heard a familiar twittering and saw a clutch of girls out of the corner of his eye.

Oh no.

Even the surly counter worker had cheered up and was eyeing him as she keyed in his order. This was Phase One. The giggle. The look.

Phase Two, assuming there was more than one person in the giggling group, included a little pushing and shoving, a contest to see who would come over first. Without looking he knew Phase Two was in motion just behind him.

"Five twenty-seven," the clerk told him, and by this time she had planted a ridiculous grin on her face. To speed things up a little, he grabbed the first bill he could find, the hundred in his pocket that he'd promised the kid at back at the Omni. The clerk's face fell.

"I'm so sorry, sir." She pointed up at a sign behind her: *No bills over $50 accepted. No exceptions.*

"But—" He could have inhaled the fries from where he stood.

"I'm really sorry." She looked it. "I would take it if it were up to me, but—"

"Hey, it's okay. No problem." He might have something else in his wallet. Probably. But when he reached into his back pocket, his heart stopped.

"Uh-oh."

He patted his pockets, right and left, then his shirt pocket just to be sure. Then all over again. But there was no mistake.

"I had it when I left the hotel," he said, his mind spinning. "I pulled out the tip and put it right back. I'm sure of it."

He began mentally backtracking, but didn't have far to go until he remembered the bump-and-run back on the street, when he'd been acting the tourist. That was it. No doubt. The counter clerk volunteered to call the police.

But wouldn't you know the girls in back would choose just that time for Phase Three. The bravest of the bunch sidled up beside him, eyes wide.

"It *is* you, isn't it?" she whispered. When he paused long enough to smile, she turned back to her girlfriends and screamed.

"It's him, it really *is him!* Jamie D. Lane!"

Her friends instantly joined the screaming, loud enough to turn heads out on the sidewalk. And if that wasn't enough, three more of the girls were already on their cell phones, speed-dialing every groupie in Chicago.

"No, no, no." Jamie gave it one last desperate shot. "You're making a mistake. I'm not who you think I am."

Girl Number One looked him straight in the eye and smiled. Her hands shook.

"Yes, you are."

"No, really. People always mistake me for that singer movie actor guy. I can't even remember his name. Jimmy something, right?"

Didn't work. By that time the phone fans had brought people in from the street, and the gal behind the counter was trying to take orders. Instead, the growing mob pushed closer, while those in the front (mostly teen and twenty-something females) pushed pens in his face and demanded his autograph. He looked over his shoulder and started to apologize to the girl behind the counter, but she had already taken off her visor and extended it toward him.

"Can you sign it for me, please?" A couple of others had gathered behind her.

"I told you it was him." The fry guy had abandoned his post. So had the burger cook.

"I knew it already," the counterperson snapped back. "I just didn't want to be rude. I mean, give the guy some space, right?"

Right. Jamie sighed and faced the crowd after he had scribbled his name on her orange visor. Then it was on to arms and legs, paper napkins—just about anything available. Best wishes, Cheers, or just a signature. One of the fan's boyfriends even waved a copy of *People* magazine in Jamie's face, the one with the star's smiling photo under the heading of "America's Top Ten Hottest Bachelors." Jamie had no idea how they'd produced that thing on such short notice.

"Man, I wish I was you," slurred the guy, leaning closer and poking Jamie in the eye with the magazine. Judging by his breath, he'd been making the rounds at a few clubs. Jamie paused with his pen in midair and asked the man his name. Rodney.

"Yeah, Rodney," he said as he personalized the magazine cover, "I wish you was me, too."

Rodney beamed as he showed his prize around the restaurant, holding up his hands like a winning prizefighter.

"What's it say?" wondered the girlfriend, but Rodney had to read it for himself.

"Get a life. Jamie D. Lane." He smiled back at Jamie and gave him an exaggerated thumbs-up. "Cool."

By that time a Chicago policewoman had pushed her way through the crowd to his side. The girl behind the counter pointed at him with both hands.

"Somebody report a stolen wallet here?" The officer did her best to make herself heard above the crowd, and then she caught sight of Jamie. "Hey, you're—"

"Don't say it." By then Jamie had signed more than his share of assorted body parts and extremities. "Can I just get a ride back to my hotel?"

"No problem. But tell you what. My niece is a big fan. Do you think you could…"

Jamie sighed and nodded. The wallet could be replaced. But he wondered what it would take to get an earlier flight to L.A.

6

You're not famous until my mother has heard of you.

—JAY LENO

Jamie checked his Rolex and tried once more to add up the hours since the ugly scene back in Chicago. Less than ten, and unfortunately none of them spent in bed. Catnapping on the Learjet didn't count; he could never really sleep in a jet, even with noise-canceling headphones. And he still wore the same shirt he'd been wearing in the Burger King where he'd been mobbed. Had that really happened? The throbbing in his eye where the fan had poked him told him it had.

At least he hadn't arrived back in L.A. too late, though he honestly wondered why he was there, what good he was really doing sitting next to his mother's bed. Mom certainly wasn't complaining. She sat upright with a couple of pillows behind her, quietly contemplating the ages. The only thing anchoring her, keeping her from drifting up through the ceiling, might have been the twin oxygen tubes tucked into her nostrils.

"She's been waiting for you," the nurse whispered from the door of Mom's room, the same one who had written him the note. *Come quick before your mother dies.* "When I told her you'd be coming, her eyes lit up."

Maybe and maybe not. The staff of the Belle-Aire were paid well to keep residents comfortable in their last days. That went for the residents' families, too, and they did a fair job of it. They'd better, given the hefty monthly bill he paid.

"Did you see your son came to visit you, Mrs. Lane?" The nurse shouted to get Mom's attention. "Your son. The one singing on the television. Remember?"

Mom gave her only a glassy-eyed stare and returned to examining her fingernails. She mumbled something about how Randy had no right to leave her, that if he left, he would never come home again except in a box. Finally, she looked over at her son, focusing on his feet.

"Randy?" she whispered.

"It's Jamie, Mom. I don't know who Randy is. I came to see how you're doing."

"They said you wouldn't be home on leave."

He had to lean forward to hear the words.

"She saw your show from London," the nurse told him. "All the residents loved it. It was a real highlight around here, Mr. Lane."

Wonderful. Jamie shuddered as Mom coughed once more, deeper than anybody could expect from a bird of a woman like Penny Lane.

Her parents had obviously never heard of the Beatles when they'd named his mother, and besides that, she was only a couple of years younger than John, Paul, George, and Ringo. But he still remembered the first shock of recognition when he'd played her vinyl copy of *Magical Mystery Tour* on their hi-fi turntable in their apartment's front room. At age nine, he liked the picture of the four men with the feather costumes and funny masks on the front. She'd laughed when he informed her they'd named a song after her.

Penny Lane. She was the original, though. He reached out and took her hand, looked down to make sure it was really hers, and wondered at his mother's paper-thin, nearly translucent skin. The ring on her finger, a delicate pearl from her own grandmother, nearly slipped off. And he started to sing for her, the same way he'd done dozens of times.

"In Penny Lane there is a barber showing photographs…"

He didn't try to sound like Paul McCartney, just sang quietly so she and no one else could hear. She closed her eyes and listened, or he thought perhaps she did, to the catchy little melody with the nonsense words about portraits of the queen and fire-engine clean, fish, and finger pies. Sometimes she used to follow along, but lately not so much. Even so, he hoped the tune could help him tunnel through the fog to the person trapped somewhere inside a mind cruelly beset by early-onset Alzheimer's.

It never comforted him to hear doctors tell him how rarely the disease afflicted a fifty-four-year-old woman. That was supposed to make him feel better? Failing that, one of the nurses had mentioned a moving novel about a woman with the disease, a mother and a wife who battled tragedy with some kind of faith. The nurse had tears in her eyes as she described the plot, something about a vow to cherish. But no, thank you; at the time he hadn't taken her up on her offer to loan him the book. Maybe he should have. But the way he saw it then, the odds had pretty much just piled up on Mom, or the gods had, or God. Take your pick. He wasn't sure which made the most sense to him, since he hadn't been to church often enough to know and didn't know anyone well enough who could have explained it to him, even if he'd known what question to ask.

Unfortunately, that was only the half of it. To make matters worse—and this part really qualified the Lanes as a true-life inspiration for a TV movie of the week—the tragedy of losing her mind had been swiftly over-shadowed by a particularly vicious onslaught of emphysema. Nothing in real life was simple, was it? Mom couldn't just slip quietly into senility; no, she had to go wheezing and hacking, fighting for each breath. Jamie never got used to the cold rattling sound, how it made him wince in pain, every time.

All he could really do was hold on to her hand and keep singing. The music was his only weapon, the only way he knew to cope. She'd taught him that. So he sang.

It didn't matter that she had brought it on herself by years of heavy smoking. Still, Jamie always cringed, always felt guilty for knowing where the disease had come from and then thinking the dirt-awful combination that had stripped her of both body and mind could somehow be for the best. No, really it could not be, and obviously he hated to see his mother fail. Despite the good days and the bad days her nurses talked about, Mom looked more frail every time he visited. But here was the rub: At least with the Alzheimer's, she wasn't so aware of what had hijacked her body. That, he supposed, was silver lining number one, if you believed in silver linings.

Silver lining number two: At least the Alzheimer's had gotten so bad, she'd forgotten she smoked, and several weeks ago the nurses had quietly removed her hidden stashes of cigarettes—in a purse, under the bed, in the medicine cabinet. The funny thing was, she never even asked. So now she didn't go sneaking out to the 7-Eleven anymore at 2 a.m. in her night-gown, barefoot, looking for a pack of Winstons. There, see? All the news wasn't bad.

They locked her room now, too.

Silver lining number three sounded even more cruel, with no way around it: At least with the emphysema, she wouldn't have to endure the Alzheimer's for long. The nurses had promised to call him when things looked particularly grim, which was part of the reason he'd received the note in London. They now officially listed her as "day to day," not expected to prevail much longer. A week, three. Not longer.

So was it wrong to think like that, as they grasped at booby-prize advantages spawned by the words "at least"? Again, Jamie wasn't quite sure, but he couldn't shake the feeling that somebody was secretly filming their melodrama, one in which he had forgotten most of his lines and his mother had certainly forgotten all of hers. She had hardly recognized him in the past five months, since she moved into the Belle-Aire. Once or twice, maybe, but he couldn't be sure.

Oh, but guilt? He'd heard somewhere that guilt was bad for the spirit.

Negative energy and all that. It had sounded reasonable at the time. So no way was he going to tell anybody about his cartload of the stuff.

Who would he have told anyway? Not Nick, and certainly not Nick's Beverly Hills therapist, who had a lisp and a nervous laugh that reminded Jamie of a raven with a head cold. Not even Mom's nurse, who obviously meant well as she served up lines like "I'll be praying for you" or "God bless you real good." Well, despite her charming Mississippi accent, either she wasn't using the right magic words, or God was busy with something more important, like world peace. Or maybe the two got their wires crossed. Whatever. But the nurse's God obviously wasn't blessing anybody at Belle-Aire real good, least of all Mom.

Forget it. Jamie had already decided he didn't have the time or the energy to stress about the negative stuff that hit him in the face every time he stepped inside Mom's room. So he thought about the good times they had shared, living in a crummy little apartment in West Covina where he'd been the only man, growing up poor.

"You remember our apartment, Mom?" he finally asked her, just to say *something*.

No answer. Fine. What was to remember anyway? Peeling paint and broken pipes? Blocks of rubbery Velveeta from the food bank?

"You remember the time I fell off our balcony and broke my arm, and you called 911 because you thought I died?"

Still, she sat silently.

"And the time Rudy Piñero and I caught all the snakes in the culvert and tried to keep 'em in the sink, but they got loose in the apartment? Mom, do you remember?"

She coughed once again, while a young nurse came in with a cart jingling with bottles and glasses.

"Time for your meds, Mrs. Lane," chirped the nurse, checking a clipboard. "How are you feeling? Do you need another pillow?"

Mom shook her head violently. Now there was a response, but Jamie had been through this before. He sighed and stood, ready to go home. Only this time his mother didn't let go, just gripped his hand fiercely as if he were a kite that would fly away. And she looked him in the eyes for the first time all day.

"Don't go, Jamie." The words came out soft but clear. Not Erving or Willard or whatever ghost from her past that haunted her thinking.

Jamie.

Jamie's mouth went dry as she looked up at him with a puppy-dog expression in her eyes.

"I'll get Dr. Lewis." The nurse flew out the door and ran down the hall. Jamie didn't move, couldn't breathe. If he did, he might blow away the moment.

"I'm right here, Mom." He took her hands in both of his. "Do you know me?"

As if to answer she pulled her hands back, slipped her grandmother's ring off her finger and held it out to him.

"I want you to have this."

He hesitated a moment. "But Mom—"

"Take it." She held it out to him. "You're going to need it."

He wasn't sure what she meant, but all right.

"Good." When he finally accepted it she smiled, closed her eyes, and let her hands fall. "Now take me home."

Of course that could have been some kind of prayer; Mom used to talk about people going "home" to Jesus, which made no sense to Jamie either.

"Mom, this is your home now."

With that she began groaning and violently shaking her head once more, and Jamie feared he'd seen all of the old Mom he was going to see.

"Home. Take me in your Studebaker. I'm packed and ready to go."

He tried to laugh, tried to say something normal. Who had a Studebaker? He wasn't even sure he'd ever seen one of those old cars before. He *was* losing her again though. Say something…

"Mom, you know I don't have a Studebaker. But if you want to go visit, sometime, maybe—"

"No!" Her eyes flashed this time, and she started to swing her tiny feet out from under the sheets. "I want you to take me there. Dinner's waiting. Barkley's waiting."

Barkley. She had often told him about her little cocker spaniel companion when she was growing up. So now he knew he was really losing her, again, when she started getting into the confused stories of her childhood, the memories and friends she had known as a girl growing up in a small town.

By this time the nurse had returned with Dr. Lewis, and Mom tried to pull out her oxygen tubes.

"Mrs. Lane, no." The nurse rushed forward to settle her patient down, while the doctor pointed Jamie to the door before barking orders about sedatives and cc's. "You need to quiet down." Jamie could only stand back and stare.

"Jamie!" his mother cried as she began to collapse once more behind her veil of coughing. "Promise me…you'll take me home. To Riverdale. Promise!"

How could he? Riverdale? Even if it were close by and not two states away. Yet even as the nurse pumped a sedative into the IV, his mother's lips continued to move, continued to mouth the words, "Promise me…"

How could he not? He gripped her ring in his hand as he backed out the door and finally nodded.

"I promise, Mom. I'll take you home. But just rest now."

Dr. Lewis and the nurse didn't notice him leave, only his mother. As Jamie backed out into the carpeted hallway, he saw her nod and smile ever so slightly before the tiny flicker of recognition faded out and she closed her eyes once more.

Home to Riverdale. Right. He almost returned to the rest home the next day and even got one of his cars out of the garage. But the haunting feeling that he'd already said good-bye to his mother would not leave him, and he knew he couldn't get up the courage to say good-bye again. In the end he stayed away, canceling all his appointments, watching the Pacific surf from his living room window, playing the *Magical Mystery Tour* album over and over, drinking strong coffee, and waiting, not returning Nick's calls. Especially not Nick's calls.

By the next day he had begun to wonder about his self-imposed house arrest, though, and he'd heard "All You Need Is Love" about as many times as he cared to in one lifetime. He poured himself yet another cup of coffee and reread the headlines of the Sunday *L.A. Times* just as his cell phone chirped again. He glanced at the number on the tiny screen to make sure before hitting the green Answer button.

"Mr. Lane?" He recognized the nurse's voice, the one who had tried to get him to read the Alzheimer's novel. "I'm so sorry to tell you, but…"

He didn't hear the rest of what she said, not really. He already knew. And then he heard himself repeating his own words, too quietly for the nurse to hear.

"I promised."

Take with you only the bare wood of life.

—CLEMENT OF ALEXANDRIA

Anne straightened the pencils on her desk for the third time, checked her lesson plan for the tenth. Attendance book? Check. First day of school insurance handouts from the office? Copied and ready. Bulletin board?

Maybe her seventh and eighth graders were too old for that kind of thing. But the photos of famous playwrights had seemed like a nice touch: Shakespeare in the middle, of course, and...well, their names were written on the backs of the photos, in case anyone cared to know. The students in her incoming English class most likely would not.

But that could change. Did she have enough scratch paper in the supply closet? Copies of *Classic Literature for Middle Grades* piled neatly in the corner?

She couldn't remember. She did, however, remember the doctor's comments before she'd been discharged from the hospital in San Francisco two years ago.

"You're going to have to adapt to certain shifts in your short-term cognitive abilities."

In other words, get used to it. Take more notes. Keep more lists. Set your alarm clock. Compensate. Cope. She glanced at her watch and paced in front of her desk. She probably didn't have time to visit the ladies' room before students were due to arrive. Oh well.

Why did I say I'd do this?

Teaching physical education to inner-city fourth and fifth graders was one thing. And that was before. Teaching seventh- and eighth-grade English was quite another.

Why did they even offer me this job?

Officially they really needed a teacher, and she really needed a job. Her parents thought it could be good for her rehab. But she also suspected it might have had something to do with the fact that the job didn't pay enough to attract anyone from the outside. Or maybe because her father and the principal, Lance Howell, often went duck hunting together. So although it did concern her that a deal might have been struck between two middle-aged men in hip waders, she didn't have time to worry any more about it as a buzzer sounded and her new students began to trickle into the room.

"Find a seat, anywhere you like," she told them. "But be prepared to stay there for a few weeks while I learn your names."

If that were even possible. She hardly remembered her own sometimes. But she did her best to smile at each child as he or she stepped in. Some smiled back, while others avoided her glance and only reluctantly peeked up at the whiteboard where she'd carefully written her name. She double-checked her blank seating chart, poised to enter the name of each child in the corresponding square.

"You're the new English teacher?" asked a lanky girl who had plopped herself into a desk chair halfway down the middle row. She would have been much taller had she ever straightened her back—much prettier. Every few seconds she tossed her considerable mane of dark hair into the face of the hapless boy sitting behind her. Maybe he liked it.

"I'm it. My name is—"

"I hope you don't make us do a lot of book reports"—the dark-haired girl interrupted her—"like Mrs. Foster used to."

A couple of kids snickered while one poked at her friend. Several more entered the room, filling up the last of the seats.

"Mrs. Foster is having a baby this year," Anne told them, "but I suppose you already knew that. I'm Miss Stewart, and some of you know my family from church or from the bakery."

"Are we going to get free doughnuts?" asked the lanky girl. When everyone laughed, Anne tried to smile along. Already she could tell this girl was going to be a challenge.

"So let's start with you." Anne ignored the laughter and turned to face the girl. "What's your name, and tell us one thing about yourself, would you, please?"

"Amy Phillips." She was clearly used to the attention. "I'm a cheerleader and I run track."

"Oh really?" Anne looked for a way to connect and tried her best to hide her limp as she moved to the front of the room. "I used to run track in high school. Riverdale Public."

"Cool." Obviously Amy Phillips wasn't shy. She looked at Anne more closely and worked on her bubble gum. "Do you still run?"

In other words, *What's the limp all about? What's wrong with you?* The question was clear, really. Amy's neighbor from across the aisle kicked at her.

"No, it's a good question." She didn't blame Amy. She just hadn't thought it would come up so quickly. *Oh well.* "Just because Riverdale is a small town doesn't mean everybody knows my life story."

So she leaned back on the desk for support and took a deep breath.

"I might as well get it out of the way, just so you know where I'm coming from." She concentrated on each word, hard, wrestling it into place before it could skitter away. "First of all, let me tell you I do not have Tourette's syndrome, and I am not mentally retarded."

Already the cheerleader's hand shot up.

"What's Tourette's...whatever you said?"

"Amy!" A guy just behind her had the answer. "That's where people can't help it, they just start cursing, like something goes wacko in their head."

"Oh, is *that* what's wrong with you?" Amy shot back, and the entire class snickered. Not a good start.

"All right." Anne raised her hand for silence. "Let me finish what I started to tell you, okay?"

Cheerleader and the gang settled down.

"I told you I went to high school here in Riverdale. I ran a lot of track. But after I graduated I went to a Bible college in San Francisco. I wanted to make a difference for the Lord—do something special, you know? I got a job teaching PE at an inner-city school."

She blanked for a moment, recovered, then continued.

"I guarantee you it was not like this school at all."

The class giggled, all eight boys and eleven girls.

"Anyway, I thought that's where God had called me. But then about two and a half years ago, I was driving home from a dinner at my church. A guy ran a red light and smashed into my car going fifty-five, totally caved in the driver's side."

Several of the kids gasped. As she said, not everyone in town had heard her story. Others leaned forward in their seats, caught up in the drama. She wiped a tear from her eye and tried to hold back another.

"Long story short, the car was totaled, and I almost died. I was in a coma for nearly three weeks."

Another girl in the front row interrupted. These kids were going to need a few lessons in classroom manners.

"I was in a coma, too, when I was a little baby. I had this fever and—"

"Shut up, Jennifer." A boy next to her waved his hand. "We want to hear the story."

Jennifer shrank back and crossed her arms. Anne started to say something to the boy about his language but changed her mind and went on. She would deal with manners later.

"Anyway, the left side of my head connected with something, they're still not sure what, probably the steering column when the car flipped, I-I don't know. The doctors call it TBI—traumatic brain injury. I won't bore you with all the gory details. That's basically it."

Was she telling them more than they wanted to know? A hand went up from behind Amy. "Yes?"

"What happened to the other guy in your…accident?" asked a round-faced boy with a troubled complexion.

Anne bit her lip at the question she had hoped not to hear, felt the old anger well up inside. Not at the boy, just…

"First of all, it was *not* an accident." She tried not to snap, but she just couldn't keep the heat from toasting her words. "The driver drank what he did on purpose, kept drinking all night on purpose, got into his car on purpose. His friends let him go, *on purpose.* Turns out his blood alcohol was twice the legal limit. None of that was an accident, like, 'whoops, sorry, I didn't mean to.' It was all a choice. I don't call any of that an *accident.* I call that a *crash,* okay? You understand what I'm saying?"

No one said a word for a very long moment, not until someone in the back cleared his throat in a guarded whisper.

"Yeah."

Even Amy shrank back at their teacher's tears, while Anne held her head as she made her way around to her chair. She'd done it again. Old Faithful had erupted, and this time in front of a classroom of seventh and eighth graders. Only this time, the display left her dizzy and spent.

"Are you okay, Miss Stewart?" asked another girl. Anne nodded, then opened her eyes to keep from falling off her chair.

"I'm sorry. It's been a few months since I…well, I thought I would be starting to get over what happened. Obviously, I still have a ways to go. I hope you'll…stick with me. I get a little emotional, sometimes, more than I ever used to."

"Is that from the CSI stuff?" a girl in the back wanted to know.

"That's TBI, and yes, that's what the doctor told me. I'm still me, just a little different than before. But then, you all didn't know me before, or most of you didn't, so you won't know the difference."

She tried to smile. How were they supposed to respond now? She would start again.

"But I didn't answer your question, er…"

"Ron Kent."

"Okay, Ron." She pulled herself together as she penciled in his name on her chart, three seats across from Amy Phillips, cheerleader and runner.

"The man in the other car…he pretty much walked away from the crash with just a cut on his arm from some broken glass. A few months in jail, and I think he had to take an alcohol recovery class or something like that."

Still the students stared at her, dumbstruck. It could not have been what they expected from their new English teacher, and this was not the way she had wanted to open her class, at all.

What had she been thinking?

"That's not fair," Amy pronounced judgment swiftly, but Anne held up her hand.

"Maybe not. And maybe we can discuss it another time. In fact, I'm going to give you a chance to read about injustice in our first book assignment. I'm giving you a choice of three books: *Julie of the Wolves* by Jean Craighead George, *Johnny Tremain* by Esther Forbes, or *Jacob Have I Loved* by Katherine Paterson."

"I knew it." Ron groaned. "A book report."

"A book report," she echoed. "What a lovely idea. And look at this: All the books start with a J."

Humor was the only way out of the corner Anne had backed herself into.

"Well, that's enough about me," she announced. "Now it's your turn, and you can certainly feel free to keep it a little less dramatic than what I just presented to you. In fact, please do. So Amy, you're a..." She looked down at her chart. "A cheerleader, right. And what else?"

"I'm in track." Amy soberly tore off a corner of her spiral-bound notebook paper and wrapped it around her gum. "Remember?"

"Of course I do." Anne nodded and looked back down at her notes. "How about you, Ron?"

Anne forced a smile as she listened to the kids and took notes as they told their stories. Part of her still wanted to run off in tears after the awkwardness of her ill-timed testimony. The other part...well, they would just have to see what kind of an English teacher she might turn out to be.

Now if she could just remember where she had laid that lesson-plan book...

Guess you ain't never had a look at me without my whiskers and all cleaned up. I bet you wouldn't hardly recognize me, that much of a change.

—HUMPHREY BOGART, *The African Queen*

Jamie awoke slowly, still remembering the dream of washing his face, scrubbing, singing in the shower. Only the washrag turned horribly sour, and he wondered why it suddenly felt like sandpaper. He shook his head and rolled over, trying to figure out which city his tour had stopped in.

Cleveland or Philly, Albany or NYC, quick over to Boston and then to a benefit in Providence.

No, that was last month—before Nick had tried to send him on that vacation. Before life had gotten in the way.

Or death, actually.

The washcloth hit him again, this time in the ear, and this was not like any wake-up call he'd ever had before. He groaned and swatted but only came up with fur.

Fur? He sat up and tried to force open eyelids glued shut by too many weeks of concert touring. Only then did the fog start to clear and the washcloth turn into a dog's tongue.

"Where am I?" At least he knew he still lived. The little dog had made sure of that, and he didn't seem to care whether he bounced on the bed or on Jamie's stomach. *Time to get up, human.*

"Get off me!" Now it all came back to him. Riding north on the

Greyhound bus, sitting next to a large woman who complained about her sinuses and consumed enormous quantities of fried chicken. That had been part of the gig, though, part of his pilgrimage, his penance. No planes, just the bus—in honor of Mom.

But this dog, this little terrier mutt? What had he been thinking?

"Okay." He sat up and looked around the tiny motel room. Despite the baby blue, concrete-block exterior, he had to admit the place seemed clean and comfortable, with a portrait of a couple of mallards in flight on one wall and a velvet portrait of another duck on the far wall, just above a gurgling little brown refrigerator. Ducks everywhere. His bed had been a little lumpy but better than most he'd suffered through on the road. All for $27.50 a night, plus tax. Monthly rates also available at the... He squinted at the personalized ashtray next to the bed. Right, the Mar-Jean, Riverdale's finest motel since 1957.

Riverdale's only motel since 1957. As the guy behind the counter in the Quonset hut had explained when Jamie had checked in the night before, it was named for the first owner's two daughters, Mary and Jeanne, who were toddlers at the time. Or maybe his daughter and his wife. Whatever. This guy introduced himself as Bud, the founder's oldest son. Said so on his embroidered bowling shirt. And by the way, they served up a great breakfast biscuit at the B&W restaurant next door. Used to be an A&W hamburger joint until Bernie MacLemore and Wayne Williams bought it out a few years back. Bernie and Wayne, B&W, get it? That was also according to Bud.

As the dog whimpered, Jamie stared at himself in the mirror and tried not to think of the panic from the night before.

"We'll put you in the Mallard Room," Bud had told him.

No number?

"Nope. My wife never liked numbers. So we have the Elk Room, the Eagle Room, the Elvis Room, the Cutthroat Room..."

Cutthroat in honor of cutthroat trout, and there would be a big portrait of a fish in that room. Of course, the Elvis Room was Bud's favorite. They used it for their honeymoon suite. Viva Las Vegas, right?

"That where you're from?" Bud wanted to know.

Jamie had done his best not to swallow his tongue when Bud had looked straight at him. And Jamie managed to mumble something about just moving there. Yeah, there were a lot of hot shows there. And no, he hadn't seen Elvis. Sorry.

"That's a shame." The innkeeper had grinned back at him as he handed over the key to the Mallard Room.

Yeah. But who else had seen the fake Nevada driver's license in Jamie's wallet? He'd only flipped it open for a moment as he'd checked in, pulling out a twenty. But today he was still Joseph P. Bradley, thirty-two years old, with short black hair (not curly blond) and dark brown eyes (not baby blue). Colored contact lenses could do amazing things. His trademark blond beard? Gone, flushed down the sink of a Ritz-Carlton suite in San Francisco. Also gone: His earring, Rolex, and gold chain. And though it didn't show on the "official" photo, he'd traded his Armani shades for a dated aviator style he'd seen in *Smoky and the Bandit,* and his expensive wardrobe for a truck-driver-chic ensemble of faded jeans and a denim work shirt torn at the elbow. All topped off with a well-worn tan cowboy hat, courtesy of Spencer the ID man.

All this trouble just so he could get out of L.A. for a few days without being mobbed? Jamie understood now why the guy with no last name had come so highly recommended, and why his considerable fee had to be paid in cash. The former FBI witness protection specialist worked quickly, asked zero questions, and made house calls. And most important, he'd assured Jamie that Nick would never know. Jamie's manager had better things to worry about, right? The only things Spencer had not been able to change were Jamie's height and weight: Six-one, 180 pounds. But not to worry. Spencer even took care of details like a new bank account under a fake name, a dedicated cash account with an untraceable debit card. Jamie could use it whenever he felt like being anonymous.

Like now.

Maybe the ring is working. Jamie smiled and cupped his hand over his mother's ring still hanging from his neck on a gold chain. To tell the truth, it made him feel a bit like Frodo in The Lord of the Rings. Or not.

After a quick shower in a metal stall, Jamie peeked out through the window at the two-lane ribbon of Highway 97 in the distance. To the right it swept south across the plateau, tracking through amber waves of grain and shimmering in the late summer sunshine. To the left and to the north, it would snake through the foothills before meeting scattered groves of live oak and Douglas fir, finally catching up to the dark shelter of a mountain backdrop. That would be the Simcoe Range, if he remembered the bus driver's travelogue correctly.

Closer to the Mar-Jean and off to the side, a little mini-golf course had once been carved out of a wheat field. Now the wheat and the weeds were reclaiming their rightful place, and the Astroturf peeled back to bathe in the sun. A bright yellow school bus, with Riverdale Christian School stenciled in bold black block letters on its side, rumbled by, bouncing with a load of kids.

"Okay, I get it," he told his little mixed-breed companion, who by this time was pacing in front of the door. "No room service at the Mar-Jean, I guess."

He pulled on a rumpled but clean set of clothes and checked the mirror, which had more ducks etched into the corners. With any luck he'd be done with his business by lunchtime and on his way by nightfall. Of course, he might check out his mother's old house, if it still stood. Or maybe the high-tech windmills planted on the foothills behind town, just above a large white cross, half hidden in the trees. Not that the cross interested him much. But afterward he'd find a car to rent for the trip home, assuming this town had a place to rent a car. He paused for a moment as he laced up his shoes and grabbed a granola bar from inside his bag. He wondered why he'd brought Mom's old photo album, tucked in beneath a pair of socks. Oh well. By now the little terrier mix scratched at the front door.

"Sorry. Didn't mean to make you wait."

The dog shot out the door and aimed for a patch of well-used yellow grass between the buildings, while Jamie grabbed a small canvas sack out of his duffel bag and followed. As Jamie stepped outside, Bud, the fellow who had checked them in the night before, glanced up from the hole he was digging. Invisible from the waist down, the innkeeper looked as if he had been planted in the middle of the gravel parking lot.

"Quiet enough for you?" The innkeeper wiped a burly hand across his forehead and leaned on his shovel. Eight in the morning, a hint of autumn in the air, and the man was sweating.

"Not bad." Jamie stopped for a moment to munch on his breakfast and feel the angled sun on his face. "In fact, I slept good. Really good."

Truth be told, he hadn't slept this well in months.

"Yeah, people always say that in the Mallard Room." Bud tossed another shovelful of dark dirt onto the pile next to his ditch, then his shovel struck something that sounded like a pipe. The dog came over to inspect. "You're not one of those government windmill engineers, are you?"

"Uh, no." Jamie did his best to remember the instructions Spencer had given him to read, from *Your New Identity.* Something like, "Be alert, but don't let them know you're afraid of being discovered." (Chapter 1.) "Jerky motions show you're scared; so does looking at your watch too often. Keep it smooth."

"What's his name?" asked Bud.

"Who?" Jamie nearly jumped as he slapped his hand to his side. Three minutes after eight. No names. No autographs. Not now. Then he remembered. "Oh, you mean the dog."

Bud nodded and scratched the terrier behind his half-floppy ears. Good thing pets were welcome at the Mar-Jean.

"Uh, no name." Jamie hadn't thought about it. "Not yet. Actually, I was just wondering… Is there a dog pound in this town? Animal shelter? SPCA?"

The man's raised eyebrow invited Jamie to finish his story.

"Picked him up yesterday across the river at the truck stop. Or actually, he picked *me* up. Just walked right up to me in front of the diner, like I was supposed to give him a ride."

"Knew just what he wanted, huh?"

"He looked hungry." Jamie shrugged. "Kid behind the counter there said he'd been hanging around for the past week out by the Dumpsters. What was I supposed to do?"

"Yeah, know what you mean." The man scratched his own chin before returning to his digging. "Sometimes you meet up with somebody, and it's just supposed to be that way. No name though, huh?"

The mutt looked up at Jamie and barked, as if trying to tell them something. Jamie had to laugh.

"Actually, I just remembered. He *does* have a name." As if that made sense. "Barkley."

The name seemed to fit this little guy just as it had fit his mother's dog. He kept his eyes fixed on Jamie, as if he surely knew they were discussing his identity. But now he had more important matters to attend to, and Bud returned to his digging.

"Hmm," mumbled Bud. "Well, I guess that works."

By this time a couple of other men had drifted back to the motel parking lot from the B&W and started to gather by their white government Suburbans. Barkley had caught the scent of a breakfast biscuit one of the government guys had parked on the hood of his Suburban next to a steaming cup of coffee. He raised himself up on his hind legs in the full begging position. This dog was obviously a master at bumming fast food.

"Here you go." One of the men, a tall guy with a navy blue ball cap, had already tossed Barkley a corner of his sausage biscuit when he noticed Jamie.

"Oh, sorry." The guy picked up his coffee and opened the door. "I didn't know…"

Barkley didn't wait for an invitation, just jumped up into the driver's seat and waited. Three of the government guys looked in and laughed.

"Think we should call him a cab, Mike?" asked one of the others.

"Come on, boy." Jamie snapped his finger and hurried over. "You've got a lot of nerve."

The men all laughed as Jamie reached in to retrieve the beggar, who only scooted beyond his reach.

"Speaking of taxis," Jamie added, "you guys haven't seen any in this town, have you?"

"Just hop in if you need a ride," the man said. "Plenty of room for you and the dog—if you're headed toward town, that is."

"Well…" Jamie figured they could probably walk from the Mar-Jean. What was it, maybe half a mile? But Barkley had already made himself comfortable in the car once more, this time in the backseat. "I just need to find the local mortuary."

Fame is only good for one thing—they will cash
your check in a small town.

—Truman Capote

Barkley finished up yet another bite of breakfast sandwich on the way into town, and the three engineers thankfully hadn't asked Jamie too many questions. During the five-minute ride he had found out a little more about the windmills though.

Started out as an experiment, said the driver, an electrical engineer named Mike Witherspoon. But they soon found that the winds in the hills above Riverdale were some of the most consistently steady in the country, what with the Columbia River Gorge and the shape of the plateau and all. "Consistently steady" might have been a little bit of verbal overkill, but that was the way these kind of guys talked. Jamie did his best to nod at the right times when they started getting into stuff like phase inverters, double redundant backup systems, and supplemental power grid additions.

Five minutes later the Suburban pulled up in front of the Vernon Young & Sons Mortuary and Funeral Home, which wasn't hard to find given the fact that nearly every business in town hugged four blocks of Main Street, four blocks of Simcoe Way, and a few scattered streets around the hawthorn-lined county courthouse square. The funeral home filled a big white Victorian building, while an older black hearse waited in the gravel driveway out back. Right next door to the Haven of Resurrection Cemetery.

Inside the funeral home a woman with a Wilma Flintstone hairdo looked over her glasses at Jamie from behind her desk. "You've arranged for shipment of the remains?" She frowned as she glanced down her nose at Barkley. Barkley returned her look with a wag of his tail.

"Actually, I've got them right here." For the first time since leaving L.A., Jamie pulled out the modest bronze urn from his little sack and set it carefully on the counter. "I understand her last request was to be brought here to Riverdale."

"I see." The woman stared as if she'd never seen a burial urn before.

"I would have called ahead." Jamie picked up a brochure about funeral preplanning, then set it back down. "But…well, it's kind of a long story. Kind of a spur-of-the-minute thing, you know?"

Maybe people didn't drop in every day off the street, holding their mom's ashes.

"I have her death certificate and everything." He patted the envelope in his backpack, just to be sure. "It's from Los Angeles, where she lived."

She held up a finger and lifted the phone. "I'm going to need to call Mr. Young. Could you hold on for just a moment?"

A few minutes later a fifty-something Will Young introduced himself and led Jamie out through a grove of oak trees to inspect the urn garden, offering his running commentary in a low, steady undertaker's voice. Barkley remained behind in the office; for obvious reasons, dogs weren't welcome on the Haven of Resurrection grounds.

"And here's our columbarium." Mr. Young slowed as they reached a V-shaped, shoulder-height brick wall opening up to a single flagpole.

"Columbarium?"

"The corner of our cemetery dedicated to cremated remains."

Right. He knew that. Jamie studied one of the little niches in the wall where they would plug the urn. Some were capped with brass plaques; others still awaited an occupant. This would be okay, Jamie told the man.

It was what she had wanted, sort of. She'd wanted to come back to River-dale, anyway, where she was born.

"Really?" Mr. Young wrinkled his forehead. "I've never heard of any Bradleys here in Riverdale."

"Bradley?" Jamie had to think for a moment. Out of habit he reached to tug his ex-beard, where it used to be. "Oh no. *My* name's Bradley. I'm just a…friend of the family. Her name is Lane. Was. Penny Lane."

"Ah yes. Lane." He nodded in understanding, which made Jamie wonder if there were other Lanes buried here or how much this man knew of his mother's past. He volunteered no information, though, if he knew. On the other hand, he didn't seem shy about suggesting the purchase of a memorial bench and tree, or at the very least a memorial bush, which at $235 sounded like a much more affordable option. And then, of course, could he suggest a slightly more appropriate urn? The genuine bronze Ballet-of-the-Sea model, for instance, measured a full 245 cubic inches and cost just $395, while the Praying Hands amphora provided quite a beautiful remembrance for the more religious person. Wouldn't that be more suitable?

By that time Jamie wasn't quite sure what he had agreed to, but Mr. Young nodded gravely and scurried off to make the arrangements, leaving Jamie by the wall. Rather, the *columbarium*.

"Sorry to leave you here alone, Mom." He wasn't sure which way to look as he lowered himself to someone's stone memorial bench, facing the wall, the urn at his feet. A robin worked the newly watered grass off to his right, tilting its head close to the ground, listening as if he could hear voices in the ground.

Jamie did the same, but he only heard the chatter of sprinklers and the distant squabble of a crow. And it seemed to him half a prayer, this listening. Only problem was, no one seemed to be saying much of anything. The robin hopped away.

"I don't know why I did this, Mom." Jamie sighed, and his eyes settled on a tiny bouquet decorating someone's ashes at the foot of the wall. "Don't know why I came here. Guess I had to see for myself what this place was all about. Plus I promised you, right?"

Right. Better late than never? Maybe not, and the tears of guilt stung his eyes, and it reminded him of a song. Not one he'd ever performed, but an Eric Clapton ballad about how he didn't belong in heaven. That wasn't hard to identify with.

"I guess this wasn't quite what you had in mind," he whispered, and the tears surprised him, but he let them water the grass beside the bench. "And I'm sorry. I'm really sorry. You did your best for me, and I wasn't there for you. I guess I didn't quite come through, did I?"

The robin came back to listen. Good thing no one else could hear him, at least no one in the cemetery.

"I don't even know if you can hear me, Mom, from where you are."

That would be heaven, naturally, wherever that was. If anybody deserved it, his mother did, for putting up with everything she had. For raising him, for always wanting more for him. But would she even know his name if he saw her in heaven? The ballad still rang in his ears. He, on the other hand, wasn't so sure he'd make it there for her to recognize him. And surrounded as he was by graves, ashes, and tombstones, the thought seemed more real than he normally cared to admit, closer than he liked. He wiped his tears with the palms of his hands, blew out a deep breath, and left the urn next to the bench.

"Good-bye, Mom." He couldn't swallow, could hardly breathe, and certainly couldn't see his steps. But he wandered between rows of stones, most old and gray and not quite level, trying to clear his head before Mr. Young came back for the urn and saw him again.

After a few minutes he caught his ragged breath and read a few tombstones to settle down: *Born 1887, died 1932. Veteran of the Great War.*

Infant son of Mildred and Oskar. Into His Everlasting Arms. He who believes in me shall not perish. Loving daughter of... He stepped carefully down the rows, unsure if he'd ever been this close to this many dead people at one time. He'd always done his best to avoid the bad luck in graveyards, something his lucky ring probably wouldn't offset. And each one seemed to have a faith slogan chiseled into the stone that marked its existence. *I am the resurrection. On wings of angels. Gone but not forgotten.*

Actually, the place wasn't all that big. No surprise, then, when he eventually located a name he recognized, a side-by-side family plot for Delay Orford Lane and Agnes Watson Lane. He stood still for a moment, just to be sure that it really was his grandparents. Yet even though his mother had never mentioned the names to him, he knew them, had seen pictures of them in the album, seen their names. The bodies of Mom's parents lay buried at his feet, a fitting distance across the cemetery from their estranged daughter. He stared at the tombstone, dry-eyed this time.

"Agnes Watson Lane," he read aloud, "devoted wife and mother."

He nearly choked on the words. Devoted mother?

Devoted?

"Except to your own daughter."

He'd seen quite enough. Jamie spun on his heel and marched back to the office, where Mr. Young still punched numbers on the front desk adding machine. The undertaker looked up with a start as the door flew open.

"How much?" Jamie demanded. The words echoed for a moment before Mr. Young caught on.

"How much? Oh, Mr. Bradley, please don't worry about payment now. We know that during the grieving time—"

"How much?" Jamie repeated, pulling out his wallet. "The family gave me cash for this. Just tell me how much you want."

Mr. Young opened his mouth a couple of times but didn't find his voice until he looked back down at his figures.

"Of course. We discussed the inurnment niche in our special Haven of Resurrection Columbarium, the upgraded bronze urn, endowment care, the setting fee, a personalized marker…"

"Just her name, that's all I—I mean the family—wants. Penny Lane. No 'devoted daughter' garbage, nothing like that."

"I understand." Mr. Young pressed his lips together and nodded as his hands shook. "So preliminarily, that comes to…two thousand four hundred twenty-five and—"

"That's fine." Jamie counted out twenty-five hundreds and slapped them on the table. "Please buy some flowers with the change."

The undertaker turned as white as some of his clients but recovered nicely.

"Of c-course, Mr. Bradley. We'll take care of everything for you."

"No obituary in the paper?"

"Not unless you want."

"I don't want. And our business today, just between you and me, right?"

Mr. Young gulped but nodded once more.

"We hold all our dealings in the strictest confidence. You can be assured of complete confidentiality in these matters, if that is your desire."

That was his desire. And Jamie didn't need to hear any more as he looked around the office. The secretary hurried in from the back room.

"Oh, there you are, Mr. Bradley," she panted. "I'm so sorry, but the gardener came in through the front door, and your dog just…well, he… he's gone."

Jamie rushed to the front window, hoping to see Barkley sniffing the bushes in front, but no.

"I'm so sorry. I couldn't stop him." She knocked over a pencil holder from the corner of the desk but ignored the clatter it made on the floor. "He just ran off toward town. I'm sure you'll find him. Won't you?"

10

Fame is a fickle food upon a shifting plate.

—EMILY DICKINSON

Why am I so bent out of shape about this?

Jamie honestly wasn't sure. After all, he'd planned to deliver the dog to the local Animal Control people as soon as he had the chance, hadn't he? Having Barkley run away again, well, that just made it easier. Saved him the trouble.

Maybe so. But that didn't stop him from walking the town, up four blocks of Main Street, down the other side, then through the alleys on either side. He checked the back door of Halcombe's Market and the American Legion Club, plus the ASC Farm Office, Wintergreen Pharmacy, and S&H Car Parts on the south side of the street. On the north side he poked through Tessa's Yesterday's Antiques and Collectibles, The Riverdale *Sentinel,* Molly's Hallmark, and the law offices of Frank Ogden. He even looked inside the little lobby of the Capri Theater, which featured a second-run film he thought he'd seen on The Movie Channel last year. And at most of the places, the response was typically like that of the pleasant woman behind the counter of Andy's Do-Nut Barn, which wasn't a barn at all, just a storefront bakery/lunchroom with a few tables that drew him in with the irresistible aroma of fresh-baked bread.

"Terrier? Yeah, actually, I think I did. He was standing by the doors for a while, looking at people coming and going. Followed somebody who gave him a bite of a cake doughnut."

"Figures."

"Was he yours?"

Jamie thought for a moment before he answered. "No, I guess not. He's his own."

Still that didn't stop Jamie from wandering the streets of Riverdale for the next half-hour. He bought himself a burger plate at the American Legion Club, the old-fashioned kind of basket with wax paper, a pile of French fries, and a pickle slice with one of those little frilly decorated toothpicks for color.

"Good burger," he mumbled to the older gentleman behind the counter. Just enough light filtered through the club—a bar, really—to make out the semper-fi tattoo on the guy's forearm. That shouldn't have been a surprise in a place like this. A sign behind the counter announced happy hour from 5:00 to 7:00. Jamie could never figure that kind of thing. Wouldn't that be happy *hours*?

"You a veteran?" The cook interrupted Jamie's thoughts as he adjusted his once-white apron. "Veterans get a ten percent discount."

"Wish I was. But nope."

"Ah, one of them windmill guys, then, huh? I can always tell an engineer."

Jamie shook his head. "I met some of them this morning, though."

Strike two. The cook's face fell, and he quickly glanced down-counter to make sure the three guys eating grilled cheese sandwiches were still okay. He would try one more time.

"Elk season's not for a few weeks yet. Some fellas like to come check the lay of the land beforehand?"

It was a question. Jamie almost enjoyed the game.

"Actually, I just came here to deliver some ashes."

He wiped the ketchup off the corner of his mouth, set down a ten, and headed for the door. But even though he explored Riverdale's quiet streets and tidy neighborhoods for the better part of the next hour, he never saw a sign of the little dog. He stopped to stare at a couple of Victorians with plaques explaining their history. A son of the first settlers built one in 1892. Another was once owned by an obscure Civil War hero Jamie had never heard of.

What to do next? The Crosby House Historical Museum took a couple leisurely hours, looking at old butter churns, Indian artifacts, and a complete printing press used for the first issues of the venerable Riverdale *Sentinel* in eighteen-seventy-something.

"Here on vacation?" The silver-haired woman dusting the postcard rack by the front door wanted to know.

"Didn't start out that way," he admitted, "but it's sort of turning into one."

Unfortunately, she hadn't seen Barkley, either, and by late afternoon he headed back for the Mar-Jean. By the time he returned, calf muscles aching at all the hiking, he noticed two bright pink While-You-Were-Out notes taped to the outside of his door.

"Nothing like a little confidentiality." The first came from Mr. Young from the Haven of Resurrection, wanting to know where he could send the receipt for Penny Lane's arrangements. Oh yeah. Jamie had sort of left in a hurry. That message he crumpled and stuffed in his pocket. But the second...

"How did he know?" He trotted to the Quonset hut office and pushed inside.

"This note on my door?" Jamie waved it like a little flag at a parade. "Where did it come from? I mean, who is this?"

The owner took the note and deliberately pulled out a pair of reading glasses. "Oh, that's Father Greg out at the abbey. He called this afternoon, wanting to talk to you, something about your dog."

"My dog?"

"You were looking for him, weren't you?"

"Word sure gets around."

"This is a small town."

Was it ever. But how did this Father Greg know to call the Mar-Jean?

"Barbie at the Haven of Resurrection said—"

"Okay." Jamie held up his hand. "I think I get it. The whole town knows I'm here, is that it?"

"No, no. I wouldn't say that. But feel free to use the phone here at the front desk. I don't think your extension in the Mallard Room is working."

"Thanks, I'll use the pay phone out front. I assume that one is working?"

A minute later he was on the line with a Father Greg MacCaulay, Abbot of Our Lady of the Hills Abbey.

"I'm so glad you called, Mr. Bradley. I have someone here at the abbey you'll be interested in knowing about."

The dog?

"Well, I apologize for doing this, but I made the mistake earlier today of offering a piece of my doughnut to this hungry-looking little dog. He did look as if he'd missed a meal or two, so I thought he was a stray."

"Professional panhandler, actually. He's very good at what he does."

Father Greg laughed, a deep throaty chuckle that made the telephone receiver vibrate.

"Well, I'm sorry to say he followed me home, but it's really only a short distance from where you are, I believe."

"You've been talking to Barbie at the Haven of Resurrection, then?"

"Actually, no. I asked Dot at Halcombe's, and she had been talking with someone who…well, I don't actually recall the connection."

"Never mind. Is there any way you can drop him off here?"

"Yes, well, that's the problem, actually. Normally I'd be delighted. But we loaned out our little truck to Jack Dorsett out at Blockhouse this after-noon, who had to pull one of his stumps, so we're currently without wheels. But as I said, the abbey is only a short distance away. In fact, if you're not doing anything, perhaps you'd like to join us for our evening meal."

"I wouldn't want to—"

"Nonsense. It's the least we can do for putting you to all this trouble."

"No trouble, really."

"All right, then. We eat in about an hour—around six, before vespers."

Jamie wasn't sure he wanted to know what vespers were, exactly, though he had a pretty good idea. And if the only way to get Barkley back was to have dinner at a monastery, well, he could do anything once.

Except, what was he thinking? Was he going to pack the dog back home to L.A.?

Well, why not?

"You find the dog?" Bud yelled out the office door. Jamie nodded and gave him a thumbs-up. This really *was* a small town. But he had one more call to make. Less than a minute later he held the receiver away from his ear to keep from bursting his eardrum.

"Of all the crazy stunts," Nick didn't need a phone to make himself heard into the next state. "You choose now to disappear. I've been calling your house for two days. Where are you anyway?"

Jamie paused for a moment.

"Jamie, are you hearing me? This is your manager speaking. I can't manage a guy I can't find. And if you keep doing what you're doing, the cash cow called Jamie D. Lane is going to dry up. You're not going to have thirty-seven cents left for a stamp. And neither is the C. J. Patterson Agency—and you know how C. J. would feel about that. Are you hear-ing me, pal?"

"I hear you, Nick. I just needed to take some time off."

"Sure, fine. We talked about that. And I had you scheduled for St. Bart's a little later this month."

"You know that's not what I wanted, Nick. I didn't want all the bodyguards and the bimbos after me the whole time. No publicity freaks passing pieces of paper under the bathroom stall door for me to autograph."

"You're exaggerating."

"That's not the half of it. All these people, they always want something. Vampires. Especially the press."

"Oh, come on, Jamie. When did you make this discovery? You've just got to suck it up. Goes with the territory."

Jamie didn't answer, afraid his manager was at least partly right. And if so…

"Besides, Jamie, do you have any idea what your little adventure is costing us?"

"I don't know and I don't care."

"You're nuts, you know that?" Nick sighed. "But I'll tell you what. Just tell me where you are, and I'll send someone to pick you up. No questions asked. We need you back right away. *Then* you can go on vacation."

"No."

"What do you mean, no?"

"I mean, I need a couple more days. Time to drive back, too."

Nick groaned. And Jamie heard himself say the words, though he couldn't explain why he'd said them. *A couple more days? For what?*

"Oh, come on. What are you doing, hiding in some hotel someplace? You're not exactly the kind of guy who can just hide without people recognizing you."

For the second time, Jamie had to admit…

"You know I'm right," Nick went on. "And in the meantime, what do I tell everybody who's knocking my door down, wondering what's happened to you? Peter from the studio wants to know. Julie from A&M. The scheduling people from all the networks. C. J.'s having an absolute heart attack. I mean, you have no idea the pain you're causing me and the agency, Jamie. No idea."

"I'm sorry, Nick. Tell them whatever you want. Tell them I'm recovering from something. Or tell them I have some family business to take care of. I'll call you again."

"Wait, wait. Listen, Jamie, if you don't get back here in forty-eight hours, I'm going to…well, all I have to do is make a couple of phone calls. You know that, don't you? I'll find out where you're hiding, and we're going to end this little cat-and-mouse thing."

"It's not a cat-and-mouse thing. I have to go."

"Yeah, well, enjoy your freedom while it lasts, Mr. *Bradley.* Forty-eight hours, no more. Got it?"

"I'll call you. I promise." But he didn't agree.

"Forget about the call. Just get back here."

Jamie hung up the phone and glanced over at the smallish front window to see Bud staring at him. Jamie waved. Must have been a sad day in Riverdale when the last party line shut down. And now it looked like time for him to check out of the Mar-Jean. Never mind that it was way past checkout time. He could leave tonight.

Forty-five minutes later he tramped up a shady gravel driveway in the wooded hills just above Riverdale, duffel bag slung over his shoulder. His feet told him he'd better be there, pretty soon. The path followed a gurgling river, where it smelled of cottonwoods and a pond that opened up in a small clearing.

Our Lady of the Hills Abbey.

Among the hills to the north, fifteen or twenty small log cabins snuggled under firs and oaks, each one commanding a view of the pond and the main lodge. The pond, which fed the stream he had already followed here, had been created by a modest earthen dam, and served as the home for a pair of regal white swans. The large cross he thought he had seen from the highway was erected here too, a rustic pair of logs some fifty feet tall, painted white and commanding a view of a clearing that looked out over the plateau. On the far side of the grassy clearing, the cedar-log lodge held its own site of honor, capped by a steeply pitched green metal roof and surrounded by an expansive deck.

"Tough duty." For a minute Jamie took it all in, waited in the lengthening shadows for the Shangri-la to disappear. He could have turned around right there and pretended he'd never seen it. But a furry streak shot out the front door of the lodge and raced toward him.

"Barkley!" Jamie bent down as the terrier nearly knocked him to the ground. "There you are."

The little dog squealed and rolled on his back in the grass as Jamie scratched him behind the ears.

"Looks like he's found his owner again." A towering man in black work pants and a tan shirt appeared at the lodge door. He grinned behind thick round glasses and stretched out his hand in greeting. "Father Greg MacCaulay. Glad you could make it. And you brought your bag."

Though the priest had the height of an NBA all-star, he looked as if he might totter over at any time.

Jamie lost his hand in the extra-large grip.

"Joe Bradley. Just headed out of town, but…you've got quite the place here. I didn't know abbeys were this nice."

"That's usually the first thing a visitor notices." He nodded, and Jamie noted his host's soft English accent. "A gift to the church, actually. A private individual had operated it as a retreat center, up until about ten years ago. He wanted it to go to the Lord's work after he was gone."

Uh-huh.

"But come with me," the abbot continued. "I'll introduce you to the others."

"You mean they can talk?"

Father Greg laughed once more, as he had on the phone, and the sound echoed off the surrounding trees.

"We're Trappists, it's true. But not all Trappists have taken a vow of silence."

That was a relief. Jamie wasn't quite ready for sign language and note passing.

"Though we do have times of the day when we practice the discipline of quiet meditation on the Word," the abbot went on. "So most people would say it's a pretty quiet place. In fact, I imagine very few people know we're here. Come."

Jamie followed, losing his chance to turn and run. And just for today, maybe that wouldn't be such a bad thing. After all, he'd made it through another twenty-four hours with no one recognizing him. No one badgering him for autographs or publicity photos. No one repeating his name, demanding his attention or his signature.

He could get used to this.

And the monk's words made him wonder too.

Very few people know we're here.

Maybe that wouldn't be such a bad thing either.

11

You feel like the same person you were before the injury. But you are not! How long will it take you to become aware of this?

—www.tbichat.org

Anne peered out the window over her sink where she finished the last of the dinner dishes. Or just *dish*, actually. She could see the willow tree in her parents' backyard, the one Daddy had planted when she was little. During the daytime she actually had a pretty good view of the mountains from out here in her little caboose cabin, especially from up in her loft lookout, the raised platform in the middle of the caboose where she climbed up to read and sleep.

Her father had converted the quaint old Burlington Northern caboose a few years ago for use as a unique guest cottage. He'd had it hauled to the back of their lot at the edge of town, painted it a jaunty yellow, and installed a compact bathroom, a loft bunk in the middle, a kitchenette, and flower boxes all around. She had added yellow checked curtains and matching slipcovers. He had probably never expected his grown daughter to return as a guest though.

Well, here she was. And with dinner finished, she would have to get at her lesson plan pretty soon. But she heard a hammering from out in her dad's garage, and that usually wasn't a good sign. Instead of cursing, Dad had a way of taking his extra-heavy hammer and giving a frozen bolt a good swipe or two. But only in emergencies. She smiled and added an extra snickerdoodle to a plate. Dad's favorite.

"Ah, just in time." He smiled at Anne as she stepped into the shop a few minutes later with her offering. "I needed an extra hand to get this old piece of the fender off. Here, you hold this wrench while I try to loosen it from the front."

Of course she didn't mind helping on his latest restoration project: a beautiful but neglected old '37 Chevrolet Sports Coupe Deluxe, with a rumble seat and teardrop headlights. He'd rescued it from a scrap heap in nearby Zillah about five years ago, but until now hadn't really made much progress, at least not anything she could see.

"You do have a minute, don't you?" He grunted, and the muscles in his neck strained as he tried to turn the bolt.

"Not really." Her nose almost touched his as she fought to hold her side of the bargain. Just like old times. "But it can wait."

He studied her face for a minute and put down his wrench.

"I'm sorry. You need to take it easy."

"What are you talking about? Give it another shot of WD-40. It'll loosen up."

"No. I mean *you* need to take it easy. Don't strain yourself. I shouldn't have asked."

She threw her wrench down on the shed's hard-packed dirt floor.

"You still don't get it, Dad. I can do anything I used to do, before the…before the wreck. I can jog, I can cook, I can do my own wash, I can feed myself. Everything the doctors said I wouldn't be able to do."

"Sometimes I forget." He grinned and picked up her tool. "You can even throw things around, which you never used to do."

"Ohhh!" She shook her head in exasperation.

"No, really, I kind of like that."

"You do not. But I can even teach." Her face fell as she heard herself crowing. "Sort of."

"Of course you can." He patted her on the back. "Otherwise they wouldn't have hired you."

"They have no idea. The class can already tell I'm not all there sometimes. But they're really good kids. There's this one girl…uh…well, anyway…"

She told him about her first class and the tricks she'd pulled to stay one step ahead of the kids. He smiled as he listened.

"You've come a long ways from when you were in San Francisco."

"I'm not sure if that's good or bad."

"You tell me." He never stopped wrestling with the stubborn fender. At least this time he didn't tell her to take it easy. But he'd opened a memory she desperately wished she had lost, along with all the others.

"God meant it for good." His words echoed in Anne's ears.

"You make it sound too easy, Dad. Like…restoring a car or something like that."

"Nobody said restoring a car is easy. And your life is a lot more complicated than a '37 Chevy, Anne. Believe me."

"It's not that. But every time I think I'm getting a grip on things—pow!—it all falls apart again. Like two steps forward…"

"Three steps back." He finished her sentence. "I know."

If you know, then why do you always drop the smug one-liners on me?

The question floored her. Where had that come from? She almost apologized before she remembered she hadn't said anything.

Yet.

"So do you have any suggestions for me? Every time I think of that guy, I'm ready to strangle the first man I see."

"Whoa! Glad I have a wrench in my hand. Self-defense is allowed, right?"

"Dad, I'm serious."

"I know, and I'm sorry. I just don't know what else to tell you. You're the college grad, remember? I just run a small-town doughnut shop and fix classic cars at night for fun. Nobody ever taught me how to be a Christian psychologist."

"I probably need one."

"That's not what I meant."

"Yes it was. And you're right. Sometimes I think my mind has been whacked so far out of alignment, it's not even funny."

"Listen to me. You are not whacked out of alignment. You just need more time. And we're all praying for you. Got it?"

She smiled and nodded through the tears but couldn't stay any longer. Without another word she laid down the tool and ran outside into the cool September night. Dad didn't follow. Good.

Or not so good. The sound of a truck's horn out on the highway made her skin crawl up the back of her neck. Funny how a dumb thing like that could bring back memories. Because every time she'd been asked to recall the crash, all she could recall was the sound of a blaring horn and nothing more.

So really, they didn't qualify as memories. Just fears. Stupid, ungrounded, unspiritual fears. Fears that hadn't completely left her, despite the fervent prayers of her parents and everyone else in church.

Come on! she scolded herself. "I'm thirty years old."

Going on nine. She scurried quickly down the gravel walk toward her little home, but the horn sounded again, and Anne found herself in a cold sweat as she slowly climbed five steps to the deck. The strange thing was, she didn't always respond this way, and it wasn't enough to tell herself how silly she was acting. She slammed the door shut behind her and leaned against it, trying to catch her breath.

12

The nice thing about being a celebrity is that, if you bore people, they think it's their fault.

—HENRY KISSINGER

All right, let me spell this out for you one more time, just so you understand." Nick raised his voice and spoke straight into his cell phone's remote lapel mike as he paced the front room of his suburban Nashville condo. The view of the rolling hills was great; the rent wasn't so. He hadn't even bothered to fill most of the rooms with furniture. What did it matter, this pretend home?

But Mitford liked it—Mitford, the large round tabby cat dozing on Nick's windowsill.

"I'm listening." The concert promoter's voice hadn't yet settled back to normal.

"The kid is exhausted, okay, Esteban? He's been on the road basically four months, living out of his suitcase, and he comes down with this, this fatigue syndrome or something, right?"

"You're saying he's sick?" Esteban Garcia matched Nick's volume, and then some. "Last time I talked to him, he sounded fine. And now you're telling me he's sick?"

"He's under a doctor's care. It's under control."

"Under control, right! I've got three venues booked, and they're all starting to get nervous after they heard Jamie missed yesterday's photo shoot. I mean, I've got crews lined up for everything. Publicity. Paychecks. Get it? The clock is ticking, and look, I'm ready to cancel here, Nick. We're going to lose a lot of money if—"

"I'm telling you it's under control, Esteban. Don't panic, okay?"

"Easy for you to say. But I don't hear boo from Jamie to make me feel better. Hey, this isn't a drug thing, is it? Because if it is…"

"Are you kidding? You're talking about America's choirboy here. He's just tired, that's all."

"I thought you said it was some kind of syndrome."

"Yeah, that too. But it's not serious. Doctor says he'll be fine, just give him a couple days."

"A couple days, huh? I'll have my secretary send him some flowers. He at home?"

"No! I mean…uh…he's at a clinic for a little while longer, just to clear things up. The man needs his privacy, you know? Part of the treatment."

"I'll have 'em sent to the clinic."

"He's allergic to flowers. You understand."

A slight pause nearly echoed on the other end.

"You don't think you're catching this thing, too, Nick? You don't sound so good yourself."

Nick hoped his laugh didn't sound as forced as it felt.

"Hey, I'm at the peak of my game. So is Jamie. That's why we're doing this little bit of preventive maintenance. It's like changing the oil in your Lexus. Do you worry every time you change the oil in your Lexus?"

"I drive a Beemer, Nick."

"Whatever. Just don't worry."

"All right, all right. But just so you know, I've been recording this conversation."

This time it was Nick's turn to pause. Who was pulling whose leg now?

"Kidding, all right?" The concert promoter snorted. "You just get your man on his feet, singing again, and we'll all be happy."

"Like I said, Esteban—"

Nick hit the red Hang Up button on his phone as soon as he heard the other end go dead, then ripped off the earphones.

"I can't believe you're doing this to me!" he railed. The cat looked up at him. It took a lot to disturb Mitford. "These people are breathing down my neck, and you're off doing…whatever it is you're doing."

He turned to his Palm Pilot and scrolled through the address list before punching in another number on his cell phone.

"Come on, come on…" He tapped on the phone as it rang once, twice. Finally…

"Yeah, Norman? Glad I caught you. Nick Anderson here."

He paused and frowned.

"Anderson. You know, Jamie D. Lane's manager? Right. We met at the Grammies a couple years ago? Sat at the same dinner table with our wives. Uh-huh… Actually, no, we're not together anymore… I don't know what she's doing now. I guess collecting alimony, right? Yeah, I send her enough of that."

He laughed but felt a familiar rock in his stomach when he glanced over at the three-year-old photo of his daughter, Emily. Funny how he once thought he was doing all this for her. He put down the pencil he'd nearly chewed in half.

"Oh, hey, don't worry about it. Life goes on. Besides, I have a cat now. Low maintenance. He's always here for me when I get home."

Calls like this reminded him why he would never, ever get himself a video-phone. He bit his lip, turned away from Emily's photo, and headed back toward the kitchen, looking for a bag of chips he'd left in the cupboard. Junk food always helped.

"Anyway, Norm, reason I'm calling is I understand you do a little investigating on the side. No, no, nothing domestic. It's just a friend, he's…well, this is all totally confidential. Goes without saying, right?"

He took a deep breath, waiting for the go-ahead.

"All right, I'll lay it all out for you, much as I can. Actually, Norm, my boss, C. J. Patterson, asked me to call you. He's really concerned—and of course I am, too—that our client Jamie has gotten himself into some kind of trouble… What do I mean by that? I mean vanished. Like that Left Behind stuff. Poof. You know?"

He located the chips, crumpled one in his hand, and went on.

"He did call, but no, he wouldn't tell me where he was… No, see, that's the problem. We *can't* just wait for him to show up. We've got too much riding on this guy. Actually we think he may be close to going over the edge. I gave him forty-eight hours to get himself home, but I have this bad feeling, you know? So we need to find him, like yesterday."

Norman asked for a few more details, things like credit-card accounts and phone-call records. So far Jamie had left no trail, but that could change overnight. Nick explained about the San Francisco hotel clerk who had seen him last. And, oh yeah, budget was not a problem.

"Why didn't I say so in the first place? Well…" He smiled for the first time. "I just wanted to be sure you could find him. Oh, I believe you. I'll let you know if I hear anything else. Good."

Nick hung up still smiling. Good call. But as he stood there in the kitchen the smile faded, replaced once more with the bitter reminder of everything he'd sacrificed for this client. From his family to his career and everything in between. He glanced at an autographed copy of Jamie's first platinum CD, framed on the wall.

That's what he got in return?

"You owe me, kid."

Mitford brushed up against his leg, and Nick wondered if anything could ever balance the scales. He bent down and let the cat nibble on some of the potato chip crumbs in his hand. Maybe...

"Maybe this isn't all bad," he told Mitford, who gagged on a larger bite.

Clarity is good, he told himself. *Careful not to press the panic button too soon.* But could he pull it off before Jamie totally self-destructed, and he was left holding...

Crumbs?

Well, the first step wouldn't be tough. Jamie had brushed her off the last time she'd called, back when they were stuck in Chicago. Hadn't he? So why not? He picked up the phone and punched in the number.

"Erin?" He cleared his throat and slicked back his hair. "Nick Anderson here. You haven't heard from Jamie, have you? Didn't think so. But listen, I was just wondering..."

"So let me get this straight." Jamie looked up and down the table at the sixteen men sitting with him. Eight on a side. Except for one, they all wore flowing white robes with a long black pullover sash and a hood in the back.

The monks of Our Lady of the Hills Abbey. As Father Greg explained it, a community of the Cistercian Order of the Regular Observance, popularly known as Trappists.

"There's no TV, no radio, no Game Boys, no cell phones, no computers, right?"

They all looked up at his question, as if they weren't quite used to a lot of predinnertime chatter.

"One computer." A bearded man to Jamie's left paused from his vegetarian lentil soup to correct him in a soft whisper. "Brother Anthony uses it for our fruitcake Web site."

"And for taking fruitcake orders." The balding brother to Jamie's right finished their sentence. "He used to be a Web designer."

"Right, okay." Jamie tried to take it all in.

He tried the lentil soup himself and took in the full, smoky flavor. Not bad. Even Barkley happily slurped down a bowl, mixed with bread chunks and apple slices. If dogs were vegetarians…

"One phone for emergencies and for taking phone orders," explained one of the brothers.

"One phone." Jamie nearly choked on his soup. "Wow. So explain this to me again. You make fruitcakes and…anything else?"

A kindly glance from Father Greg quieted the brothers, and he offered their guest a plate of sourdough rolls and a slight grin.

"You're more than welcome to stay and find out the answer for yourself, rather than hear one of us try to explain it in words. Oh, and by the way, we normally take our meals in silence."

"Yikes." Jamie swallowed. "Sorry. I didn't know. I mean, I-I'll shut up now."

He returned to the soup and finished his bowl without slurping or pinging the side of his bowl. Soon afterward he helped clear the dishes and followed the brothers as they trooped out of the little dining room. Of course he was welcome to rent one of the empty cabins for a while, Father Greg explained.

Why not? Jamie thought about it, wondered how long he might be able to pull it off. Well, he sure didn't have to go back tonight anyway, and he didn't have to call a taxi to fetch him. For one thing, it was getting later than he thought. And for another, he kind of wondered about what went on at this odd place. And more than that—but he wasn't quite sure about that *more* part, just yet.

"You guys have a pretty tight schedule then, huh?" he asked. "I never would have guessed just by looking at you."

Father Greg smiled as they reached the little cabin where Jamie and Barkley would be staying the night. "It's ordered to bring us into closer union with Christ."

Whatever that meant. But if it worked for them, Jamie was fine with that.

Or he would have been, if he hadn't awakened in the middle of the night to the sound of footsteps outside the guest cabin. He flipped on the lamp by his modest single bed and squinted at his watch on the bedside table.

Three-twenty?

Naturally, he would have rolled over and returned to his dreaming. But Barkley decided to scratch at the door and whimper. And then he heard another set of footsteps outside his window, and another.

"All right, all right." Jamie groaned as he slipped out of bed and into a pair of jeans. "I guess everybody's making a run for it. Let's go."

He wasn't sure if he would need a flashlight until he peeked outside into the cool dew of the morning. Had he ever been up this early in his life? A bobbing line of tiny lights led the way around the glass-still pond to the chapel.

"Hey, what's up?" he asked the next hooded monk passing by. He would have to follow them to find out.

"I know you guys talked about early morning vigils," he whispered, trotting to keep up with the dark shape. "But you weren't talking about *this* early, were you?"

A bell rang from the chapel, once, twice.

"I guess so. You guys aren't messing around."

He wasn't quite sure why he still followed, just that he'd come this far, and he supposed he would have to see what they were really doing. By this time he found himself standing behind the circle of brothers in the candlelit chapel. He was going to tell somebody that it was a good thing he left the dog outside, but decided against it. And when they started reading from the Bible, he couldn't be sure who was reading, only that it sounded soft and mystical, like a chant or like music. Even so, he understood the words clearly:

> If I ascend to heaven, thou art there!
>> If I make my bed in Sheol, thou art there!
> If I take the wings of the morning
>> and dwell in the uttermost parts of the sea,
> even there thy hand shall lead me,
>> and thy right hand shall hold me.
> If I say, "Let only darkness cover me,
>> and the light about me be night,"
> even the darkness is not dark to thee,
>> the night is bright as the day;
>> for darkness is as light with thee.

And so it went, each monk reading another portion steadily and quietly, as if he meant it. Good for them if they did. And yet he had never heard anything like it, these men breathing in the words as if they had just survived near drowning. Eating the words as if they were passing around the waffles, serving up steaming stacks with maple syrup. All the while the ghostly beautiful singing flowed from inside the hoods, never stuttering, a command performance for a hidden audience.

He didn't know what *Sheol* meant, and he had never heard of this kind of nightlight God—if that's who they were reading about. He assumed yes. But what did he know about spiritual stuff like this? Nothing, not a thing, which may have explained his slack-jawed wonder at the reading.

At the same time Jamie's stomach growled, and he hoped they didn't hear, hoped they didn't suddenly realize he had come and that he did not belong. Because he obviously did not, and the trespass felt so blatant. But it made him wonder, and he settled in a hard wooden seat, back against the far wall, legs pulled up against his chest.

He listened to the music of the words, in a strange way far more beautiful than he could have guessed or expected. And who was there to hear them? One half-awake, burned-out singer, hiding from the world and searching for something that even he couldn't quite recognize. He would know when he found it, though, and it made his hands shake to think he might be closer here in this chapel than he had ever been before.

One thing for sure, though: He would need to stay in Riverdale a little longer.

Crazy, the things that went through his head, and it had to be because it was still only four in the morning. The reading continued, and maybe that's why he slept so soundly, why he didn't wake until Father Greg tapped him on the shoulder a few hours later.

"Hey, breakfast time?" Jamie snapped awake. He hoped vegetarians served good breakfasts. No problem with the lentil soup, but...

"I'm sorry. Breakfast was over an hour ago. We thought you were in here praying and didn't want to be disturbed."

"Praying?" Jamie did his best not to laugh. His dreams of country flapjacks and sausage dissolved, *poof.*

"Yes, we work from 8:30 to 11:30. Several work on the fruitcake baking, several on the mailing, and a few help maintain the grounds. Brother Aaron could use a hand staining the porches. Perhaps if you're not doing anything else?"

Jamie thought about it for a second. Why not? As long as he'd come, this was his chance to live like a monk for a day or two. He'd try anything once. Besides, the quiet felt good. And Nick could wait.

"Actually, Brother Aaron says we're out of stain. Would you be willing to cycle into town to pick up a gallon? Normally we send someone into town once a week for supplies, but—"

"No problem, Reverend father-brother."

Father Greg smiled and shook his head at his new helper.

"The bicycle's over by the shed. Brother Aaron will tell you what he needs."

13

It's too bad I'm not as wonderful a person as
people say I am, because the world could use a few
people like that.

—ALAN ALDA

This was good.

Anne squared away her desk for Day Two of the Great American Rehabilitation Experiment. Day planner ready with sticky notes attached at
strategic spots? Okay. Seating chart completed with names and photos
clipped from last year's yearbook? Done. Handouts ready and duplicated,
arranged in descending order by period? Almost.

An envelope on the corner of the desk caught her eye. Someone had
scrawled "Miss Stewart" on the front. A card? Garfield with a thermometer in his mouth. Cute.

"Dear Miss Stewart," she read quietly. The students must have slipped
it into the room during first or second period, her prep periods today. "We
hope you'll be feeling better soon, and we want you to know we'll be praying for you. Thanks for being our teacher. Love…"

And then the kids had all signed their names, which she couldn't see
of course because of her tears. Oh dear. She looked for a tissue in her
purse, couldn't find one, and decided to make a run for the restroom
down the hall. The wall clock above the door said 9:40. Plenty of time.
She snatched the handout masters and limped for the door.

"Oh, hi, Miss Stewart!" A bright face peeked in the door just as she reached for the knob. The lanky girl from the front row. "Did you get the—"

That's when she noticed Anne's face.

"—card? Oh, are you all right?"

Anne brushed the tears from her cheeks and forced herself to smile.

"Yes, I got the card." Act like nothing had happened. "It was very sweet of you all to think of me. I was just heading down to make some copies."

"Need some help? Mrs. Foster always let me help make copies and stuff."

"No! I don't need—" But Anne swallowed her words as soon as she heard them. She guessed she looked as startled as...what was the name?

"I'm sorry." Anne smoothed the edge off her voice. "I appreciate your asking, but I'll take care of it, um…"

"Amy." The girl clutched her books to her chest and turned to go.

"Amy. Right. Thanks again, Amy. Maybe you can help me another time. You should be in class now, shouldn't you?"

Amy nodded as she shuffled down the near-empty hall. She dangled a wooden bathroom pass around her finger. Now with less than twenty minutes until her next class, Anne hurried to the workroom—and promptly jammed the copy machine.

"Oh brother." She slammed down her notebook and yanked the side of the machine open. "Does it always do this?"

"At least once a day."

The answer made Anne jump, which brought a giggle of surprise from the other woman at the door.

"I'm sorry. Didn't mean to startle you. You need a hand with that thing?"

"I've got it." Anne smiled over her shoulder. She couldn't quite remember her name, but the older woman taught the fifth-sixth combined class, just two doors down from Anne's room. They must have been on morning recess at the time. "Yeah, I've got it."

And she did have it. One more yank and the shredded paper came out of the machine's innards. Unfortunately, it took a little plastic thingie with it, sending a cloud of black toner dust all over the carpet, all over Anne's hands, and all over the front of her blue jumper.

"Oh, oh, oh, *no!*" she shrieked. But the more she tried to dust the mess away, the worse it became, and the more of a clown she felt. She glanced up at the clock. Ten minutes till class. Now what?

"Oh, Anne." The fifth-sixth teacher came up beside her. "We've been complaining about this dumb machine for years. I'm sorry—"

Anne tried a damp paper towel, which did nothing but smear the horrible black smudge, making it look as if she had been shot in the gut and had started bleeding black blood all over herself. She looked at the clock once more—her lesson plan didn't include anything about exploding copy machines.

"Please, dear, don't try to wipe your tears with your hand." The woman took Anne by the shoulders. "I don't know if that's mascara or toner. But listen. You just run home and change. Take as much time as you need. I'll cover your class."

Anne tried to breathe, but the dust started to make her sneeze. And cry between sneezes. And oh, what an awful mess. She nodded her thanks and stumbled down the hallway just as the bell rang. She tried but could not sidestep the waves of anger that now shook her as she stumbled outside.

No. This would not have happened with the old Anne's steady disposition, instead of this new cry-a-minute personality. Who had she become anyway?

And it wouldn't have happened if she wasn't so clumsy now.

Or if that idiot hadn't plowed into her car, robbing her…oh, there she went, one more time.

Whining.

As in, *God, why did you let him do this to me?*

She didn't think it hurt to ask. Once again God remained silent, though, and that was his option, but on days like this, she would definitely have liked an explanation. Something other than "My strength is made perfect in your weakness" or "He who began a good work in you will be faithful to complete it," and so on, which were wonderful. But they had somehow lost their fizz in her life, though she would never admit that to anyone. But for once she wished God would tell her something new, something she hadn't heard since she was four years old in Sunday school, something she could sink her teeth into, like a wonderful new recipe she'd never tried before.

By the time she climbed into her car she'd finished crying for the time being, but she just wanted to punch somebody. Hard. Preferably the drunk, but at least he was in California, far enough away. She made sure she avoided downtown, though in a town like Riverdale, she probably could not avoid seeing someone she knew.

She circled around to the Little Klickitat Road, near the old gravel road that led up to the monastery, and congratulated herself. So far, so good. She'd taken the long way, but she'd get home. Through the woods and over the hills if she had to, but she'd get home.

A moment later she stopped congratulating herself. A guy on an old bicycle suddenly appeared from the old gravel road, out from a grove of firs. A monk, had to be, messing with something in the handlebar basket—a doll, no, a dog! He didn't see her Volkswagen, either, at least not until it was almost too late. He slammed on his brakes and nearly dumped his cargo, then managed to put his foot down and stared at her from the middle of the road.

She punched her brakes as well, screeching to a stop maybe three feet from the bicyclist and his dog. Maybe four. And for a long moment they stared at each other. His eyes widened, and he had to see her mascara-streaked face, her Halloween mask.

Funny thing, though. He looked strangely familiar, but only in the vaguest sense. He didn't look at all like a monk. For one thing, he wasn't wearing the plain dark work trousers she'd seen them wear when she had toured the fruitcake bakery with Dad. His haircut didn't look like a monk's, and he wasn't wearing a monk's standard beard. She assumed he wouldn't be wearing a robe for cycling—but not jeans and a Nike Swoosh T-shirt. Definitely un-monkish. Maybe he was a new recruit.

Even if he wasn't, she put up her hands in apology before she quickly averted her eyes and waited for him to wheel slowly away. He would not see how red her ears had become, as they burned beneath her straight dark hair. Yet his stare never left her, wide-eyed and gap-mouthed. She could feel his eyes on her, the incredulous stare, and she would not be able to explain that exactly, but she knew it to be true. He did finally manage to wheel himself and the dog out of the way and off to the side of the road, however, so without rolling down her window she sped away in the direction of home.

At least she had never seen him before in her life—and with luck might never see him again.

But never mind. Five minutes later she paused for a moment in the safety of her bedroom, took a deep breath and prayed for peace to take hold of her once again. And in the cozy walls of her caboose retreat, she heard once again the hint of silence, read the counted cross-stitch quote on her wall, the one her grandmother had once made in careful deep red thread: *As for me and my house, we will serve the Lord.*

She took a deep breath and tossed the ruined jumper in a hamper. *There. That's better. Enough of the tears.* And she might have been tempted to stay there the rest of the day, curled up on the observation window seat with the latest Francine Rivers novel she'd been wanting to read. But as she pulled on a clean skirt and blouse, she peeked out through the shade and noticed the rural mail carrier's car swerving down the road. Marie had arrived early today, but that was okay too. Anne straightened her skirt and hurried outside.

"Bill, bill, bill…" Their carrier handed over her mail as Anne reached out her car window. "And a letter from your friend Jennie in California."

"Thanks, Marie." She smiled and tossed her mail on the passenger seat as she turned her Beetle back to school, this time taking the quickest route back. Her class waited, after all. But by the time she reached the school and parked in the gravel under a shady line of elms, she couldn't resist just sneaking a quick peek at Jennie's carefully handwritten letter. Ah, good, and far better than any e-mail. Tonight she'd have time to savor her friend's news over a cup of tea. Jennie always made her laugh. For now, she'd enjoy perhaps just the first couple of paragraphs…

She didn't get that far. A name halfway down the page caught her attention, instead, and it made her catch her breath.

Him.

As much as she wanted to immediately crumple the letter and not read the news, she could not. And to her credit, Jennie apologized three times for even mentioning the man's name in print. But she thought sure Anne would have wanted to know that he had been released early from Folsom State Prison on parole, released early for good behavior.

Good behavior? Anne finally tossed the letter aside, slammed the door, and hurried back up the stairs to the brick school building. Ignoring her limp, she hurried through the side door as she fought back a fresh wave of angry tears.

14

Like you, I once thought I was free.

—CYPRIAN OF CARTHAGE

So, Brother Aaron"—Jamie did his best not to drip paint on his shoes as he worked on the spindles of the back deck railing—"you ever been to Bermuda?"

"Bermuda? I'm from Boise." Brother Aaron laughed as they worked their way across the deck, section by section. At this rate it might take them another day and a half. And these September days weren't getting any longer.

"I take that as a no." Jamie smiled as he worked the paintbrush back and forth, up and down. Dip, splatter, brush, and over again. After morning and afternoon work sessions yesterday, his arms seemed a little stiff, but other than that, it really wasn't so bad. "You ever wanted to?"

"Maybe." The freckled first-year novice shrugged and wiped his brow on the sleeve of his khaki work shirt. "But I like it here. I like the routine. The worship. The quiet times. The swans on the pond, you know, or the stars. Every day is different."

Jamie shook his head. "Well, I admire you guys. But really, you don't mind getting up at three every morning?"

"At first it was a little rough." Brother Aaron chuckled as he painted. "I fell asleep the way you did the other day. But you get used to it, and then you really can't imagine any other way."

"That, and the fact that you guys get to bed so early. I haven't turned the lights out this early since I was in the first grade."

"We're glad you could join us for a while. The work is good with two people."

"Right. The work is good." That felt strange to say, but it was true. "Anyway, it sure beats singing…"

Jamie's voice trailed off, and though Brother Aaron looked up, he didn't ask for the rest. Of course, he hadn't asked anything else about Jamie, the way most people would have. No "What do you do for a living?" or anything like that. So far it had just been painting and God.

"You'll be at vespers again tonight?" Brother Aaron talked about it as if it was the latest Hollywood release. "Father Greg is almost finished reading *The Practice of the Presence of God.*"

They'd been talking about that nonstop, and Jamie had a hard time figuring how they had so much to say about a little book written by a monk back in the 1600s.

"Uh, maybe." A couple of vespers services were fine, and the monks were friendly and all. The singing might have sounded better with a little bass and a beat, but who was he to say? "Actually, I thought after work time, I'd borrow the bike and ride around town. Maybe catch some dinner at a restaurant, see if there's a show playing. You don't want to come, do you? You guys have another bike?"

Again Brother Aaron flashed him that patient smile, the same one all the other brothers wore when Jamie asked another dumb question.

"We only have the one bicycle," he reminded Jamie, looking for a rag to clean up his brush. "You're sure free to explore as you like."

In other words, thanks but no thanks.

"Sure." Jamie surveyed their work. Not bad for a singer and a monk. "Maybe I'll do that."

Just like the day before, afternoon work ended promptly at 3:30. According to the daily schedule, their vegetarian supper would follow at 5:00. So by 4:00 in the afternoon, Jamie pointed the monastery's rusty bicycle toward beautiful downtown Riverdale, following his nose. Barkley rode in the basket once more, his nose pointed into the breeze like a figurehead.

"Full steam ahead, huh, Barkley?"

For a moment Jamie remembered what it was like to ride his bike around West Covina in the waning days of summer, when all he had to worry about was when the fifth grade would begin and how to make enough money to buy Slurpees at the 7-Eleven. He closed his eyes as he crunched down the path, letting the aroma of cottonwoods and firs wash over him. He didn't want to think about Nick trying to find him, or about all the people waiting for him back in L.A.

"A guy could almost get used to this kind of life," he told Barkley, who looked back and slobbered on his hand. But Jamie couldn't help feeling that his new freedom was like the freedom of a three-minute Disneyland ride, and a pretend native with a pretend spear would pop out of the bushes, just like on the Jungle Cruise, his favorite when he was a kid.

He snapped open his eyes, remembering the crazy woman in the VW bug who almost ran him over the other morning.

"Freeee-dooooom!" Jamie gave the yell his best Mel Gibson Scottish accent. But never mind that. They made quick time with Barkley watching for traffic and Jamie pedaling toward the prospect of a USDA Prime sirloin steak, medium-rare, please. That would be the first order of business: Scope out the nearest steakhouse, or at least the place most likely to serve some beef. Baked potato with extra butter and sour cream, maybe a side salad with blue-cheese dressing. Yeah, he was early, but the monks would be eating supper soon back at the monastery. Why not the folks in Riverdale?

Bucky's Ponderosa wasn't open until five, but in the meantime Jamie had no trouble following his nose to Andy's Do-Nut Barn. Barkley seemed to agree that half a dozen glazed hors d'oeuvres sounded just about right.

"Don't move," he commanded the mutt, who could not have jumped out of the bicycle basket if he'd wanted to. Barkley sat obediently and watched Jamie step into the little bakery and coffee shop. Bells on the front door tinkled hello.

"Ahhh…" Jamie had to stop and take a deep breath before he reached the glass counter. Even at this time of day, the heavenly aroma of fresh doughnuts hit him squarely in the face. He had never smelled anything better in his life.

"Everybody does that." The aproned guy behind the counter half-smiled as he waited for Jamie's head to clear. Judging from the gray moustache and receding hairline, he looked to be pushing sixty maybe. But the size of his arms told Jamie the baker probably also pushed a lot of weights. "Can I get you something?"

"Yeah," Jamie said, half-serious. "You need to bottle and sell the atmosphere in here."

"You're not the first person to tell me that. I'm still trying to figure out a way."

Jamie nodded as he sidestepped the spinner stand of religious booklets that corresponded to the simple cross hanging around the baker's neck. What was it about this trip? The big cross above the town, the brothers of Our Lady of the Hills, and now this. *Oh well.* "Holy" doughnuts would taste just as good, he imagined. Maybe they blessed the flour. He zeroed in on a neat stack of old-fashioned glazed behind the glass, next to a hand-printed Help Wanted sign.

Wouldn't this be a great place to spend some quality time. He wondered what a real job would be like, one without agents and producers and persnickety sound systems and screaming fans tearing pieces of his clothes and hunks of his hair.

Never mind the booklets. The heavenly smell more than made up for them, as did the row of very cool framed classic auto photos rimming the upper wall.

"Duesenberg Model J," Jamie whispered as he looked at the cars. "'56 Chevy Nomad…"

"Hey, that's pretty good. Not too many people know the difference between a '55 and a '56."

"Pretty obvious when you look at the taillights."

"I have an old '56 in my garage." The baker rubbed his hands together. He'd found a fellow classic-car buff. "If you're interested…"

The door bells tinkled once more, and Jamie looked up to see the girl who had nearly run him down the day before.

"Anne!" The guy behind the counter vaulted around the side to help her with a box. "I don't want you lugging in heavy boxes!"

"It's just napkins, Dad. Relax." She tossed the box over to him and at the same moment noticed Jamie staring at her. She had obviously cleaned up since the last time he'd seen her.

"Oh." She glanced quickly back through the glass windows at Barkley in the basket, who was following every move. And her forehead wrinkled, as if she was trying to remember. "You're the…"

Maybe she wondered how much she wanted to say. *Too late.*

"…the monk I almost ran over the other day. Or maybe I'm thinking of someone else?"

"No, it was me, but—" He couldn't remember ever seeing such penetrating brown eyes before, even back in L.A., where colored contact lenses and Hollywood makeovers could put a million-dollar face on the girl next door.

This looked different. Not perfect, just real. Her limp and the prominent scar across the left side of her forehead did nothing to dampen the beauty.

"I'm really sorry about that," she squeaked.

"No, no. It was my fault actually."

"It wasn't."

"Don't worry about it. Really. Except—"

Her eyebrow arched in a quizzical expression.

"Except I'm not a monk. I'm just staying at the monastery…for a while."

"Oh. I didn't know…regular people could do that. It's a beautiful place up there, isn't it?"

He nodded as the words left him, and he had to turn his eyes away. Funny, women had never affected him quite like this before.

She turned to her father. "Have you seen Mom?"

"Stopped by church for a minute on her way here. We've really got to find somebody else to take the night shift. She can't be doing this every night. And Wanda only wants to do a couple days a week now."

Which explained the Help Wanted sign.

The baker turned his attention back to their customer.

"I'm sorry. What can I get you?"

Jamie started to point at the doughnuts again when a crazy thought crossed his mind. Not for the money obviously. But for the experience… and just for a few days. Just for the experience. Just to run into the brown-eyed baker's daughter.

Why not? And so he decided to expand his little experiment in small-town living, dipping his toe in the waters of a normal life. Maybe Mom had hung out here. Who knew?

"Actually…" Jamie had no idea if he could pull it off, no idea the words would actually come out the way he thought they might. "I could use a…a job."

He pointed to the sign. "You need somebody for nights? I'm free."

And now that it slipped out, he would have sewn his lips shut if he could have. What was he saying?

"Really?" The baker looked him over. "Well, obviously we need the help. And you seem to know your classic cars, which is a good thing. You ever worked in a bakery before?"

"Oh, sure." This time Jamie tossed out the lies without hesitation, like lines in a play or a performance. "Back in Nevada. I did day shift, night shift"—what else would sound good?—"down shift. You name it."

"So you've worked on one of these machines?"

The baker led him to the back room, where a hulking machine lay idle along one wall. The dough-pumping apparatus anchored one end, a cone-shaped stainless steel bowl topped by a gaggle of blenders, heaters, and rotors attached to a four-foot trough for hot oil. How a doughnut made it through all that machinery, Jamie had no idea. He had never seen anything like it before in his life, never been closer to a bakery than right now.

"You bet I've worked on these." Jamie springboarded from one lie to the next. "Yeah, these"—he leaned forward to see the label—"these Lil' Orbits are great machines. Only the one we had was probably not as big."

"Well, let me show you how this one works." The baker turned to Jamie with his hand extended as the brown-eyed girl came back and grabbed a folded apron off a shelf. "By the way, I'm Andy Stewart. This is my daughter, Anne."

"Joe Bradley." Jamie caught his breath when Anne offered her hand, which felt cool and smooth, and for a moment Jamie didn't want to let go. But he finally pulled away and turned back to the doughnut machine lesson.

Be still my heart, he told himself. For the first time he thought maybe he'd made the right call about staying in this town a little longer. *With natives like this...*

For his part, Andy must have been too excited about finding a night shift doughnut maker with bakery experience. Of course *Joe* could turn in his résumé in a couple of days. Considering all of his good experience, he could even start right away, and they could tidy up the paperwork later. They just needed his Social Security number and a peek at his driver's license. His wife, Elaine, would be thrilled that she could attend women's Bible study tonight after all.

"You have no idea how much this means to us." Andy pounded Jamie on the back once more, the grin ear to ear. "I'd actually planned to close early, but I think God had something better in mind. This is an answer to prayer."

"Definitely." Jamie tried not to stare at the boss's daughter. "It's an answer to mine, too."

He glanced over nervously at the Lil' Orbits Model SS1200, Andy Stewart's gleaming stainless-steel monument to modern doughnut crafts-manship. Jamie should probably have taken notes as Andy explained everything, except that would have made him look as if he didn't know how to run it. He most certainly didn't, but he thought maybe when he was all alone in the kitchen…well, how complicated could it be?

"You're sure you can handle it now?" Andy had already gone through the instructions a couple of times. They would need twenty-five dozen for the morning—including five dozen regular and ten dozen each of glazed and chocolate-covered—which shouldn't take much more than two or three hours, four at the most. He'd be finished no later than ten o'clock.

No problem. Jamie's stomach rumbled, a low reminder of the dinner he'd missed. The mutt was probably going crazy outside by this time too.

Andy shook his head and said at least three times that he'd never hired anybody like this, on the spot, right off the street, but that he knew an honest worker and a fellow classic-car buff when he saw one. Jamie swallowed hard and nodded while his new boss promised to maybe check in on him a couple of times if he needed it.

Not to worry. Enjoy the Bible study, or whatever he needed to do.

All the while, Anne leaned against the doorjamb, arms crossed, a crossword-puzzle frown on her face. She'd made sure Barkley had a couple of plain cake doughnuts for dinner, and maybe that didn't measure up to a Bucky's Ponderosa steak, but it was close. Jamie kept an eye on her as well.

"I've got some papers to grade," she finally announced before straightening up and limping for the door. "Good luck."

"Like I said," continued Andy as he followed her out, "don't forget the nutmeg. That's what brings people back. Except for the chocolate-covereds…"

15

All sorts of personalities enter the monastery…the cool and the clueless.

—Fr. James Orthmann

The ingredient list already swam around in Jamie's head as he did his best to mix up the first batch of doughnut batter: eggs and sugar, melted butter and buttermilk, soda—was that Pepsi or Coke? Flour and…something else. Whatever. Already he wondered how he was going to act his way out of this one. He'd been hired, sort of, sure, but as soon as they found out he couldn't fry his way out of a potato-chip bag…well, he'd get to that when it happened. For starters, he looked up at the recipe tacked on the wall, noticing that the bottom was ripped off.

No problem. The cookbook on the shelf had a recipe any dummy could read:

Sift the flour, baking powder, and salt together and set aside. Good. He could do that. Sift was just a fancy word for mix, right? *Mix the sugar and shortening together.* Got it. *Add the beaten eggs and mix well.* Beaten. That would be like scrambled eggs, and he'd made that before. Or he'd seen someone make it before, in a buffet line. Okay. *Add the dry ingredients to the sugar mixture.* He could do that, but maybe it would save time if he added the wet ingredients, too. Couldn't hurt. *Heat oil to 315 degrees.* Then just turn it up.

"Hey, hey!" He wasn't quite sure how much to mix. But Andy had said something about eight cups of flour…per batch? That sounded like a good place to start. He sifted, mixed, beat, and poured until it all looked…not as lumpy. Only problem was, it sort of flowed out the top when he tried to pour the entire mixture into the hopper. Did that matter? Probably it would all turn out fine, but when he finally turned on the machine it somehow reminded him of one of the three books he'd actually read in grade school. Something about a boy who has to take care of an automatic doughnut machine that won't stop, and the doughnuts are piling up all over, and then a rich lady loses her diamond ring in the batter, and they think it's baked into one of the doughnuts.

He watched the doughnuts drop into the hot grease, sputtering and sizzling and bobbing, but he still couldn't remember the name of the book. *The Mouse and the Motorcycle*? No. Each newborn doughnut made its way down the grease canal, slowly but surely, getting a tan, until they were flipped over by a wire mesh contraption halfway to their destination. Finally, the first one dropped down to a wire basket on the end.

There! Nothing to it. So what if they were a little lumpy?

"*Homer Price!*" He remembered with a snap of his fingers.

"I don't know who you think you're fooling." The voice behind him made him nearly jump into the dough hopper. Anne Stewart made his heart stop, for more reasons than one.

"Have a doughnut?" He picked up the first one, still hot, and fanned it with his fingers.

"You've never done this before, have you?"

"Sure I have. Back in Nevada. Ah, I guess it's been awhile, but—"

She took the offered doughnut and winced at the first bite, as the badly overloaded blender began to grind and wheeze.

"Salt." She hit the Off switch to prevent further damage. "You poured way too much batter in there, and you forgot the salt besides. A couple other ingredients, too, I think. Did you ever read *Homer Price*?"

"How can you tell?"

Obvious question. She didn't answer, just fetched a ladle and started to remove the mix from the stainless steel hopper. Next, she fitted another blender to the bowl, sprinkled a generous tablespoon of salt into the mess, then nutmeg and a couple of other ingredients before she began to smooth out the lumps with a whisk. Jamie stood dumbly behind her, watching every move, trying to memorize it all for next time.

If there *was* a next time. Right now, he couldn't be sure.

"I feel like an idiot," he finally admitted. She didn't stop blending, didn't look up, didn't tell him he wasn't.

"Sometimes we just need a little help, that's all." She blew a dark strand of hair to the side, away from her cheek. "Just don't leave out any of the ingredients, and make sure you blend it smooth. It takes time to get all the lumps out."

"I'll remember that." Finally he took the whisk from her to continue the blending, and she looked away when his hand brushed hers. "So what do you do for a living? I mean, besides rescuing fools and offering wise advice about lumpy batter?"

"I'm a PE teacher." When she frowned the fire flickered in her eyes. "Or I used to be. Right now I'm teaching English."

"No kidding? I used to hate English."

Smooth move! Insult her right off. She'll love you for that. But Anne didn't seem to mind the foot in his mouth; she even smiled a little.

"I do too, sometimes."

"You mean you don't like what you're teaching?"

She started to open her mouth, then apparently changed her mind and shrugged.

"I'm grateful for the job. They gave me a chance. But you don't even know me, and here I'm giving you the story of my life."

"I wouldn't call telling me about your job the story of your life."

"Yeah, well." She rubbed her palms on her hips and paused to look around the kitchen. "The rest you probably don't want to hear."

"Oh, I don't know…" He whacked at another batter blob and did his best to keep the conversation going. "I don't mind."

But by that time she had already turned to go.

"Wait a minute." He tried to think of something to say. Anything. "Weren't you…looking for something when you came back?"

"It's not important." Color crept into her cheeks. "I…I don't even remember."

He picked up a binder and textbook next to the blender and held it out to her.

"Yeah, that's it," she said, and a hint of a grin returned. "Thank you."

With that, she snatched up the books, turned on her heel, and limped away.

16

I'm never going to be famous.... I don't do anything, not one single thing. I used to bite my nails,
but I don't even do that anymore.

—DOROTHY PARKER

Hey, Mrs. Stewart!" Jamie coasted the two-tone white and sky blue '63
Studebaker Lark to a stop in front of the Do-Nut Barn and stomped
down the emergency brake. One could always hope it would hold. At least
no door locks were necessary in a town like Riverdale, which, in the case
of Jamie's near-classic, was a good thing. Well, after two weeks of his riding the monastery bicycle, Mr. Stewart had given him a good deal on the
car, hadn't he? An employee discount. It just needed a little work. But
Mom would have been proud. Come to think of it, for all he knew maybe
his mother had once owned the car.

"Joe." Mrs. Stewart held out a corner of a doughnut for Barkley, who
was hanging expectantly out the passenger-side window. Though Anne's
mom rarely said much, she did often carry a treat for the dog. "We have
a special order tonight for the Methodist Church. They're doing a
women's breakfast in the morning, and they want four dozen assorted on
hand."

"That all? No problem." Jamie hopped out and scanned the bakery
for any sign of Anne as he hitched up his faded jeans. Okay, so they were
a couple inches too big in the waist, but they looked like what the locals
wore. Probably because the Salvation Army Thrift Store collected from

the locals. Consider it another unique experience, another part of his relocation. Jamie didn't mind the secondhand fit as much as he'd thought he would.

Getting his laundry done, however, was another story—at least at first—since he'd only brought five pairs of socks and underwear with him from L.A. Sure, he could toss them in the wash with the brothers' robes, but if this experiment in anonymity was going to work, he knew he would have to tackle this issue himself.

Hence the Pink Elephant Laundromat, Saturday morning. He had slipped out early that day. Well, early by his clock, not the monks'. By doing so he thought he might avoid the crowds, if there were any.

Yeah, right.

"You need some help, young man." Her name was Velma Cartwright, and her washing machine at home had broken down. In 1968. Since then she'd planted a nice assortment of marigolds and petunias in the washer, and everyone seemed to think they were quite lovely. And though she had since given up hope of the repairman ever showing up, she told him she didn't mind going to the Pink Elephant every week, especially not since her James had gone to be with the Lord.

After all, she said, her grandkids never came to visit anymore. The fact that Ross had moved away to Cleveland with his wife and Vickie had gotten a job in Reno may have had something to do with it.

Jamie looked up from reading the label on the box of Tide, and later he figured out that his puzzled expression must have signaled how much trouble he was in. So she pulled up a folding chair and showed him all about permanent press and colors, cottons, hots and colds, and how long to dry each one. She also told him which dryers were the hottest and which ones gobbled quarters without a second thought.

"Piercey, he doesn't give a rip." Piercey was the owner of the Pink Elephant, along with a dozen modest rental homes scattered around

Riverdale. Last year some kid jammed a wad of gum into one of the coin slots, and you could still see it even though she'd called Piercey to fix it at least five times already. She did clean all the lint from all the dryers though.

"He ought to hire me." When Velma smiled she revealed a considerable gap in her front teeth, just big enough to drive a pickup through. But at least, she pointed out, they were still hers and all hers. Unlike some other women she could mention, who relied on makeup and hairdressers and even things like silicone implants in the most embarrassing places, if you could believe that. She'd heard about those things, anyway. Never met anyone who'd actually…well, you know.

"Me, I never went in for such stuff." She grinned proudly. "It's all Velma. Nothing more, nothing less."

"That's good, Mrs. Cartwright." Jamie measured out a cup of soap the way she had showed him and slammed the lid. "I like that."

Thing was, he actually did. Because somehow the old woman's transparency felt pretty good to be around, after another full phony day of being himself. But which did he prefer? Jamie the phony L.A. superstar or Joe the phony Riverdale nobody?

He wasn't sure which was worse. And he didn't want to think of Nick blowing a gasket trying to find him. He hadn't dared call since that time back at the Mar-Jean Motel, when he'd first told his manager what he was doing. *I'll just be gone for a couple of days.* Now he was having too much fun.

"Sorry, Nick."

"What's that?" Velma leaned over and tilted her ear his direction. "I don't hear so well with all this noise."

Who did? Jamie just hadn't realized how hypnotic the spinning dryers could be. He straightened out and shook his head.

"Nothing."

Nothing, right. His manager would never believe how Jamie spent most of his evenings (making doughnuts), where he slept (in a monastery), where he hung out Saturday mornings (the Pink Elephant), what he drove (a battered '63 Studebaker), or where he ate most of his meals (again, the monastery).

Nick might also never believe that even after two and a half weeks, no one had yet recognized his most famous client. For proof, all Nick would have to do was visit Juno's and check out the vintage jukebox. Jamie had checked it out the first time he'd visited, two weeks earlier. Not too many places still had these kinds of old players, with the lights that changed from blue to yellow to red and green, the bubbles coming up through the colored tubes.

Don't panic, he'd told himself as he scanned the jukebox titles. Plenty of vintage Frank Sinatra, Willie Nelson, and the Eagles. Hits from a few generations ago, like "Blue Eyes Crying in the Rain" and "Hound Dog."

And definitely no Jamie D. Lane.

He wasn't sure if he was disappointed or not. Nick would have collared Juno's manager and demanded to know why the world's leading pop baritone didn't have a place in this two-bit jukebox, or why they didn't have a parade and call it Jamie D. Lane Appreciation Day. Jamie actually had a theory to explain why no one in Riverdale recognized him.

First, the disguise. Okay, so technically it wasn't a disguise, just a bit of a makeover. But obviously that was enough, at least so far. Even people who knew exactly what he looked like with his beard might not expect the clean-shaven version, especially with the darkened, shorter hair and darker eyes. No, he didn't look anything like his last appearance on the cover of *People* magazine. (But come to think of it, he'd better freshen up the hair color around his roots.)

Second, the context. After all, Jamie had hidden so far from his regular turf. Who would be thinking they'd find him in a small town, working the night shift at Andy's Do-Nut Barn? This would be the last place they'd expect to see him. So they didn't.

And third, the small town. One look at the jukebox told him who was still hot around here. *Can you say country?* Face it, he didn't exactly have a big fan base in this place. Maybe if he wore a white cowboy hat and carried a guitar.

So they didn't recognize him. Yet. Jamie smiled and punched "Hotel California," happy that his name wasn't listed anywhere in this music lineup. Well, duh. None of his double-platinum hits (all six of them) had ever been released on vinyl forty-fives either.

17

Can't shake that dream of you and me in some
little town.

—BYE BYE BIRDIE

Good afternoon, Andy's Do-Nut Barn." Jamie balanced the phone on
his shoulder while he found a pencil stub and jotted down the order.
"…and two dozen crème-filled, for the party. Gotcha."

He tried not to laugh out loud at the request.

"No, sorry. I don't think 'Happy Birthday Samantha Joy' would fit on
the doughnuts, even if we could do that sort of thing."

Samantha Joy's mom wasn't giving up though.

"Yes, we have maple bars, but you want me to sing 'Happy Birthday,
Dear Samantha Joy' when I make the delivery? Uh…I'm really sorry, but
that would be cruel and unusual punishment. You don't want a lot of trau-
matized little kids." He laughed. "Believe me, you really don't want me
singing out loud."

She went on, and he finally nodded.

"Okay, then. I'll have them to your house tomorrow morning, Mrs.
Akers. But no singing."

He still chuckled as he hung up the phone. Andy paused from adding
a column in his black book.

"You sure know how to handle those tough customers." The owner
chewed the end of his pencil. "Pretty soon you'll be after my job."

"Not a chance. I already have all the fun. Three days a week afternoon counter, night baker…"

Anne stepped in ahead of the after-school crowd and tossed a stack of music on the counter. She looked at her father as if she had just run over a pet cat on the highway.

"You won't believe what I just volunteered to do."

Andy groaned. "Not again. Anne saves the world."

She opened her mouth to protest while Andy explained.

"My daughter is the all-time sucker for a sob story. You lock this woman away when the Girl Scouts come knocking, or the back room will be full of Thin Mints."

"I think I had Girl Scout mints," said Jamie with a smile. "Once."

"She was like that in school before she left," Andy went on. "Volunteered to do just about everything. Student government, special events… you name it, Anne has volunteered for it."

"What can I say?" She held up her hands. "I hear a story and I just want to help."

"Well, what did you say yes to this time?" Andy picked up the sheet music and wrinkled his nose. "What's this *Bye Bye Birdie*?"

"You know, the musical where the singing idol visits a small town, and—"

"I remember." Andy nodded. "Always thought that was a pretty flimsy show."

Right, thought Jamie. *Singing idol comes to a small town. How realistic is that?*

"Dad! It's not flimsy. You're looking at the new director for this year's Riverdale Christian School musical."

Andy didn't respond right away, just took off his glasses for a better look.

"You sure you know what you're getting into? I mean…a *musical?*"

"What do you mean? I acted in four different plays in high school, or did you forget?"

"I didn't forget. But that was *before*, Anne."

She glanced over at Jamie, who naturally had no idea what her father meant.

"What was I supposed to do?" she snapped. "It's a fundraiser for the Mexico mission trip, which is why we're doing it for the fall semester, rather than this spring."

"That's great, but—"

"And you know Mrs. Walters retired this year, and she said she can't do it anymore."

"Can't or won't?"

"Come on, Dad! She's in her seventies. And no one else would volunteer. So I figured—"

"Can't you talk her into just coming back and playing the piano for you? Just this one time?"

Anne shook her head. "She and her husband are taking their RV to Arizona for the winter. They're leaving a little early this year. I think three weeks from now."

"Well, then. This is going to be interesting, isn't it? Only thing I would say is it doesn't exactly seem like the kind of musical you'd want to do at the Christian school. Aren't some of the songs kind of borderline?"

"They're fine." Anne set her jaw. "We can change anything Mr. Howell doesn't like."

Andy scratched his chin as if trying to think of some other way to talk her out of it.

"Wait a minute. If Mr. and Mrs. Walters are gone, who are you going to get to play piano?"

"Uh…" Anne rubbed her forehead. "I'm sure we can find somebody.

Lots of people play the piano. It couldn't be that hard."

"I don't know…" Her father obviously didn't believe a word of it.

For just a moment, Jamie had a déjà-vu-all-over-again feeling, just like his last moment of insanity, when he'd applied for the bakery job. He felt the same kind of craziness taking over as he watched his hand go up without even asking it to.

"I play a little piano."

They looked at him as if they'd never seen him before in their lives.

"You?" they both echoed. Anne looked at her dad for a little help.

"Well…" Jamie shrugged. Who knew if she'd allow him to volunteer? If nothing else, though, it would give him a better chance to keep an eye on the elusive Anne Stewart. That in itself would be worth it, even if it was just for a few weeks. Who knew what it could lead to? Besides, wasn't this something a normal person would do? A normal person with a normal life?

"Looks like you've got yourself a volunteer," Andy said. "Better than doing it alone, right? I'll give Lance a call if you want. Kind of clear the way, if you know what I mean."

"You don't have to do that, Dad." Anne held up her hand.

"I don't want you to get the wrong idea." Jamie thought he'd give them a way out, just in case. "I wouldn't land any Nashville gigs. I play just enough to be slightly dangerous. And I'd do it the afternoons I didn't have to work, or whatever. I'd be willing to fill in until you find somebody else. That is, if you think it's a good idea."

Apparently they did, or maybe they just didn't have any other crazy helpers. Or maybe—for whatever reason—Anne's dad worried about her taking on the job by herself. The next afternoon Jamie found himself standing in front of a turn-of-the-century brick building. "Riverdale Grammar School" and "1904" had been chiseled in the sandstone Roman arch spanning the entry, a contrast with the newer Riverdale Christian

School sign planted in the leaf-littered front lawn.

Riverdale's public school kids had obviously outgrown the classy but cramped little building, but it seemed to suit the small private school just fine. And it reminded him like so many other places that...

Mom used to come here.

Where else? He turned around slowly on the front steps, imagining, wondering which memories might have been hers, too. A laughing bunch of junior high–aged kids in matching red sweaters came tumbling down the walk, while a mom or a teacher pointed the way to the music room for him.

Ten minutes later he found himself behind a horribly battle-scarred ancient Baldwin piano in the crowded music room, plunking out a tune from the *Bye Bye Birdie* sheet music, trying his best not to hit all the notes exactly the way they were written. No use calling any more attention to himself than he already had. Anne's introduction only made things worse.

"This is Mr. Bradley," she told the group of junior-high and high-school kids. "He's volunteered to help by playing the piano for us."

Thirty-five students had reported to the music room after school to try out for the play. Jamie didn't see the point of auditions, since there had to be at least that many parts to fill. Maybe Anne figured if they cared enough to come to auditions, then they cared enough to do a good job. Jamie wasn't so sure.

Jamie waved at the group as Anne continued. He could sit there and listen to her clear voice all day.

"Mr. Bradley is new to the area. Where did you say you were from, Mr. Bradley?"

"Uh..." Jamie's mind wandered. One of the kids stared at him with a look that seemed to say, *Don't I know you from somewhere?* And suddenly he wondered if coming here to play had been such a good idea after all, Anne or no Anne.

"Mr. Bradley?"

"Oh right! Sorry. Could you repeat the question? I mean, Nevada! I'm from Nevada." What if someone recognized him and blew the whistle? "Yeah, big place. Northern, southern, big city. I'm new around here. I guess you could say that. I'm new. That's right."

Well, that sure made a lot of sense.

"And he's working right now for my father at the Do-Nut Barn. He's an expert with machines." Anne leaned hard on the word *expert*. In fact, she seemed to enjoy putting him under the microscope. And by then he knew he should not have come. One of the kids in the front whispered to her friend before raising her hand to ask a question.

"Mr. Bradley, were you ever on TV? Kelli thinks she's seen you someplace before, like on a commercial."

Jamie groaned inwardly and wondered how to come back with a funny crack.

"Yeah, I did infomercials for Jenny Craig." Best he could do on such short notice. "Used to weigh five hundred pounds. Dropped it all in six weeks."

Everybody giggled, even those who weren't sure he was kidding, but Jamie knew he should have prepared better for this. He smiled and swallowed hard. Nice joke, right? A couple more hands went up.

"Why don't we save our questions for a little later?" Anne said, and Jamie was glad for the rescue. "Right now we need to get on with the auditions so we can get you kids home sometime before dinner. Otherwise your parents are going to start wondering."

Whew. Too many more of those kinds of questions and… Well, he started up the music once again.

Anne parked herself on the edge of a table, tapping her foot in time to the overture while the students stood ready up on a small stage. This would be the musical part of the tryouts, and Jamie plowed through the intro as best he could so they could all get a feel for the music. It took a small town like Riverdale for him to pass himself off as a pianist, even a second-rate one at that. At least the piano lessons he'd always rather hated, the ones his mother had made him take, had finally come in handy.

"That's good, very good." Anne smiled at him as she looked up from her copy of the score. "You're full of surprises, Mr. Bradley. I thought you said you didn't play very well."

"Trust me, I don't." Just to make a point Jamie wandered off on the lively chorus for "Crocodile Rock," the old Elton John pop hit, before he remembered where he was and stopped short.

"Whoops, sorry." He hit a dead spot when one of the ivories stuck in the down position. They seemed to do that a lot with this sorry excuse for a piano, which had surely been worn down and broken when his mom had attended grammar school here. He poked at the key with his little finger and they both laughed. "Is that kind of stuff allowed at a religious school like this?"

"You mean dead notes or Elton John?"

"Who's Elton John?" asked one of the kids. His friend shoved him out of line playfully.

"Come on, Avery. Haven't you ever heard of Elton John? He played for the Trailblazers."

"How's I supposed to know that?" Avery, a tall kid wearing basketball shoes at least three sizes too big, shrugged and held up his hands. He looked at Jamie for the answer, but once again Anne ran interference.

"Don't worry about that." Anne waved her hand at the girl standing in the front of the line as she turned back to Jamie. "And I'm sorry about the old piano. It's the best we have right now, until the school administration or the PTA can come up with more funding. I think music is pretty far down the wish list though. But please go on, er…"

"Stacey." The girl twirled a strand of dark hair around her finger as she balanced first on one foot, then another. Once more she rearranged the music perched on the music stand in front of her.

"Right. Stacey. I knew that. So let's start at, uh, from the top. Where it says, 'Can't shake that dream of you and me in some little town'?"

Stacey took a breath, but Avery in the oversized basketball shoes had something else to say.

"Maybe they should have come to Riverdale." A few other people in the line giggled. "That'd take care of any dreams."

Jamie couldn't help it. He stopped the music and rested his hands on the keyboard. "So what's wrong with Riverdale?"

"Nothing really." Avery stepped out of line. He looked like half the other boys in the school, with his red and white Riverdale Knights sweatshirt and bleach-tipped hair. "It's just there's nothing for kids to do here."

"Nothing?" Anne lifted her eyebrows.

"I mean, no offense, Miss Stewart," the boy went on, "this is a cool play and everything. It's just that unless you count the four lanes at the Center Bowl, there's zip here for kids our age."

"Besides chess club, fishing in the river, biking, track, soccer, baseball, basketball, youth group, 4-H, and..." Anne probably could have gone on.

"Yeah." Avery didn't hear her. "Soon as I graduate, though, I'm outta here. I'm going to the city."

Jamie studied Anne's expression as a couple of the other kids mumbled their "me, too's." They were going to join the army or run off to college or go to beauty school. Anywhere but here. Obviously, the kids had hit some kind of nerve because Anne turned away, and Jamie started up the music to lighten up their moment of melodrama.

"I'm sorry," she told them, straightening. "Let's keep going."

18

You know, I used to live like Robinson Crusoe,
shipwrecked among eight million people. Then
one day I saw a footprint in the sand, and there
you were.

—JACK LEMMON, *The Apartment*

Whatever did I get myself into? Two afternoons later Anne backed up
four measures and launched into the "Bye Bye Birdie" chorus for
the…well, she'd lost count of how many times. But in this number, a
group of screaming girls fawned over Conrad Birdie, the Elvis-like hero of
the story played by Sean Merchant, and Sean was loving every minute of
it. If teaching English was hard enough, though, directing this musical
had to be…

She rubbed her forehead and prayed no one had noticed how she'd
once again lost her place in the score. This was only the second afternoon
of practice! Who was she trying to fool?

He'd noticed. Joe looked up from behind the piano, grinned slightly,
and nodded at her as he started back into the song, right where they were
supposed to be. She had to admit he wasn't the finest piano player she'd
ever met, but he had warned her he wasn't. He knew his way around the
music, but his fingers weren't quite practiced enough to prove it.

He made up for his lack of finesse with a generous dollop of heart,
though. For one thing, the way he grinned and pumped the keys like a

circus organ grinder made her giggle, and the kids besides. In two practices he'd already made friends with nearly all the cast. And he always knew just where to step in, how to rescue her from getting lost, without anyone else noticing. If she had known how to play the piano—which she most certainly did not—she would gladly have switched chairs with him right then and there. *Here, you can direct this crazy musical, okay?*

"Miss Stewart?" Amy Phillips stood waiting for someone to tell her what to do after she had sung her lines. "Did I do okay?"

Anne had no idea as she wrestled her focus back to the now.

"Um…I think that sounded very nice, Amy."

When she glanced over at Joe, though, he gave her a tiny shake of his head, almost imperceptible if she'd not been looking for it.

"But…let's try it one more time just to be sure." She smiled as Joe launched back into the last measure, hitting hard the notes where Amy had gone flat. He showed Amy how to better support her singing voice from the diaphragm, how to avoid nasal tones, how not to scoop through the notes from below.

He's obviously done this singing thing before, Anne thought, though she had no idea where or when. Not that she didn't ask at the close of practice.

"I guess you could say I've always been into music." That's about as specific as he got, though not nearly as artfully dodged as when sweet little Leah Wilson asked him about the condition of his eternal soul a few minutes later.

"How long have I known the Lord?" Joe seemed to turn the question around in his head a time or two before smiling slowly over his keyboard. "For as long as I can remember, I guess."

Well, okay. Leah took that as an answer, though she might have wondered after their new accompanist was asked to open in prayer at the start of practice number three.

★

"Open in prayer? Me?" Joe's eyes widened the same way they had when Leah had asked about his faith the afternoon before. "Uh, sure."

But Anne noticed that he seemed to recover well enough. He might not have been expecting that sort of thing after all. Some folks from the more privately devotional denominations balked at praying aloud in public. He could well have been one of those Lutherans or Methodists who simply wasn't used to the way they talked to the Almighty at Riverdale Christian School, or next door at the Riverdale Community Baptist Church, which sponsored the school and where most of the staff attended. Anne understood though.

He cleared his throat and looked around before shifting uncomfortably on the piano bench and bowing his head. Maybe he was setting his denominational reservations aside, if that's what they really were, during the longer-than-usual pause. Finally he spoke up. "Uh, thank you God for…the rain outside. A little chilly today, and I don't know where that nasty wind keeps coming from, but that's okay. We don't mind, I guess. We're looking for another good practice though. Thanks in advance."

He caught Anne's eye as he looked back up, and with a wink he added a chorded "ah-men" on the piano, almost singing the close to his prayer. Almost, but he seemed to catch himself when music slipped from his mouth and the girl who played *Bye Bye Birdie*'s Kim brushed by his piano.

"You're funny, Mr. Bradley." She shook her head. "But I still think you look like somebody I should know."

"Of course I'm somebody you should know." His cleared his throat for a moment, as if she had said something far more embarrassing. "I'm your volunteer voice coach. Now how about putting some more feeling into that line, 'I'll cry, Birdie!' Okay? We're talking about a rabid, foamingat-the-mouth *groupie* singing this to her absolute favorite singer in the world. Do you know what that's supposed to be like? Do you know the pain this girl is going through?"

"No sir." Kim backed away in confusion as she took up her music to begin.

"Well, I—" he began, but then seemed to change his mind. "I don't either. I mean, neither of us know any famous people, right? But I think we can figure it out. Here…"

And so a moment later he switched back to his coaching and joking, his one-liners and his shtick—all of which seemed to cover something far deeper.

Anne tried her best not to stare, focusing instead on the kids as they sang. But still she couldn't help wondering, *Who is this man, really?*

After practice number four, Jamie thought he had a pretty good idea what it felt like to be an arsonist who lit the fire and then came back to see the building burn. Not that he'd ever had any problem playing with matches. Torching things had never made much sense to him. But the rush of adrenaline that hit him each time he practiced with Anne Stewart and her students told him he was edging closer to the fire, close enough to singe his eyebrows. For Pete's sake, one of the kids told him he looked like someone she should know!

But he knew there was something else, too. Not the heart-thumping feeling of skipping up to the ledge and staring straight past his toes down into the Grand Canyon, of almost being recognized but not quite. No, this was different. He felt it every time Anne looked his way, waiting for him to start the music.

So never mind his less-than-average keyboard skills and all the sour notes (some accidental, some on purpose). Never mind the pathetic piano with half the ivories missing and three dead keys. (This was the best they had?) Something else was happening here, same as it was happening at the Do-Nut Barn and at Our Lady of the Hills. He promised himself that before he left this town, he would find out what it was.

Only if he did find out, then what?

He didn't know how to answer that question either. But he'd grown pretty good at convincing the students he was one of them. Even when Mark Lambert started talking about their Mexico trip, which threw him a little at first. Why would a group of kids like this want to go to Mexico anyway? At first Jamie thought he knew.

"If you go down there, you'll have to check out the Yucatán. There's all the Mayan ruins right there, real educational, and a lot of people say it's got some of the best resort areas on the Gulf Coast."

"That sounds cool, Mr. Bradley, but"—Mark looked around at the others—"I don't think we're going to be staying in any resorts."

"No kidding?" You go to Mexico, you stay at resorts, don't you?

"We're just going to Tijuana."

"You're kidding, right? That's a dump!" Jamie laughed, then wished he hadn't when he noticed the looks on their faces. These kids were serious.

"But that's where we're gonna be working." The smile returned to Mark's pimpled face first. "We're supposed to help build some cool little houses and do VBS with little kids who live in the…dump."

"You're not kidding, are you?" By this time he *knew* they weren't. It would be awhile before he could extract the foot from his mouth, and he would just pretend he knew what VBS stood for. Very Big…Something?

In the meantime, Anne seemed happy to explain to him that this play was all about fund-raising. Nickels and dimes so they could all go sleep in some kind of dorm and work their tails off.

"So tell me the truth." He looked up from his piano at Mark. "You're really looking forward to this?"

"Can't wait!" Mark didn't hesitate for a second.

Jamie was catching on. And he was pretty sure he knew how to answer when Darcy Fellowes asked him between scenes, "What are you reading in your daily devotions, Mr. Bradley?"

That seemed like a pretty personal question, but first of all he had to figure out what daily devotions were and what kind of reading that represented. *USA Today* or superhero comic books probably didn't qualify. Most likely she was talking about the same kind of stuff the guys back at Our Lady of the Hills read at vespers. So the best strategy? Turn the question right back around.

"Well, the brothers and I get up at 3:30 every morning for devotions," he told her, which was partly true, if they'd been talking about his first night at the abbey. And what was that book Brother Aaron had mentioned? "We've been going through a book called…uh…*Practicing God*. What are *you* reading?"

"You mean *The Practice of the Presence of God*?"

"That's it." See how close he'd come? "I knew it had something to do with practicing."

So he survived that line of questioning, thanks to the good brothers at the abbey. The kids would want to know more about that place, too, since none of them had ever set foot on the grounds.

"After all," admitted Amy, "we don't know too many…you know."

That would be *Catholics,* and he'd gathered that much.

"Well, the hills are full of 'em." He tiptoed around the Catholic-Protestant thing, not entirely sure if there were any religious land mines he might step on in the process. "And they eat pretty well. Brother Anthony is a good cook. You ought to come up for a visit sometime."

That brought a nervous laugh from Sean Merchant and a couple others gathered around the piano. Like, sure, they would stop by on their way to the outer planets of the solar system.

"So are you…" Amy barely whispered, and she looked around the room to see what had happened to Miss Stewart. "Are you…*Catholic* too?"

The way she said the C-word convinced Jamie it was not a usual part of the girl's vocabulary. By that time he knew he stood dangerously close to one of those mines.

"Uh, no." That seemed safe enough to say. "I'm not."

"So what *are* you?" asked Sean. These kids were not giving up. Jamie's mind raced to remember one of the denominations represented in the half-dozen churches here in Riverdale.

"I'm a Luth…" he began, "a Luth-bap-terian."

Which got a pretty good laugh until Anne returned with a parent in tow, Barb Miller, whose daughter sang in the chorus.

"All right, everybody!" Anne called. "I know we still have weeks to practice, but Lindsey's mom needs a cast photo for the *Sentinel.* So everyone line up at the edge of the stage, tall people in back, and you, too, Mr. Bradley."

Not a chance. Jamie had headed for the door the moment he noticed Barb Miller pulling a camera from her handbag.

"Tell Miss Stewart to go ahead without me," he mumbled on his way out to one of the guys. "Gotta go to the restroom."

Besides, he told himself, *it's probably bad luck to have your photo before the performance. Isn't it?* He touched the ring hanging around his neck. *Especially this far before the performance.*

"We can wait for—" the boy replied, but Jamie had already slipped out the door. As much as he had enjoyed the view over the edge of the cliff, he knew what would send him tumbling over the edge.

"Excuse me." He bumped shoulders with Mr. Peet, the science teacher, but didn't slow as he trotted down the hallway, slid into the staff restroom next to the main office, and bolted the door behind him. He didn't even bother turning on the lights, just stood in the little room, catching his breath and feeling his heart thumping in his chest.

"This is stupid," he whispered. Outside he could hear the squeaky wheel of Mr. Loving's cleaning cart rolling down the hallway, and he wondered how long it would be before the photographer left, how long he would have to hide.

19

People seldom go to the trouble of scratching the
surface of things to find the inner truth.

—JIMMY STEWART, *The Shop Around the Corner*

Practice going pretty well, Miss Stewart?" Mr. Loving smiled at her as
he pushed his cleaning cart past her room.

Anne glanced up from her score at the twenty-some kids gathered for
after-school rehearsal.

"How are we doing, kids?" she asked.

"Awesome!" they yelled back, and it almost sounded like a *Bye Bye
Birdie* chorus.

But they were right. What was this, the fifth practice? No, sixth. The
end of the second week of their ambitious Monday through Thursday
after-school practice schedule. Anne had no idea how it was all coming
together so well, except for *him*.

Meanwhile, Mr. Loving whistled his way back down the hall, which
only brought a chorus of groans from several of the kids.

"Bad luck to whistle in the theater," explained Ginnie, holding her ears.

"Yeah, but this isn't the theater yet." Josh always had an answer for
everything.

"Who's been telling you these things?" Anne was pretty sure she
already knew.

"Mr. Bradley." Of course Josh would set her straight. "He's got a million of 'em. Did you know that if a black cat walks *toward* you, it's good luck, but if it walks *away* from you, it's bad luck?"

"Really?" Anne shook her head. *Oh, come on.*

"Yeah." Josh went back to studying his script. "Not that anybody believes that kind of stuff around here."

"Right." Anne had to grin. Come to think of it, Joe had mentioned something about a lucky acorn once. She hadn't paid attention, or she'd forgotten…but come to think of it, what had happened to Joe?

"Don't you remember?" Ginnie looked up at her with a puzzled expression. "You sent him off to the cafeteria with Amy and Sean to work on a couple songs."

Right. And maybe it was time to check up on them. So she left her kids for a minute to see how Joe and the others were doing.

Amy and Sean, she reminded herself. Sean had a pretty good voice, which was why she'd chosen him for the lead role, but Joe seemed to think Amy could add a little more emotion.

"Try it one more time." Joe's voice drifted in from the cafeteria. The cheerleading squad must have left for the afternoon. Anne paused behind the double doors in the hallway, listening, as Amy delivered the line about finding out what life is all about.

"You'll need someone who is living just for you," she sang, and it sounded pretty good to Anne.

"Okay, but why don't you try it this way," Joe replied, clinking out a slightly different cadence on the out-of-tune piano in the cafeteria. Amy asked him something Anne couldn't make out, and Anne leaned in closer to hear his response.

"All right." He didn't sound too happy. "I'll sing the line for you, but just this once. I want you to give it your own emotion."

Anne was not prepared for the voice she heard next: clear and vibrant, holding the high note an extra moment, stopping her heart. This was their volunteer piano player? She had to see for herself and slipped into the room to make sure.

Amy and Sean wore the same dropped-jaw expressions.

"I couldn't sing like that in a million years, Mr. Bradley," whispered Amy.

"Are you sure we can't have adults in the show, Miss Stewart?" asked Sean. " 'Cause I nominate Mr. B. He can really sing. Did you hear how he sounded? That was awesome."

She had. And it probably rated a little higher than awesome, but Joe obviously wasn't going to let it get any further.

"Forget about it." He rubbed his eyes and studied his keyboard. "I just wanted to help with that one line. The timing's a little tricky is all."

"Next time maybe we should charge admission to have people come hear you sing," suggested Amy.

Joe only shook his head and pointed to the music in front of him with his left hand before tracing the melody on the piano with his right.

"Not a chance. This is all about you guys, not me. So let's begin from the top of page six. Ready? One, two, three, four…"

How could I be so STUPID? Jamie ground his teeth as Amy stumbled through her solo one more time. He didn't hear a word, only wondered what had possessed him to sing that one line. *I promised myself I would not do that!*

Maybe this was how people fell back into a drug habit. From now on he would keep his mouth shut. Still, it had slipped out, and the kids had reacted the way he was afraid they would. What was it, some kind of weird subconscious need for the spotlight? Now they'd figure it out for sure, and he'd have to leave his experiment in normalcy. He flubbed the note again and stopped in the middle of Amy's line about "That's the way it should be..."

Oh, man. Now it went from bad to worse. The off-tune piano echoed in the room as they all turned to stare at him. And then of course he had to hold up his hands to apologize.

"My fault. I'm sorry." He searched for the words that would tell them *no big deal.* "I guess I'm not feeling so good this afternoon. Do you think you could finish up by yourselves this time?"

"Sure, Joe, but..." Anne didn't finish her sentence.

He stood to go, tried to avoid her piercing brown eyes but couldn't. Now he'd really done it.

"I'm really sorry," he mumbled again before he escaped.

"Dad likes him," Anne explained, and in Riverdale she knew that carried a fair amount of weight. People had been elected mayor on account of those three words. If Andy Stewart recommended someone, you could be sure he had a good reason for it. Sure enough, her father's friend Lance Howell, principal of Riverdale Christian School, nodded behind his bifocals and leaned back in his leather desk chair, listening carefully.

"I just want you to be completely comfortable with the situation," he went on, and Anne knew exactly where he was going with this. She had known when he called her into his office before school the next day. "He's a volunteer, so we treat him as such. You know the policy. And you know we're not required to get an FBI check on someone like that."

"He's never alone with anybody, if that's what you're thinking. I make sure there are always at least two students."

"I'm not thinking anything. I've heard nothing but good reports so far. But what do you really know about him?"

"Just that he's from down south, Nevada somewhere. He's pretty quiet, never talks much about himself, but the kids love him. As far as I can tell, he has some kind of musical background. I suppose Mrs. Phillips was a better pianist, but he knows music, especially voice. You know he works for my dad..."

Mr. Howell nodded as he followed the conversation.

"...and that he rents a room up at the monastery."

"Really?" The school principal came to attention in his chair. "I didn't know that part."

"I don't think he's Catholic, as far as I know."

"That's not a concern. Despite what your father tells me, I'm more concerned about the fact that we really don't know more about this man. But what *is* he?"

"You mean as far as his faith? I'm not quite sure."

"Hmm." Mr. Howell frowned. This might have been easier if the guy had been a card-carrying Baptist or something like that. "I just want you to feel free to tell me if you ever have any misgivings. Any at all."

"None so far. Dad says—"

"I know what your father's said about the man, and I appreciate his judgment. Sorry for interrupting by the way. But we still need to be prudent. It's our job to protect those kids, after all."

Prudent. Of course. She nodded as she got up to leave. And she left out the part about his world-class singing voice, since she didn't know what to do with that fact either.

"Oh, and by the way, Anne."

She stopped.

"I just got a phone call from a parent of one of the kids in the musical."

"A call? You mean... Is there a problem?"

"No, no, not exactly. She just had a concern about some of the words to one of the songs."

"Oh, is that all?" Anne sighed, but she should have seen it coming. "Which song would that be?"

"I'm really not sure. Something about…well…kissing. I think they're concerned it may be a little suggestive for our audience. But I'd like to see the score again. See it for myself. Maybe we can modify the lyrics just a little, without hurting the meaning."

"Right. Maybe we can just have one of the kids blow an air horn every time we get to a word somebody doesn't like. Or we could give people a free pair of earplugs with every ticket, right there at the door."

He laughed.

"Really, Mr. Howell," She said it with a half smile for his benefit. "It's pretty tame."

"That's what I like about you, Anne. Always so diplomatic. Especially now, since…"

He dropped his gaze.

Anne knew what he'd meant to say.

"That's okay. Just call me Ambassador Anne. I'll have one of the kids run you a copy of the score right away."

"Good. Don't forget, if you have any reservations or problems with your volunteer, you be sure and let me know. Anything at all. I told your dad we'd be looking out for you."

"I appreciate it, Mr. Howell." She paused once more on the way out to notice the little orange speck of ladybug crawling about on the sill of the principal's east-facing window. Looking for the last end-of-season warmth, several more had spent their last ladybug hours on this side of the glass. But one of them flittered away from the window to land on the carpet right in front of her. She pulled up quickly.

"Oh," she whispered. "Bad luck to kill a ladybug."

Mr. Howell laughed once more as she sidestepped the bug and walked to the door, while she wondered where she had picked up such a funny little superstition.

She only had to think about it for a moment.

Joe Bradley.

20

If I ever go looking for my heart's desire again,
I won't look any further than my own backyard.

—JUDY GARLAND, *The Wizard of Oz*

Good thing The Dalles was only a short drive down the hill and then west along the Gorge highway. Jamie enjoyed the view as he turned west to follow the winding Gorge Highway, weaving in and out of Portland-bound trucks and a minivanned family stopping to snap scenic photos at a bend in the river. Still pretty pleasant for the first official day of autumn.

Out on the wide ribbon of slate blue Columbia River, a barge headed upstream, followed by its three-story pushboat. Like a tugboat, only in reverse, and tall enough for the driver to see over his load. Even higher, a V-flock of Canada geese banked overhead in the dull gold morning sky, headed south, or wherever it was that Canada geese headed when the morning chill signaled it was time to go. He thought he heard distant honks as they signaled to each other, *Fly on.*

Good thing he didn't have to travel quite as far as the geese; the right front wheel of his Studebaker had started humming and vibrating on the way down the hill to the gorge. That gave his steering wheel the shakes, too, and not just his own hand. He probably should have had another cup of coffee this morning. Or maybe it was just the little bumps at the edge of the twin-lane divider. A guy in the car next to him honked a warning.

"Keep your shirt on." Jamie mumbled out the side of his mouth and glanced to the side without moving his head. The driver of the silver Honda next to him left him in a puff of gray exhaust.

So, yeah, here was his chance to clear his mind and check out the neighborhood. After all, he had plenty of time before he was expected back for his night shift at the Barn. No play practice today either. *Good.* But he wondered what Anne would be doing today, and even more than that, he wondered *why* he wondered.

So he reached over and rolled down the passenger-side window to let the watery scent of the river wash through the car, to help wash away the confused swirl of questions he'd been packing around since he first arrived in Riverdale.

Questions like, How long could he hide in this little town?

Why did the people here matter so much to him all of a sudden?

What would he do if anybody found out what he was doing this morning?

Deny it, probably. And so he practiced a couple of lines to himself: "I have no idea where it came from." Or how about, "I had nothing to do with that."

That should work. If all else failed, claim ignorance. He did know one thing: He was hardly closer to finding answers today than he was the first day he arrived, a few weeks before. And these were bigger questions. Where did I come from? And where do I really belong? They were questions he never even thought to ask before, much less answer. So he drove on, ignoring the gentle but constant shimmy of the wheel. He figured it would hold.

He also figured he would have to be very careful when he walked through the door of Mike's Music & Piano, a small, glass-fronted shop on the outskirts of The Dalles, between a Burger King and mattress outlet warehouse. Sure, he still looked different without his beard and not nearly as recognizable with his hair a darker color. But this wasn't Riverdale. He scooted the sunglasses up on his nose.

Another fifteen minutes brought him to Mike's—"a complete selection for all your performance and school band needs" was what the Yellow Pages ad had told him. Too bad he couldn't have just ordered this thing over the phone. Maybe he should have tried. Well, too late. With a deep breath he stepped out of the car and past the aging oak tree guarding the front of the store.

A jingle bell on the door tinkled as he entered the store, and he made his way through a forest of red and gold electric guitars, while a blue-haired college student behind the counter looked up from her fashion magazine and said something about letting her know if he needed any help. No problem; he could do that, especially since she obviously had no idea who he was. And he started to relax until he stepped up to the six-foot posters in back of the drum set display, part of an old record-label promotion with a half-dozen other performers like Luciano Pavarotti and Vince Gill. He had thought his own poster featured a terrible smirk, but they'd already been printed before he could protest.

And now, apparently, a few small-town music stores still thought it cute to decorate with the "Voices of the Century" collection. *Puh-leez.*

Please don't be here. If he ran into a full-sized cutout of himself on the wall, well, he would be out of there in a heartbeat. His own heartbeat didn't settle down, though, until he'd made sure it was just Luciano and Vince. Good. They didn't have all the rest of the posters. Of course, one never knew.

"Looking for something in particular?" The blue-haired girl had obviously sneaked up on him.

"Oh!" He tried not to look as startled as he felt. Maybe she just thought it was funny, since she didn't apologize.

"Pianos," he finally managed. "I'm looking for a piano."

He wouldn't be able to tell her why, especially since he still wasn't sure himself. And what about price? features? style?

"Yeah," he answered, even if that didn't make sense. After comparing three or four instruments, they all started looking the same. The Baldwin seemed nice, but then so did the Yamaha, only he couldn't tell the difference between the Florentine Light Oak and the Georgian Mahogany. The girl with the blue hair, whose name turned out to be Maya, nearly pressed her nose into the wood, trying to find out for herself.

"They're pretty close, all right," she decided, returning her gum to her mouth. "Guess it depends on which one you like better."

That sounded pretty profound. A quick glance up at Luciano reminded him that it didn't really matter, that he just needed to pay for one of these pianos quick and get out. So he settled on a nice Kawai Model K-18 in high-gloss mahogany, with a modest forty-four-and-a-half-inch rise. Not the largest upright piano on the floor, and not the most expensive, but clearly not the cheapest either.

"This one." He tapped his finger on the top of the piano. "This is the one I want, as long as you can deliver it to Riverdale."

"Whoa." She checked her watch. This customer obviously wasn't wasting any time. "You want some fries with that?"

"No, thanks." He tried his best not to grin, but come to think of it, this had turned out better than he'd thought. "I do need it delivered though."

"This is extremely cool." She scampered over to her counter. "I've never sold anything except drumsticks and sheet music before."

Why did that not surprise him? But he had to stare at the delivery paperwork, trying to decide. Maya leaned across and pointed to the first line.

"Your name goes there," she told him. "See where it says 'Name' right below the line?" She returned to her calculator, and he chewed the end of the pen for a moment before writing "Anne Stewart" in careful block letters, followed by the school's street address. He couldn't remember the number, but that wouldn't matter. "Riverdale Christian School" on Simcoe Way would be just fine. And the grand total, including the $124 delivery and setup fee, would add up to $5,402.11. No sales tax across the river here in Oregon, which was nice.

"Forty-one, forty-two, forty-three…" He quietly counted out hundred-dollar bills while Maya paused, her eyes wide. She didn't take her eyes off the growing pile of cash, not even when the phone rang.

"Mike's Music, where you get the mojo and a whole lot more. This is Maya, can I help you?" All while watching him count: forty-six, forty-seven, forty-eight… She brushed off the call with a quick "Hey, can I call you back? I've got a customer, and I'll tell you about it later."

"Actually," he told her when she hung up, "that's something I need to work out with you."

Fifty-three, fifty-four, fifty-five.

"Whatever you say. But like, you're not some kind of bank robber, are you? 'Cause if you are, you know I'd have to tell the cops no matter how nice you are. Nobody ever pays cash for this kind of thing. And all these hundreds feel like you just printed 'em up."

"No, no, no." Jamie shook his head. "Nothing like that. But this has to be anonymous, understand? It's for the school, but they can't know who it's from."

"Oh, anonymous. Sure. Whatever you say."

"Meaning this is just between you and me, okay?"

She nodded and he leaned into his straight-faced warning.

"So even if somebody from the school calls up asking who paid for this thing"—he shook his head—"I need you to keep this to yourself. That's really important. You understand that?"

"Sure, Mister…uh…" She swallowed hard and glanced down at the paperwork. "Oh, I take it you're not Anne Stewart."

He smiled his yes. "But it's all paid for now, right? So all you do is drop it off, and—"

"And when they ask, I just tell 'em Merry Christmas early, and he wanted it to be a secret?"

"No! Don't even use the word *he*. You say the donor wishes to remain anonymous, period. Something like that. Confidential. You don't describe me or anything like that. And that's all you say. Even to your girlfriend, there."

He pointed to the phone to remind her of what she'd said.

"Wow." She nodded. "I saw something like this on *Law & Order* once. Only it was drug money, right? And the dealer—"

"You don't have to worry that it's anything like that. By the way, though, do you get a commission?"

"You mean like on sales? I wish. Mike is kind of tight like that."

"Right." He nodded as he turned to go. "Well, I appreciate your understanding."

So there. Past the watchful gaze of Luciano Pavarotti, he escaped to the relative safety of the gravel parking lot, where a freshening breeze peeled golden leaves off an oak tree next to the gravel parking lot.

"Gotcha!" He reached out to catch a leaf just before it spiraled to the ground, and he couldn't remember when he had ever been able to do that before. A good sign. But out of the corner of his eye, he noticed Maya had followed him outside.

"Hey, mister!" She skidded to a stop behind him. "You didn't take your change, and you paid a hundred too much!"

"That's your commission." He turned to hand her the leaf. "Did you know that if you catch a falling leaf on the first day of autumn, you won't catch a cold all winter?"

"Really?" she squeaked. "That's cool. I didn't know…"

"My mom always told me that." He turned back toward the car, which he'd parked at the far end of the Burger King lot, just in case. Even at this time of the morning, though, the burger smoke smelled awfully good. Like freedom.

Maybe he would get some fries after all.

21

What kind of place is this? It's beautiful! Pigeons
fly, women fall from the sky! I'm moving here!

—ROBERTO BENIGNI, *Life Is Beautiful*

Funny what kinds of things made the front page in a little town like
Riverdale. Things like that highly anticipated record-breaking pump-
kin raised by a Mrs. Sally Enderson of 407 East Main. Funny how much
poor old Mrs. Enderson's face resembled her squash, wrinkles and all. Or
the fifth-grade poster contest won by Alicia Marschall, daughter of Ron
and Judy Marschall, and it was pretty obvious that Mr. and Mrs. believed
their little prodigy was headed straight for the big time. Just look at the
realistic way their Ally drew those hands, and never mind the six fingers.

Or the late-breaking item right down at the corner of the page. In the
photo Anne Stewart stood stiffly next to a Kawai Model K-18 upright
piano in high-gloss mahogany from Mike's Music & Piano in The Dalles,
right there in its place of honor next to the stage where the horrible old
beater piano used to be, may it rest in peace. Jamie hoped they would find
a good home for the old instrument though. Maybe they could let it go
at the top of the boat launch down at Maryhill State Park and sink it
straight into the deepest part of the Columbia River.

But the photo of Anne looked pretty good, considering the flash in her
face. Jamie made sure no one else in the Do-Nut Barn saw him when he
carefully tore out the article and the picture. He reread the headline: *Santa
Arrives Early: Mystery Donor Delivers New Piano in Time for Musical.*

It hadn't taken a front-page news article for everyone in town to talk about it, though, ever since the piano had been delivered last Monday afternoon in the middle of play practice. Jamie had done his best to pretend he was as shocked as everyone else when the kid came running into the room, yelling about the delivery truck from Mike's Music & Piano. And as he'd watched the piano movers unload the Kawai, another strange thought had occurred to him—strange enough to make him laugh, which fortunately no one noticed.

When can I do this again? he had asked himself, and the thought would not leave him, not even now, two days later.

"I still can't believe that answer to prayer about the piano." Andy came around the corner with the bank bag in hand, ready to close up for the afternoon. It looked a little more plump than usual; maybe because people had been sitting around the bakery all day, jabbering about the piano mystery and buying enough coffee to float Main Street.

Oops. Too late. Andy had seen him with the article, and Jamie felt his cheeks redden a bit. Still, he folded the paper over to hide the hole in the front page before tossing it aside.

An answer to prayer? If they only knew.

"Yeah, it's pretty crazy," Jamie managed.

Well, that was true in more ways than one. But Jamie had practiced what he would say when people brought it up, like "I can't believe it either! Nobody has a clue where the piano really came from?"

He didn't mind hearing all the stories again, didn't mind reading the article in the *Sentinel* over and over. The funny part was, anyone who had discussed the mystery over doughnuts and coffee for the past two days—and that included at least half the population of Riverdale—well, they all had their own theory, their own guess about the identity of the shadowy piano benefactor.

Ideas ranged from the good guess to the bizarre. More than one suspected a rich alumnus, someone who wanted to soothe some kind of sentimental need to give something back to the school. Only problem was, no one could come up with the names of any alumni with any kind of money. Especially since the school had only been founded fifteen years ago.

Thanks for playing, contestants. We have party favors for all you losers.

What about some kind of 'grant? That sounded like a good idea, except the *Sentinel* had quoted principal Lance Howell in its article, saying flat out that no one on his staff had applied for any grants, that he had no knowledge of any such awards. So much for that theory.

Parents and grandparents of the cast members were fairly high up on the suspects list, until you looked a little closer. The Clovises regularly received surplus government cheese to help feed their daycare kids. The Rands nearly lost their wheat farm last year. The Brezinskis rented their little home on Grant Street and shopped at the Salvation Army Thrift Store downtown, just like a lot of other folks. And the list went on. Not one of the families looked to be in any position to drop the kind of cash required for the new piano. Because Barb Miller *had* uncovered at least one fact in her article for this week's *Sentinel:* The mystery buyer had paid in cash. Fresh, crisp hundreds, according to a young clerk at Mike's Music & Piano, who preferred that her name not be used and wouldn't say another word about the entire deal.

The best ideas were variations on the theme that someone in the church had been feeling generous, or they needed a tax write-off, or they'd come into an inheritance and passed it along to the kids. But while a few church folks *might* be able to drop that kind of gift in the offering plate, the puzzlement remained: How could it have been done so quietly? Because at Riverdale Community Baptist Church, even the pew Bibles had inscribed on the front inside cover the names of those who had donated funds for these Scriptures *for the glory of God.*

That according to Andy. He didn't explain how much God might care about the donation of a few pew Bibles to the church, though, compared to a piano for the kids at the school. Which did God like better? Maybe the comparison wasn't fair. God was supposed to have written the Bibles after all. On the other hand, Jamie wondered…well, no offense intended, but wouldn't kids appreciate a Kawai Model K-18 a little more than books?

He wasn't sure of the answer, wasn't sure if lightning would strike him for asking. And once again, he wasn't even sure where the wondering came from. It didn't seem the sort of thing he had ever noodled about before. Then again, he'd thought about a lot of weird things since he arrived in Riverdale.

At least no one had pushed any alien or conspiracy theories. And nobody had reported seeing Elvis buying the piano. Those stories would come soon enough, though, and would probably hatch at the American Legion's bar after dinner.

"I still think it's a former student." Andy tossed the cash bag on a table by the window and turned around the Open sign to Closed. "Somebody we don't know about, maybe from a few years back. Somebody who came through the school, then moved away, and everybody forgot about him."

"Maybe you're right." Jamie had already agreed with a dozen different theories since breakfast, and he was prepared to agree with a dozen more. But no one was more puzzled than he. Obviously not about whodunit. Rather, he had no idea how this had become the single most important thing he had ever done. The Grammy Award and the platinum albums had seemed to fade into the distant past. The sold-out concerts and the appearances on *Barry Rice Live!* too. Never mind all that. Without a doubt, this dumb little anonymous gesture with the piano had leapfrogged to the top of his Top Ten Personal Best list, right up there with Ditching My Agent and Meeting…

Jamie stopped short. For one thing, he hardly knew her. And for another, he had about as much chance as a monk of getting to know her much better in the time he had here. Enough said.

By far, the strangest part of all was knowing that nobody knew who had done this…but it didn't matter. He didn't care, and this was not like him at all. Except that everything seemed to fit into the pleasantly anonymous life he'd discovered here, working in a bakery, sleeping on a brick-hard mattress in a Catholic monastery, pretending he had no idea where the new piano had come from, just like everybody else in the town.

If Nick only knew. Jamie smiled at the thought of his manager, still clueless about this crazy vacation to nowhere, this place that reminded him of his mom, and he knew this was one performance she might have been proud of. In a strange way, it suited him just fine. He looked at his watch and imagined what Nick might be doing. Most likely he had left the office by now, which would be perfect. When Andy left, he picked up the phone and punched in his long-distance code and the office number. Of course, Nick was either away from the phone or out of the office, so he would leave his voice mail.

"Nick, it's me. Sorry I missed you again. I'm not always by a phone. So, anyway, just wanted to let you know I'm doing fine, and I'm going to be a few more days, maybe…well, maybe longer. But I'll keep checking in; I promise. Don't worry about me."

22

Penny Lane is in my ears and in my eyes.

—THE BEATLES

Are you here with Mrs. Abel's school group?" A couple days later, the gray-haired woman just inside the front door of the Crosby House Historical Museum stood by her guest book, ready for Jamie to sign in like everyone else. Not that it mattered, but he sighed with relief to see it wasn't the same woman as before, the one he'd met when he'd visited the museum his first day in town.

"Not exactly." Jamie stepped aside as another gaggle of fifth graders came piling through the front door, shedding the rain much the way a Labrador retriever shakes off after a dip in the pond. Adult chaperons shed their rain slickers and hung them on a pair of coat trees by the door.

He thought about coming back later, but the rest of the schoolkids crammed into the parlor so tightly that turning around soon became nearly impossible. No, he didn't really want to venture out into the drizzle again real soon. Besides, he'd come here for a reason.

"Everyone!" A woman up front signaled with her hand in the air for their attention. To their credit, most of the kids quieted right down while she explained the rules, what they couldn't touch, how to take notes on what they would learn about the history of the Crosby House mansion and Klickitat County. Jamie clutched his own notebook, but for different reasons.

He already knew Riverdale had more than its share of attractive turn-of-the-century homes, especially along Horse Heaven Lane and off the end of Main Street. Several had even been restored pretty nicely, often trimmed in creative shades of blue, pink, and violet, colors the original owners would never have dreamed of. But none matched Crosby House with its audacious twin turrets and grand gingerbread style, a house that compelled anyone driving by to stop in for a look. Dr. Emmett Crosby had seen to that when he built the grand home for his young bride in 1897, and at the time he'd spared little expense in the rich paneling and detail.

"Apparently he wanted to impress his new wife," explained the museum docent, "since she came from one of the better families in Boston and her father seemed publicly skeptical about her moving away to the Wild West. After all, Washington had only just become a state, and Riverdale was pretty much in the middle of nowhere at the time."

Was? Jamie didn't dare say it aloud as their volunteer tour guide went on to explain how the home's proud builder had obviously come out on the winning end of several big land deals in the area. He brought up craftsmen from San Francisco, and at the time it had been the most expensive new home outside Seattle. All to impress his father-in-law? Poor Mrs. Crosby would never live in the home, though. She'd been laid to rest in a Boston graveyard several weeks before she could board the train west.

"That's a shame," Jamie told the woman who had met him at the door. Her name tag read "Aggie Myers, Museum Volunteer." "She would have liked it here."

Aggie seemed to agree, but you could forget about trying to hold a conversation until most of the group had split up and moved on to other rooms, to the kitchen and dining areas, to the library and then upstairs to the bedrooms. He waited for a moment, staring at the big poster of a thermometer mounted on the wall, just above the plastic mayonnaise jar half full of small coins and a handful of one-dollar bills. Just eight thousand more dollars to go to replace the old roof? Okay. But right now they had a quiet moment before the kids came back.

"I'm looking to find out about my…friend's aunt," he blurted out to Aggie. "Kind of a long story, but it's for a family history project."

At least the last part was true. This was about his family history. And it was a project. And wasn't this also the official Klickitat County Historical Museum?

"Your friend's…"

"Aunt. A distant aunt."

"Distant. I see."

Jamie probably shouldn't have added "distant." Even so, Aggie seemed willing to help him.

"She lived here between forty and sixty years ago," he added, "so I don't know if that qualifies as historical. But anything you can dig up would be great."

"Let's see what we can find." The woman smiled at him and adjusted her bifocals. "Though I have to warn you, I've only lived here for the past ten years, so I'm still something of a newcomer and don't know all the local names. But let's start with her name, shall we?"

"Oh, right. Penny Lane. Her name is…was Penny Lane."

"Penny Lane. Her maiden name or her married name?"

"Her only name."

Aggie nodded and motioned for Jamie to follow her into a sort of added-on workroom/library, where floor-to-ceiling shelves were stuffed with family histories, local farm histories, church histories, the history of the rural electrification efforts in the '30s and '40s, a guide to arrowheads discovered at the ancient campsites of the Klickitat Indians…

"Wow." He took in the room. "Looks like if there's any local history around here, you've found it."

"Mm-hmm." She nodded absently as she ran her finger along a shelf.

"Can you tell me anything else about this aunt? Do you know what church her family belonged to? What her father did? Where they came from?"

No, sorry, and no. He heard a plinking noise and looked over at a kettle on the floor in the corner, catching rainwater that dribbled in from the ceiling. This room obviously didn't have another floor above, but no wonder they were trying to raise money for a new roof.

"It's going to take a lot of nickels and dimes to reroof this old place." She shook her head slowly. "Not that we aren't thankful for what comes in. But at the rate we're going, it's going to be another five or ten years."

He glanced up at the ceiling as she went on.

"And every time it rains through like this, there's more damage. But there's nothing else we can do. Now…"

Agnes pulled a book from the shelf, this one the history of the Riverdale Methodist Church.

"Another place you might look is the *Sentinel* office," she told him. "You can look up every issue published since 1910, 'cept for a couple, here and there. Problem is, there's no index, so you have to be persistent to find what you're looking for."

"No index." Jamie could just imagine himself pawing through ceiling-high stacks of old newspapers, trying to find something with his mother's name on it. A story about a school play, or maybe a list of honors students. Who knew? He could be searching for weeks. But if that's what it came down to…

"I-I don't see anything right offhand." She pulled down another book about the history of the valley as a herd of kids tumbled down the stairs. "But I'll tell you what. If you give me a couple of days, I'll look around some more and let you know if I find anything. Penny Lane. I like that name. Can I call you at the bakery?"

The surprise must have leaked out into his expression.

"Did you say…at the bakery?"

"Small town, you know. I've seen you working there."

"Oh, right." He recovered. "I'll bet you know my Social Security number and where I was born, too, right?"

He said it with a smile, but she backed up as if he had bitten her.

"I-I'm sorry," she stammered. "I certainly didn't mean to imply—"

"Whoa." He held up his hands and did his best to backtrack. "Just kidding. Leave me a message at the bakery anytime you want. I appreciate it."

She nodded and stepped over to empty the kettle—just as the thought occurred to Jamie that maybe he had just found his second—what to call it? Victim? Not by any stretch. Cause? That sounded far too righteous. So let the newspaper call it whatever they cared to. He studied another rain bucket, listened to the plinking, thought about his mom trooping around in the drafty old museum house, maybe when she was the same age as the kids here today. And he smiled.

What if?

"Thanks again!" he called out to the back porch where Aggie was emptying her bucket. She returned his wave. Better to wait until later to carry out his plan, though, so no one would suspect.

Later would mean the next night at 11:15, after his evening shift at the bakery and a quick trip to an anonymous bank in The Dalles. The only problem was that the cop in Riverdale's lone patrol car might notice. Jamie kept an eye out for the squad car as he tiptoed up the steps and onto the museum front porch. Good thing no one heard him giggle, and good thing no one knew what he was about to slip into the mail slot in the front door. Eight thousand dollars in hundreds plumped the manila envelope a little more than he'd expected. He paused for a moment in the shadows, wondering why he was doing this, worrying how he might explain it if anybody noticed him slinking around the shadows. He checked the front of the envelope again, just to be sure.

For the roof.

He had labored over the lettering to make it as generic as possible, nothing like his handwriting that anyone would be able to recognize or trace back to him. Is this what it would feel like to write a ransom note? Maybe he should have cut and pasted letters from a *Sentinel* headline. Hmm. That was a thought, but no. Sighing, he stuffed the envelope through the slot and listened to it plop onto the wood floor. With his luck, he'd probably set off a security alarm. No? He pulled back into the shadows as a pickup lumbered by. Funny how good it felt to get rid of money this way. And he couldn't help wondering...

Will it make the paper again?

23

If you do not tell the truth about yourself, you cannot tell it about other people.

—VIRGINIA WOOLF

It figured. The monks of Our Lady of the Hills didn't have time to be reading the local paper, not even if the front page featured a rather large photo of Ms. Aggie Myers at the museum, standing on the front porch with the mayonnaise jar in one hand and a large, rather goofy smile on her face. A hard-to-miss headline, almost as large as the smile, announced: *Angel Revisits Riverdale.*

The story told how someone had slipped a large amount of cash through the museum's front-door mail slot three days before, how the mystery donation was more than enough to pay for the badly needed roof, all that.

And who did Aggie think was the mystery donor?

"We don't know where this incredible gift came from," the museum lady was quoted as saying. "But we want everyone to know how much we appreciate their donations, no matter what size they were. It's everyone's museum, and now we're going to keep it the way it's supposed to be kept."

That sounded fine and good, and Jamie wondered if he had done the right thing at the museum as he trundled another fifty-pound sack of flour from the abbey's storeroom into its bakery kitchen. No worries about his hosts finding out, though; without a newspaper, the brothers had no idea what had happened, or even what was going on in town. Jamie even thought of leaving the paper somewhere, front page up, so they would all read it, but later he changed his mind. He had only the one copy, after all, and what would he do if he lost that one? Besides, they were probably too busy trying to fill all their fruitcake orders, from mixing and baking to wrapping and mailing. They were too busy trying to fix a broken-down mixer, too.

That would be a large commercial mixer, the hub of Our Lady's fruitcake kitchen. It stood about as tall as the men who operated it, with a stainless-steel bowl the size of a washing-machine tub. The faded lime green paint and the funny writing (Hamilton & Sons) made it look sort of like a Model T. And this piece of antique equipment resembled an ordinary kitchen-size mixer about as much as a Bengal tiger resembled a newborn kitten.

Jamie guessed the abbot had tired of taming cats, though. Father Greg wiped the sweat from his brow with the back of his hand and barely looked up from the pile of metal gears and parts that had once been their large industrial mixer. A large bowl of half-mixed dough and sugar had been pushed off to the side, and Jamie slipped the sack of flour off his shoulder to dump it onto the kitchen floor.

"Problems?" he asked, but he already knew the answer from the look on the abbot's grease-streaked face.

"We've had this thing apart too many times to count," explained Father Greg. "It has to be at least as old as I am. But this time I think the motor is totally burned out."

Brother Michael over by the prep tables looked up at his flood of orders, each one on a three-by-five card tacked onto a corkboard mounted over the table. The timing of the mixer's demise could not have been any worse.

"But the Christmas orders!" Brother Michael said. "Can't we buy a new one?"

Father Greg shook his head. "I've already called the restaurant supply in Yakima, but there's nothing in the budget for a new piece of equipment like this until at least three years from now. And even then, I'm not so sure."

"Yeah, but how much could it cost?" Brother Michael still didn't get it. "A thousand? Two?"

"They tell me ten or twelve. Maybe more."

"Thousand?" Brother Michael whistled.

Father Greg nodded. "These industrial mixers are expensive, unless we can get a deal somewhere. Even then. But I'm sure something will work out."

You're sure? Jamie looked at the mess on the floor and on the table. This didn't look as if anything was working out. Father Greg just grinned and wiped his greasy hands on a rag.

"Wait a minute." Jamie rested hands on his hips. "Your main mixer breaks down, and Christmas orders are piling up like crazy. We're out of inventory. You have no money for replacing the equipment. And you say it's all going to work out?"

"It always does."

Jamie stifled a groan. Over the past several weeks, he had come to like Father Greg, really like him. But if he heard any more right now about how God answered prayer...

"Okay, I'll tell you what you're going to say next." Jamie held his finger up in a prediction. "I bet you're going to say that you're going to pray and wait for something to fall out of the sky. Is that it?"

Father Greg grinned once more, as if Jamie had just learned a secret. "You're starting to catch on."

"I was just kidding."

"I'm not. Reminds me of something Clement said, though."

"Somebody you know?"

"Clement of Alexandria, the early church father. Lived in the first century. He had something to say about a lot of things."

"Like broken mixers, I'll bet."

Greg laughed, and though the joke was on him, Jamie almost felt himself laughing along.

"Not exactly. Though he did say something about disciples learning to train themselves to see, hear, speak, and act spiritually." He closed his eyes, as if remembering. "Something along the lines of 'We do not insist that God answer prayers, or bless us, in order to "prove" he is Lord.'"

"Uh-huh."

"I think he called it 'fleshly-minded darkness, and a counterfeit form of our faith.' Something like that."

"In other words, God can give you a new mixer or not, and you don't care."

"Of course I care." The priest tossed another twisted, blackened mixer part into a box. "The point is, we don't need a new mixer to convince us that God is God. He doesn't owe us anything."

For a moment Jamie thought it made perfect sense—but only for a moment. *It's going to work out?* He studied the abbot and the wrecked machine for a moment, shook his head, and retreated before Father Greg could bring up any more first-century wisdom.

This time the decision seemed easier, though, as he made the phone call a couple of days later. He would wait until the brothers were off at prayer. Still, his heart thumped just as loudly as it had when he'd walked into the music store or when he'd dropped the money for the museum's new roof through the mail slot. He looked around the monastery office one more time just to be sure no one was listening in, and then he dialed the number for Johnson's Restaurant Supply Center in Yakima, an hour's drive over Satus Pass.

"I thought you said you had it in stock." He did his best to keep his voice neutral and bland, so there would be less to recognize later. *Don't sweat it.* "Can't you get it here sooner than Friday? I mean, for fifteen grand I was thinking you'd include a little speedy delivery in the deal."

"As I told the other priest, we're talking fourteen thousand, seven ninety-five." The person on the other end of the line corrected him.

Whatever. The way Jamie saw it, even God would have to take notice this time. Especially this time. Considering the mystery gift would go to a bunch of dirt-poor monks, wasn't it worth a few brownie points? And delivery by tomorrow morning would only sweeten the deal. *Are you listening, God?*

Finally, the girl at the other end of the line saw it his way, they'd settled on payment, and she had the story, too.

"When we deliver the new mixer, I just tell 'em we heard what they needed and that Johnson's Restaurant Supply wanted to make a donation to the monastery."

"Perfect." That would help throw off anyone who got too curious. "And when you say that, act as if you let something slip. Like, 'Oh, whoops. I shouldn't have said that.' You know what I mean?"

She giggled and seemed agreeable to the diversion. But even with a red herring in place, the thought occurred to Jamie after he had hung up the phone that his pattern was starting to get a little too obvious.

Coincidence number one: He plays a little music for the Christian school musical, and suddenly a new piano appears.

Coincidence number two: He visits the historical museum, and—*bam!*—the museum suddenly receives enough money for a new roof.

Coincidence number three: He stays at Our Lady of the Hills monastery, and they receive a new commercial mixer to keep their fruitcake operation going.

If the *Sentinel*'s reporter hadn't connected the dots yet, she surely would tomorrow. So the only thing he could think of was to muddy the waters a bit. And come to think of it, that shouldn't be very tough to do. He leafed through the phone book once more, and a new plan began to take shape in his mind.

24

The best thing about the future is that it only comes one day at a time.

—ABRAHAM LINCOLN

Anne checked her list one more time just to make sure. And even though Steve, her physical therapist, had warned her she would probably need to rely on written lists for the rest of her life, well, he had told her plenty of things that hadn't necessarily been so. Like "Don't expect to walk without a cane, Anne."

That had been the first of his predictions she'd proved wrong. Nothing had ever tasted sweeter than when she'd walked down the aisle of the San Francisco rehab clinic—limping, but under her own power.

Or "You'll probably want to think of another kind of job, Anne."

She remembered almost punching him when he'd said that. But changing professions was not even an option. She was a teacher, after all. Although she had considered joining the circus a time or two. "Step right up, ladies and gentlemen, to see the Amazing Anne with the Head Injury! She stumbles! She cries! She immediately forgets why!"

She didn't forget insult number three, however. "Most people will get used to the way you'll speak."

The way you'll speak? Please. Never mind that it had taken her three months to say the words "North Meridian Road" without stumbling over her reluctant tongue, so it was a good thing she didn't live anywhere near that street. And though she'd never told anyone, she'd been privately hor-rified the first time she heard her own voice on a phone answering ma-chine. That had been by accident, twelve months after, and it had only made her attack her speech pathologist's lessons even more fiercely. Poor guy…whatever his name was…had never known what hit him. Anyway, these days the slight tongue-tied feeling only snuck up on her late at night, usually after a long day of work, and most people could easily excuse that sort of thing.

Except her.

No, she would not and could not excuse any of it. She knew exactly who to blame, and she didn't need a list to remember that. But she had left all that anger behind, hadn't she?

Plenty of times. Tearing her list into tiny pieces made her feel a little better.

Not really. She fished the pieces from the wastebasket in the corner of her caboose living room and pieced them back together. In fairness to Josh and the other therapists, they'd told her she would be angry, that it was natural. They'd told her it should diminish over time, fade into the distant past. And she supposed they were partly right. They just hadn't told her how long it would take. Three years? Five years? Ten?

Even worse, they hadn't warned her that the anger would yo-yo right back at her, hot and fast, most times after she'd given it to the Lord and already felt it drain away, the way it was supposed to.

But God, please take it, again, she prayed, still piecing her list puzzle back together. *One more time?*

The best part was that up to now he always had, and once again that fierce bitterness that consumed so many other crash survivors left her, lifted as if by some unseen hand. Only how long, she wondered, before she would reach up in an unguarded moment to snatch it back? She was good at that—had perfected the technique, in fact—and she trembled at the thought that she could resemble one of the walking dead she had met during rehab in San Francisco.

People like Kara, the pretty dark-haired girl who'd lost the use of her left leg and arm, and whose hard, cold stare gave Anne chills. *I will not end up like that*, Anne had promised herself, but she knew she had broken the promise over and over, in small but painful bits and pieces.

Or like Mike, the guy in the wheelchair who talked so much and so bitterly about what he had lost to the drunk driver. As if he was the only person in history to have been robbed? With Mike it was never "Hi, how are you?" but "I'm Mike, and I'm ticked at the whole blankety-blank world."

Oh! When that kind of bitterness splashed over her, she could nearly taste it, and she shuddered at the all-too-familiar bile. Now *bile*—there was a good word. The bitter yellow green stuff that was supposed to stay in the stomach. And it had, before the crash. Now she knew the feeling of that bitterness just behind her tongue, waiting for the right unguarded moment to come flooding back, corroding everything it touched with its pungent, life-draining power.

Once in a while the thought crossed Anne's mind that maybe she, too, could survive on such an acrid diet. And when she actually dreamed for a moment that it could help her blow past the disappointing dead ends of her new life, she remembered Kara and Mike. She remembered the way the nurses at the rehab center walked by them a little more quickly, and that was enough. The cold splash of reality always jerked Anne awake, and sometimes God would gently prod her: *Wake up, silly.*

Of course, she couldn't always be sure if it was God or just her God-trained conscience. But it did seem like something God would say to her. Like bright, living sticky notes from Someone who loved her even more than her daddy, which was saying something.

With time, Daddy had told her week after week, all the times he'd come to visit her in San Francisco. Wasn't what she wanted to hear, exactly, but at least he delivered the message in person. Mother, of course, said she had to stay home and work the bakery. Someone had to. So that left Daddy to remind her of the scriptures she'd memorized as a kid, like the one about God lifting us up in due time. First Peter five something. She might have preferred to hear one of those jolly verses from the prophet Isaiah, like "Be strong, do not fear; your God will come, he will come with vengeance; with divine retribution he will come to save you." She'd discovered that gem leafing around in her pocket Bible one night when she couldn't sleep.

No. Better to camp on the "due time" verse, though she honestly never quite understood what "due" time might be. Not until those little things happened to her, like at dinner the other night.

Since the crash she'd learned to compensate with her left hand, much more so than Dr. Moore or Josh or any other doctor-type had expected. And that worked pretty well, though it seemed a bit awkward sometimes passing the salad or the potatoes at the dinner table. She'd temporarily misplaced much of the coordination she'd once enjoyed—mainly the kind it took to jump rope or water ski or sprint to the finish line at the River-dale 10K race. Things she used to do before. So she would just sit still at dinner, trying not to remind herself.

Except this time she had happened to look down at her leg, and there it was: the little nervous bounce, up and down on her toe, the way she used to be able to do all the time but then couldn't. Up and down and up and down, faster and faster. Such a dumb little thing, but she had also learned since the crash that dumb little things were neither. And she just stared at her bouncing leg, smiling because she couldn't do anything else, wondering if the leg was really attached to her body.

"Look at that!" she shrieked, not wanting to jump up and risk ruin-ing everything, not knowing if it was just a freak thing, or whether she had just reclaimed one more piece in the mixed-up puzzle of her life. Hey, she'd take whatever pieces she could get. Her physical therapists had taught her that much. And her family, who also understood that little pieces were good, gathered around to watch her leg bounce.

So yes, the little sticky notes from God were nice. She just wondered when her dreams would return, when she would not wake up in the morning feeling spent and bored, and only wanting to sleep even more. But dreamless sleep was just another nasty side effect of the crash, and no one could explain it to her. So was constant fatigue.

She couldn't take a nap at school in front of the kids, though, and she couldn't take a nap at the bakery where Joe Bradley could see her. And no, she wasn't sure why it mattered so much about him, though it probably wasn't about him at all.

Yes, it was. But she wouldn't try to figure it out, because it wasn't worth it. Joe Bradley would probably disappear by next week anyway. She may have lost some of her short-term memory, but not her woman's intuition. The way he talked? She had no idea why her father trusted the man. Why…

Why she even worried about it. Guys like that were simply not worth it. So she jockeyed the last piece of her list puzzle into place, and everything lined up: the to-do's, the names, the phone numbers. Everything she needed to live her life today right there on paper, because she certainly could not trust trivial things like "order more napkins from Johnson's Restaurant Supply" to her world-class memory, could she? She yanked the phone receiver from its wall cradle and nearly broke her short fingernail as she jabbed in the number.

"You want to buy something for the monks in Riverdale too?" The young guy on the other end of the line sounded a little too chatty for nine in the morning.

"What's that?" She stopped her finger midway down the list.

"I'm sorry. Nothing!"

Well, whatever it was, it couldn't have been too important.

None of the brothers had ever asked him why he wadded up his dirty clothes in a backpack and hiked all the way down to the Pink Elephant every Saturday morning. He had his part-time job at the Do-Nut Barn, after all, and they knew he filled in for a few different shifts. But even though they had their own washer and dryer on the grounds, no one ever asked. Not Brother Aaron and not even Father Greg.

Maybe they've just never noticed, he figured. But the regulars at the Laundromat noticed, and that was good. In fact, he'd come to realize that being noticed at the Pink Elephant was one of the best things he could do for his act. He lined up three quarters in the washing machine slot, wondering what it would take to hit the jackpot. He reached into his pants pocket and froze.

How many loads of dirty laundry could five thousand dollars buy? Make that five thousand in one-hundred-dollar bills, all in a roll. He removed his hand from the cash and looked over at Velma Cartwright, seated in a plastic lawn chair reading a dog-eared five-year-old copy of *Mademoiselle* magazine. The same one she'd been reading the last time he did his wash.

"Um, can I ask a favor, Velma?" He cleared his throat, and she peeked up past the edge of *Mademoiselle,* her bifocals balanced on the tip of her considerable nose.

"Help yourself." She nodded at a pile of quarters next to her dryer.

"Thanks." He smiled and let out his breath. "I'll pay you back when I get paid next week."

She dismissed him with a wave, but inwardly he smiled even more. After this kind of performance, who would ever guess?

25

You never really understand a person until you
consider things from his point of view, 'til you climb
inside of his skin and walk around in it.

—GREGORY PECK, *To Kill a Mockingbird*

All right, so maybe someone else could have found something on him. Anne
chewed on the end of her pencil, one more thing she had never, ever
done before the crash. For that matter, she had never left socks on the
floor, unwashed coffee mugs in the little sink, or dust bunnies in the corner either. Ask her if it mattered now. But the Internet search? All she had
really learned was how many thousands of men around the world were
named "Joe Bradley."

Joe Bradley the Hall of Fame football player, for instance. Joe Bradley
the mortician. Or Joe Bradley Chevrolet, with the widest selection and the
best prices on SUVs in the greater Atlanta area. She guessed she could
have searched at least a hundred pages of Joe Bradleys if she'd wanted to.

"Joe Bradley, Joe Bradley…" She clicked absently on link after link,
wondering if she might come across a photo of *her* Mr. Bradley. Though
it didn't necessarily have to be documented on the World Wide Web, just
about anybody she knew—anybody under thirty—turned up sooner or
later. The man had to have a past, didn't he?

Joe Bradley Investments. Joe Bradley, Attorney at Law. Joe Bradley…
who played opposite a character named Princess Anne in a black-and-
white classic movie called *Roman Holiday.* Actually, that would be Gregory

Peck playing opposite Audrey Hepburn, but Anne laughed out loud at the discovery when she reached a thumbnail description of the film:

"Hepburn shines in her first role as Princess Anne," she read quietly, "the sheltered royal who escapes her keepers during an official visit to Rome. While she hopes to discover the simpler pleasures of life, she doesn't expect to fall in love with Joe Bradley (Peck), an American reporter with plans to cash in on an exclusive interview with the wayward princess."

That might be worth renting sometime, she told herself while jotting the title down in her notebook. And for a few moments—just a few moments—the thought of tracking down one man's identity on the Internet left her as she clicked through a movie-quotes site, graced by photos of the perky actress sitting on the steps of a Roman cathedral, eating an ice-cream cone. Hepburn's first big movie role, and look what she did! Anne made another note to ask the *real* Joe Bradley if he knew he'd been named for a movie character. Or not. She studied the note a full minute before hastily crossing it all out.

Why would she want to do something silly like that? She tore off the bottom half of the note paper—the part with her scribbling—and winged it toward the small wire wastebasket in the corner. Missed. How long had she been sidetracked? A few moments? Maybe a bit longer. But one more line from the movie caught her eye, a brief exchange between Princess Anne and Joe Bradley.

Anne: I could do some of the things I've always wanted to.

Joe: Like what?

Anne: Oh, you can't imagine. I-I'd do just whatever I liked all day long.

Funny how an old black-and-white movie can hit so close to home, she thought, sketching a quick star next to the movie name on her list. She would drop by Sid's Vids on the way home from class today, see if they had a copy of the film. And if he didn't, she would order it off the Internet, like at Amazon.com or something. But he had a pretty good section of classics, Sid did, at ninety-nine cents for three days. She glanced at her watch to see how much time she had before class.

Class started at—she checked her notebook for Wednesday—9:20. Problem was, her watch told her it was 9:05. Not possible! And here she sat, surfing the Web in her pajamas, Googling photos of Gregory Peck and Audrey Hepburn.

Since Andy had added a few hours to his schedule, Jamie didn't mind the late-morning shift at the Do-Nut Barn so much. It didn't interfere with afternoon play rehearsals. He just had to help the brothers in the fruitcake kitchen for a couple hours early, then drive here with Barkley. And business sometimes picked up when it turned cool or blustery outside. Not always, but sure enough today—with a little freezing rain thrown in besides. As if everybody wanted to get out into the driving wind…just so they could come back into the warm?

Or maybe just to take in the smell in the Do-Nut Barn. Even when the SS1200 doughnut machine wasn't fired up, the just-baked aroma persisted. Jamie liked to watch people when they stepped in out of the cold and the wind rattled the doorbells behind them. They'd pause for just a second as they unbuttoned a grease-stained work jacket or a wind-blasted coat, and lean down to pat the dog. Then their noses would sort of quiver, and you'd see a half smile cross their faces before they hung up their stuff and joined their friends. No one could argue that a new car smelled any better than Andy's Do-Nut Barn.

And anyway, the work wasn't at all hard: lots of pouring coffee, a little bit of serving doughnuts. Mostly the clientele that time of day were gray-haired folks with nothing to do and plenty to talk about. Today's topic would be the ice, which had made an extra-early appearance this year. The

freezing rain had laid down a slippery floor overnight, and it wasn't melting fast enough. Oh, and politics. So working the morning shift helped
Jamie keep up on current events, at least current events from the perspec-
tive of conservative Republican wheat farmers and retired ranchers.

"You seen this week's *Sentinel*?" One of the older guys waved the day-
old newspaper at his buddies as he stuffed another bite of hot, fresh
doughnut into his mouth. Yeah, they'd seen it already. But Charlie Wright
wouldn't let something like that stop him, no sir. He would insist on reading Don McNair's editorial to them, whether they wanted to hear it or
not. How did they know? The bifocals came out of the case in his shirt
pocket, and he perched them on his nose as he swallowed the last of his
doughnut and got to his feet.

"Says here, 'Our phone at the *Sentinel* has been ringing off the hook
since it was learned that an anonymous donor has provided a valuable
piece of kitchen equipment to the monks of Our Lady of the Hills
monastery.'"

Charlie paused and looked out over his spectacles at Jamie. "You're
staying out there, aren't you, kid?"

"That's right." Jamie paused from his coffee-pouring to measure out
a response. "I rent a little cabin."

"So what do they think about it? The new equipment, I mean."

"Oh, they say it's…you know how monks are. Answer to prayer, that
sort of thing."

"Hmm." Apparently satisfied, Charlie adjusted his glasses once more
and returned to his paper, while Jamie's heartbeat slowly returned to normal. From what Jamie had gathered, Charlie used to own the local AM
radio station, KRIV (which, by the way, was running its own special cov-
erage of the Riverdale Angel story). Years ago, of course, but he still owned
the kind of voice that could sell used cars and get people's attention at the
Toastmasters meetings held every Tuesday at noon in the Do-Nut Barn.

So whatever else worked against him—years, for instance, or the polite indifference of his audience—he did his level best to work a home-field advantage.

"You know we all get the paper, Charlie." One of his buddies tried to cut it off, but Charlie wasn't hearing so well these days. Or maybe he just had the floor and didn't care to yield just yet.

"There's more." Charlie was obviously just warming up. "Goes on to say, 'Hazel Lott called the *Sentinel* office to say she found a twenty-dollar bill under one of the cushions of her davenport, while she was vacuuming. She says she vacuums that same piece of furniture almost weekly, and it's never been there before.'"

"Sure, she does!" another of Charlie's friends, Dale something, hooted. Jamie had only heard their first names as they'd been tossed about in greetings. "I sat in that davenport before. Springs poked me in the hind end something fierce. Bet it was my twenty fell out of my pocket."

Another laugh from the others, but Charlie stared Dale down and continued. If he'd been born a few centuries earlier, Jamie decided, this man would have been the town crier, rather than the former president of the Toastmasters.

"Let me just finish: 'Virginia Partlow called in to say her high-school daughter, Jennifer, received an A in chemistry, far beyond what they had been expecting. And she received far more money selling her Subaru wagon than she had hoped.'"

"Yeah, that's a miracle, all right," Dale added. "I seen how that rig burned oil every time she ran it into town."

This time Charlie hardly slowed down at the comments from the peanut gallery, he just kept reading in his stentorian baritone.

"'So the list of minor miracles goes on, each with a different possible explanation, all of them seemingly inspired by the latest exploits of the Riverdale Angel.'"

The Riverdale Angel? This was getting better all the time. Jamie covered his smile with the back of his hand and poured the group refills all around. No decaf here, no sir. That violated their religion in this town.

" 'But what is really going on?' " the grand editorializer's voice rose to the climax. " 'A number of people we've spoken to credit the Lord or simply believe they shouldn't look a gift horse in the mouth. Maybe we shouldn't. But in the absence of a better explanation, we urge caution. For instance, what if the mystery donations are in some way connected with drug money?' "

Jamie nearly choked when he heard that one, but he pasted on a concerned look to match that of his customers.

" 'So while the Riverdale Angel is certainly welcome here, we would like to know more. And to that end, the *Riverdale Sentinel* is offering one hundred dollars to the first person who can supply any credible information leading to the positive identification of our angel.' "

Charlie Wright finally finished his reading and slapped the newspaper against the counter. And despite the hoots and interruptions to the reading, he'd gained a respectable audience.

"A hundred bucks!" he bellowed and held up a finger of warning as Jamie warmed up his mug. "I'll tell you one thing: I'll know if that Riverdale Angel ever crosses my path."

By this time everyone else egged him on. "How would you know, Charlie?"

"Because I can spot an angel a mile away, that's how."

Of course that brought a laugh, and everyone there had to find out what Charlie's angels might look like. Blonde or brunette? How good-looking were they? How about inviting them for doughnuts? And so on. This could get out of hand, given the man's first name.

But the way Charlie said it almost made Jamie believe he was serious. Even if he hadn't been, maybe this angel had danced a step too close to the fire. No use toasting his wings, even if Charlie Wright was just spouting off. And Jamie wasn't so sure he liked wading through this conversation, given the subject.

"Hey!" Suddenly Charlie rose to his feet, grabbed a napkin, and mopped at his knee.

Jamie looked down in horror at the overflowing coffee cup and stopped pouring.

"Oh, wow." He grabbed a dishrag and threw it at the table to stop the spreading flood of coffee. "I'm sorry. I'm really sorry."

No harm done, and the accident only brought more laughs. But in the cleanup flurry that followed, one thing did cross Jamie's mind: At least no one had accused this clumsy waiter of being the Riverdale Angel. But not because he'd designed it this way, not on purpose. Not like the other stuff: living in a simple room at the monastery, doing his wash at the Laundromat, eating pizza at Juno's. Just a regular Joe, right?

Come to think of it, his clumsy shtick fit in perfectly with the rest of his act—the hiding, the pretending, the lying. But how long could he keep living this lie? Another day? week? month? Maybe it didn't matter, since he'd just traded one act for another. Of course, the Jamie D. Lane gig sure paid a lot better than this one. But he didn't mind the work. And he didn't mind when the phone rang behind the counter, giving him a good excuse to run off to answer.

"Come again?"

A guy yelled even louder through the snaps and pops of a bad cell-phone connection.

Something about an accident and a ditch.

26

Well, here's another nice mess you've gotten me into!

—OLIVER HARDY

You sure you don't want me to call for a tow?" Jamie just wanted to make sure, while Barkley snuffled around the accident.

"I already did." Andy grinned at him as he knelt in the slush, passing the rope to Jamie as they secured one end to Jamie's rear bumper. "You're it."

Anne was still in school, and Mrs. Stewart had driven to The Dalles for the morning. That left Jamie and the Studebaker to pull Andy home.

Not that the bakery's delivery van, a ten-year-old Ford, had ever been much to look at. But it ran. Or rather, it had run, until Andy had hit a patch of ice and spun headfirst into the end of a concrete drainage culvert. Now the front end had crumpled in on itself like a poor little pug dog hit by a slammed door. One of the wheels skewered out to the side, fateful evidence of an axle hopelessly bent. Amazing that Andy had walked away from this the way he had. They would have a hard time just towing the wreck the two miles back to town.

"I shoulda known better." Andy stood at the side of the road, hands on his hips. "Had my nose in the rearview mirror when I should have been looking ahead. Kind of like life, right?"

"Life?" Jamie didn't get the connection, not right away.

"You look back too much on all the garbage in your past—and we all have some—and that's when you lose control and crash. But me, I just need to look ahead, focus on the Lord."

Jamie imagined a bearded Jesus like a road marker in the road ahead, but he wasn't sure if that's what Andy meant.

"But once I hit that little patch of black ice," Andy went on, "just couldn't do a blessed thing about it. Couldn't brake, couldn't steer, couldn't do nothing. Ice just took me for a ride."

Jamie nodded and made his freezing fingers pile another knot onto the end of the towline.

"You weren't a Boy Scout, huh?" Andy poked at the pile of knots with his boot toe and grinned. Funny thing to be grinning about, especially after he'd just totaled his vehicle. Jamie shrugged as he straightened and stuffed his hands in his pockets.

"Never mind." Andy wiped his nose on his sleeve. "Just try to ease it out when I tell you."

Which they did—or tried to. Jamie started the car and slowly pressed on the gas. He felt the rope tighten until he thought it might rip off the back end of his old car. Barkley yipped at the commotion. He rocked the car back and forth a couple of times, but his rear wheels only spun and whined.

"A little more!" yelled Andy, and without warning, the truck dislodged and dragged up behind him on the icy road. Which might have been a good thing except for its sad condition. Jamie stepped out gingerly and looked Andy over once more, just to be certain.

"You sure you're okay?" he asked. " 'Cause this van... I hope it's covered."

"Not worth it." Andy shook his head and held the back of his neck. "I dropped the comprehensive last spring."

"Hmm." Jamie didn't know if he could drag it back into town. So much for the van. But Andy? "I think we should stop by the clinic, Andy, maybe let 'em take a look at you."

Andy might have wiggled out of it if Anne hadn't pulled up in her Beetle just then, concern painted across her ashen face.

"Dad!" she cried. "I called the Barn on my break, and they told me. Your van—"

"—is history." He rubbed the back of his neck. "But I'm doing okay. Just a little pain in the neck. So who are we gonna sue?"

"Thanks, Joe." She gave Jamie a look that he'd never seen from her before, one that somehow made it worth it, as they helped Andy into the passenger side of the Studebaker. And one more look at the poor van gave him the idea.

Why not? Andy obviously needed a delivery vehicle to stay in business, while Jamie needed his job at the Do-Nut Barn to stay in Riverdale. And Jamie needed to stay in Riverdale to…

To what, exactly? To discover his roots? To live a quiet new life, out of the spotlight? Or just to see more of Anne Stewart?

Maybe all three, but mostly the Anne part, if he was honest with himself. And as far as his career was concerned—well, it could wait, despite what Nick said. Besides, Jamie had to admit he enjoyed the rush he felt every time he pulled off another big giveaway.

Arranging for the new four-wheel-drive truck was the easy part. The dealer seemed more than willing to go along with the script when Jamie showed him how much cash came with the deal. The hard part? Keeping from busting up when a college-aged guy from the dealership first strolled into the Do-Nut Barn with a clipboard and a set of keys, barely a week after Andy's run-in with the drainage ditch. It was a Saturday morning, three days before it all came out in the paper, when the sleet had turned to slush, but the wind off the gorge still whistled through town.

"Whoa." The kid checked out Andy's neck brace, then jerked a thumb at the rig parked out at the curb. "They told me you had an accident. You sure you're ready to drive that bad boy?"

Andy rubbed his chin and looked up from the cash register. "Come again?"

"The big black Silverado four-by out there." He slid the clipboard across the counter. "Canopy, cruise control, CD player. It's yours, courtesy of Yakima Chevy-Cadillac. You just have to sign these papers."

"Hold a minute." Andy volleyed the clipboard right back. "Nice truck. But I have no idea where you get the idea that I bought it."

"You didn't buy it. You won it. Like I said, it's all yours. No strings."

"Won it?"

By that time the rest of the Barn regulars had gathered around, adding their two cents and more, until no one had any idea what was going on—except that it had been some kind of contest at the county fair. Andy had entered the contest, hadn't he?

"Sure I did." He didn't look so sure. "I think… Well, to tell you the truth, I entered so many drawings, I have no idea. You know how it is at the fair. Vinyl siding. Gutter guards. Super orange cleaners."

"Don't look now, Andy." Ritchie Snediker, one of the regulars, couldn't take his eyes off the shiny new truck. "But I don't think you got yourself a bottle of orange cleaner parked out there."

Jamie could only keep it together for so long; he turned away in a fit of fake coughing. No one noticed, not considering the vehicle parked outside. No one except Anne, who studied Jamie from across the bakery with the kind of curious gaze that chased him out into the street to inspect the prize with the rest of the gang.

Well, he couldn't just ignore it, though of course he'd been the one to pick it off the showroom floor in Yakima. With his smudged white apron still on, he had to mill around the prize with everybody else, oohing and ahhing. Pretty soon Barb Miller from the *Sentinel* arrived with a camera strapped around her neck, flushed in the face as if she had just arrived at the scene of a fire.

Another angel event? Everyone had their own version of the story, complete with where they were sitting in the Barn when they heard the news, how Andy had reacted, and what they thought it all meant. Barb did her best to scribble down everything the Do-Nut Barn gang told her, even when it came from six directions at once. Eventually she recorded Andy's story about the contest he supposedly entered, but it looked as if the truck would join the list that included a new piano for the school, a new roof for the museum, and a new mixer for the monks. Somebody said this had the angel's fingerprints all over it, and Jamie did his best to laugh along with everyone else. He made sure to stay out of the pictures though. Obviously, the last thing he needed was his mug shot in the *Sentinel.*

"Man, I wonder what's next?" Ritchie ran his hand across the smooth-as-glass jet black fender. Barb's flash went off again, and Jamie flinched.

"Yeah, Joe." Anne still had that look on her face, arms crossed and eyebrows raised, as she leaned against the front-door frame and watched everything. "What *is* next?"

Anne wished she knew for certain what she had only suspected when the new truck arrived. Because it all made sense. Or none of it made sense. Take your pick.

She wrote it all up on her whiteboard after class Monday to keep track. At the top on the left: "Reasons Why Not." And on the other side: "Reasons Why." A black line straight down the middle from top to bottom separated the two.

Reasons why not? Obviously broke. Drifter. Clueless. No motive. Drives old car. Does laundry at the Pink Elephant. Asked Dad for advance on paycheck. (Marilyn the bookkeeper had let that one slip.) She could go on, but reason upon reason piled up in the same direction. No one could even begin to suggest that Joe Bradley could have anything to do with all this. None of it made any sense. Not even close.

Reasons why? Mystery gifts started right after he arrived in Riverdale. He knew about need for piano. He knew about need for mixer. He knew about need for truck. All circumstantial, sure. The only "angel" thing that didn't match up to this man was the museum roof, which Walters Roofing was busily at work on right now. But she wondered…what would it hurt?

Her heart jumped when she heard footsteps out in the hall, and she grabbed for an eraser to scrub away all signs of her little investigation.

"You still here?" Sarah Welsh or Walsh, a seventh-grade teacher, poked her head in just as Anne wiped the last evidence clean.

"Just leaving."

And she would be after she made one quick phone call from the teacher's lounge—a none-too-tidy back room littered with forgotten Tupperware and stacks of extra science and math textbooks. Alone for now, she found the slim local directory and located the number.

"Klickitat County Historical Society and Crosby House Museum," answered a pleasant-sounding woman. Anne could hear roofers pounding in the background.

"Oh, hi, Aggie. It's Anne Stewart. Just looking for Joe Bradley. You know the fellow who works for my father? You haven't seen him there at the museum lately, have you?"

She did her best to sound casual, matter-of-fact. A co-worker at her father's bakery.

"Sure, I know who you mean, dear. Only I haven't seen him since he came by a few weeks ago."

"A few weeks ago?" Anne's radar powered up, and she wondered how to ask the next question without sounding too obvious. "You mean, like back when the big donation came in?"

Aggie thought for a moment. "It was the day the fifth graders came through on their annual field trip, so yes, I believe that was the day right before. Is there something—"

Bingo! One more connection.

"No, nothing urgent, Aggie. I'm sure I'll see him at the Barn. I can talk to him then."

"Actually, I'm glad you called. You can tell him I did a little research for him the way he wanted, and found out a little something about his friend's distant aunt that he might be interested in."

"His friend's distant aunt." Anne scribbled a note on the back of a stray napkin. This was getting even better. "Sounds a little odd. She lived around here?"

"Oh yes. Born just over in The Dalles. Went to school here. Let him know I'll make some photocopies for him. Her name was Penny Lane."

"Penny Lane." Anne hung up the phone, more convinced than ever that there was more to their stranger than they knew. She just wasn't sure how much she wanted to find out.

27

I'll get you, my pretty…and your little dog, too!

—MARGARET HAMILTON, *The Wizard of Oz*

isten, Jamie, you are *killing* me! Do you understand what I'm saying? Are you listening?"

Jamie smiled as he held out the phone receiver as far as he could. Maybe he shouldn't have called Nick after all. He wished he hadn't. But he'd promised to check in once in a while, hadn't he? He could still hear his manager screaming through the phone almost as if he were standing next to him.

"Sure, Nick, but I—"

"Is this your way of making some kind of statement, pal? Because if it is, I hear you, okay? You just tell me what you need, and we can work something out. I know we can. You want to renegotiate the agency's percentage?"

"Nothing like that."

"Then what? I don't mind telling you you're acting crazy here, my friend. But I can get you some help. Let me get you some help. What do you say?"

"I don't need any help, Nick. I don't need anything except more time."

"*Time?* How long has it been already? People are seriously starting to wonder, and I'm hitting the panic button. I get at least five media calls a day asking the same question: Where's Jamie? Where's Jamie? What do I tell them? That he's off on some kind of secret assignment for the CIA, that he's changed his identity, that he's living with his wife and three kids in Cleveland now? Come on, kid!"

"We had a little break in the concert schedule. And performers take vacations all the time."

"Not like this. The vacation story only worked for a while. Now we have concerts and recording deadlines staring us in the face."

"We might have to cancel a few."

This time Nick didn't answer right away. Jamie could just imagine the look on the man's face. The shade of purple in his cheeks. When Nick finally responded, his voice shook with emotion.

"Tell me you didn't mean to say what I thought I just heard you say. Tell me."

"Nick, all I mean was—"

"*I know what you meant!* In case you forgot, I've been your agent and manager since you were nobody. Since you were singing backup to all the has-beens who now want what *you* have. And now you're in very real danger of throwing it all away, Jamie. No, correction, you *are* throwing it all away. Will you just listen to me for once in your life?"

"I'm sorry, Nick. I just have to find—"

"What is this, the sixties? You're searching for yourself? So find it already and get back to L.A. Yesterday would be good."

The sixties comment was mainly lost on Jamie, though he got the drift. Still, he couldn't quite explain why he had stayed so long or what had kept him here. The only thing he knew now for certain was that he wasn't going to find whatever he was looking for in Southern California.

"And by the way," Nick added, his voice softening a notch, "Erin keeps asking about you too, you know."

"Oh." Jamie rolled his eyes, glad his agent couldn't see him. "Her."

"Yeah, that's what I thought you'd say. So I'll see you back here right away?"

"I can't promise that, Nick."

Norman Adelstein cradled the phone receiver between his ear and shoulder as Nick droned on. Ah, the life of a private investigator. If this guy wasn't paying him so well…

"Stop panicking, would you?" He stalled for time as he moused through another window on his laptop. "Why don't you ask me for something simple, like your ex-wife's checking-account balance. Or how about her credit report; you want her credit report? *That* I can get for you. Late payments, traffic tickets, I can even get—"

He paused at Nick's lippy response.

"Hey, I know you're not paying me to investigate your ex-wife. All I'm saying is this job is a little more complicated. But I'll do it, okay? I said I'll do it so I'll do it."

That should have settled it. But this guy had way too may questions, too many weird requests.

"How was the phone call? The phone call was good. You kept him on the line as long as you could, just the way I asked you to do. I can't promise you, but I might be able to trace it. Not instantly, but—"

Another pause.

"Wait a minute, Nick. Back up. Rewind. You did *not* just ask me that question, okay? Do I sound like a lawyer to you? Trust me, you do not want to know if any of this is legal or not. 'Cause as far as you're concerned, this is all perfectly legal. If anybody ever wants to know if we discussed it, that's your answer. Got it?"

Nick's voice only raised another couple of notches in response.

"I hear what you're saying, but is it my fault your boy never calls you? I maybe could have done this weeks ago. But the ball was in your—"

Norm frowned. This client was getting downright difficult—and a little bit oddball.

"Hold on. I'm not following. First you told me your boss wants me to find your singer right away. The next time you said hold off a little, the timing's not right. You remember that? So I hold off a little. Now which is it? What do you mean, you never said that? What kind of screwy operation are you?... No wait, you listen to *me!*"

Norman held the receiver away from his ear. Wah-wah-wah-wah...

"Hey. All I'm trying to explain is that it's not my fault. None of this is my fault. If he's not using his credit cards, if he's paying cash or going by a phony name, we're going to have a much harder time tracking him than you told me at first. What I don't understand is why somebody hasn't recognized him out there yet and reported it to the tabloids. I figure he's either out of the country or hiding in a very small town in the middle of Wyoming or something."

He paused while Nick let off a little more steam.

"Listen, I can't help it if your guy is melting down. That's not my problem. All I can tell you is you gotta have a little more patience. You give me just a little more time, and I'll have it for you, I promise. Phone number, address, location of phone booth, cell phone, whatever it is. Yeah, I'll call you by Friday. Take your girlfriend out to dinner. Go see a movie. Don't worry, be happy."

Click. Norman hung up and squeezed the roam phone in his hand like one of those foam stress reducers. Life would be perfect without schizo clients like this guy. But it was time for damage control. And without a twinge of guilt, he immediately punched in the number of the girl at *Entertainment Insider,* the contact he'd cultivated for just such a time, and drummed his fingers on the kitchen counter as the phone at her New York desk rang. His place here in El Segundo was nice enough as homes in El Segundo went. But when he pulled this off, he'd be moving down to a place right on the beach. He already had it picked out.

Imagine, getting paid twice for the same information. What a concept. The only problem was juggling the two, giving them both what they wanted at just the right time.

"Hey, Darlene?" He smiled. "About that celebrity story I promised you…"

Anne rubbed her eyes and sat back in the desk chair. Who said this teaching job was only part time? Could have fooled her—especially on days like today when she wrestled with residuals.

Residuals. Those left-over gremlins from the crash that gleefully came back to haunt her feeble attempt at a so-called life. The gremlins that made off with her memory and gripped her tongue. The gremlins that sat on her eyelids and wouldn't get up. The gremlins that…

"Miss Stewart?" Amy Phillips broke into her daydream. "Do you want me to keep reading?"

Anne tried not to jerk her head awake, but she may not have done such a convincing job of it.

"To the end? Of course, Amy. Your story's excellent, as usual."

Excellent, sure—despite Anne's struggle to stay awake. Safe to say that just about anything Amy wrote turned out excellent. Her first book report on *Jacob Have I Loved* had been head-and-shoulders-above-the-crowd excellent. Her journal entries, excellent, just like her research paper on the life and work of Robert Frost. And now this creative-writing assignment about a day in the life of a Holocaust survivor. Excellent again.

So Amy read on, caught up in the world she had created on her paper.

Her only problem was reading her own labored handwriting, messier than most, probably because her thoughts seemed to sprint ahead of her pen. Although there had seemed an obvious fix for that, Anne had made the mistake early on of asking if Amy would rather do her work on a word processor. Amy had simply shaken her head no, and that had been the end of it.

"Her dad just got laid off at the aluminum mill," Ron Kent had whispered to the bewildered teacher after class that day, as everyone else filed out. "Now they can't even afford cable TV."

Oh. To Ron that must have meant the ultimate in squalor. No Game Boy? Worse yet, no television? How low could you go? Of course, no one in Riverdale needed to worry about making the *Forbes* magazine Top 100 Wealthiest Americans list, not even Ron's family, who ran Bucky's Ponderosa Restaurant and did all right for themselves.

Unfortunately, the same could not be said for the state of technology at Riverdale Christian School in general and Miss Stewart's room in particular. The only computer in her classroom had been used up and donated many years ago, so it had only been able to produce a foul-smelling puff of smoke and a horrible screeching noise the first time they'd tried to boot it up. Joe had laughed when she'd told him that story, which made her try to think of other ways to make him laugh. She'd had a number of chances to do so, since she often found herself at the Do-Nut Barn even after her occasional shift ended.

"You, again?" He had looked up from his dough mixing with a grin, a couple of days later. "I didn't know your dad scheduled you for tonight."

"Not exactly." She pushed past him and pretended to look for something in a catchall drawer. "I was just looking for a…"

She found a Sharpie marker. Yes. That would do.

"That one's dry." He came up beside her, and she could feel the blush rising in her cheeks when he looked into her eyes. Goodness, those eyes! "Here. I think this one works."

Zap!

She jumped and yelped at the static spark when he handed her a marker and their fingertips touched. Of course then she giggled to see him jump too.

"Just electricity." She laughed, but she knew it was that, and more. Now it was his turn to blush. She didn't know he could do that, too. He turned away.

"I'll get back to my dough."

"Thanks." She held up the marker. "I was just going to…decorate the old broken computer monitor in my classroom."

"Oh. Right. You mean like turn it into a fishbowl or a sculpture?"

That seemed like a good idea, so the next morning she painted a smiley face on the old green monitor with the marker, and one of the kids decorated the lifeless plastic hulk with fake cardboard sunglasses and a green clown wig perched on top. They called him Percy PeeCee. Somehow it seemed appropriate.

The school's small computer lab wasn't much better off. The kids complained that the third and fourth graders were always in there doing keyboarding and Math Blaster drills. So much for high tech at Riverdale Christian School. After their fun with Percy, they had more book reports to read.

"Thank you, Jules."

Jules Partlow finished his reading with a flourish, and a couple of the kids applauded quietly. Sara Harris asked if she could open the window because she was going to faint from the heat.

Anne would have opened the door to the hallway as well—if Lance Howell hadn't beaten her to it. The principal poked his head in the door with a look on his face that Anne didn't recognize. A smile curled at his lips, but she could be in big trouble too. Since she couldn't read his expression, she told the class to continue reading on their next book-report book and hurried out to the hall to see what was up.

"Anne." He started to say something, opened his mouth, and then changed his mind with a shake of his head. At least he could chuckle about it, which was probably a good sign.

"Did I do something?" She still couldn't tell. So he pointed down the hallway toward the office and the main entry, where two young men stood with their arms piled high with boxes.

"These gentlemen are from Klicki-Tech Computers, and they're saying it's a delivery for Miss Stewart's classroom."

"Delivery? Delivery of what?"

"Six brand-new laptop computers. Know anything about it?"

Anne's jaw dropped; obviously she didn't. But by that time a couple of kids had slipped to the open door and were buzzing the news back to their classmates. Anne pointed at them to return to their seats.

"There has to be some kind of mix-up." Anne held up her hands in surrender, but she had a feeling this situation was about to spin out of control. "I have no idea what this is all about."

Neither did the two guys from Klicki-Tech, the computer store in The Dalles. But they had their orders and were not about to walk back out the front door without making their delivery.

"If you're Miss Stewart," insisted the older of the two delivery guys, "these are yours."

"No, no, no." Anne could just see it now, the five-figure invoice. "I can tell you for a fact I did *not* order any computers. How would I pay for them? And *six?*"

By that time the entire class had crowded around the door, everyone jockeying for a better view of the drama in the hall. Not to mention all the other classes along this stretch of hallway; curious heads started popping out of several doorways.

"They're Macs," explained the second delivery guy, who up to that point had let his partner do all the talking. "Each one has a seventeen-inch screen, a DVD burner, and a wireless network card built in. So you can use them all over the class—no wires—and still surf the Net, print, or do e-mail. You kids are going to love 'em."

That did it. Ron Kent started whooping when he saw Mr. Howell shrug his shoulders and step aside to let the delivery through. When the rest of the class joined in, the entire town could probably hear them through the open window.

And yes, the computers were all paid for. But no, the Klicki-Tech guys couldn't explain how or who had done the paying. They didn't know, said the first guy with a grin.

"Unless you happen to know any angels," he added.

28

A man has only one escape from his old self: to see
a different self—in the mirror of some woman's
eyes.

—CLARE BOOTHE LUCE

I t's like I'm self-destructing, Barkley."

Barkley seemed like a ready listener as Jamie paced by his mother's
wall plaque at the Haven of Resurrection Cemetery in the late afternoon
gloom. The November days were growing shorter. He kept Barkley on a
tight leash; the cemetery folks probably wouldn't be too thrilled about this
kind of visit, considering the way they kept their lawn. Good thing dusk
nearly hid the two of them from view.

"And I'll tell you something else. This wasn't how it was supposed to
happen."

So how *was* it supposed to happen? *That* he could answer. He could
count it off on three fingers.

First, he was supposed to deliver his mother's ashes to the small town
where she had grown up. Who could argue with that?

Second, he would look around for an afternoon or so, get a feel for
Riverdale, just to satisfy his curiosity. Roots are good. Family ties and all
that.

And third, he would turn right around and get back to his life. Period.
End of story.

Only it wasn't the end of the story. That was the problem. The script didn't say anything about getting emotionally tangled up here. Barkley sat down on the grass and scratched his ear before looking up again as if to say, *Too late, buddy.*

"It's just that she's so different. I mean, different good. Not like the girls Nick always tries to hook me up with."

He unwrapped the little bouquet of red roses he'd picked up at Halcombe's Market, pulled one out, and looked for a place to leave the rest. The thoughtful folks at Haven of Resurrection had built little shelves next to each niche, obviously to accommodate his mother's favorite flowers. He wasn't sure what the checkout lady at Halcombe's thought about his purchase. Maybe she didn't care as much as she had cared about his scooping up all twenty-two copies of the *Entertainment Insider* from the rack at the checkout counter. What else could he do after he noticed a little story about how pop singer Jamie D. Lane had canceled his last three concert dates and had then been sighted in an Acapulco drug rehab center?

"Not quite," he chuckled. "I'm living in a monastery."

At least the horrible photo of him stepping out of a limo on a bad hair day was hardly recognizable. Though the caption said the exclusive photo had been taken this week south of the border, he recognized the setting: three years ago after a grueling concert set in Miami. The one where he'd sung through a sore throat, and Nick had blown his top about a less-than-perfect sound system. The paparazzi had been lurking outside the stage door long after everyone else had given up.

So he was glad to locate a Dumpster for the *Insider*s, followed by an easy "hasta la vista, baby" before chucking them in and slamming the top shut.

"Anyway," he mumbled, making sure his voice didn't carry through the cemetery, "I'm kind of stuck. Nick is having a cow. I'm going to miss a concert tour. My career's fast-forwarding straight down the tubes. And obviously I don't belong here. But…"

But what? The question clung to him like wood smoke to his sweater, wouldn't let go and yet wouldn't let itself be answered. He leaned closer to the columbarium in the dim light from a distant streetlight. But instead of getting the creeps, he could see an almost-clear reflection of his own face. For the first time he could see another question almost reflected in his face, a mirror image of what he'd heard before.

But do I belong back there either?

"Hey, I don't know anymore." He crossed his arms to keep warm and started pacing once more. "The longer I stay, the confusinger it gets."

And then who would answer the question? Somebody like Father Greg might know the answer; maybe Andy. Andy could look straight at anybody who walked into the Barn and make mind-reader pronouncements, like "Jim, you need a good cup of coffee." Or "Hey, Tommy, looks like you've been sneaking a cigarette."

Anne probably got it from her dad: that piercing "I can see right through you" look that was giving Jamie heart problems lately. She'd step into the back room with a look in her eyes that said she knew exactly who the Riverdale Angel was, only she wasn't telling.

And what about this angel thing? Where would his next hit come from? His next rush? The questions told him he was surely addicted. But once more, the shadows of answers only teased him from somewhere beyond his grasp. Maybe he'd buried them in the columbarium wall with his mother's ashes. Like those answers, she would certainly not allow herself to be exhumed. Because she belonged here, even if he didn't.

So he still had no answers. What had he expected? He bent down to pat Barkley, who responded with a *thunk-thunk* of his tail against the niche wall. Finally he turned to go, holding his single rose. His mother would not mind.

"I'll get you a full dozen next time, Mom," he whispered as he hurried back to the car and tossed the flower in the backseat.

"Don't step on the flower," he warned Barkley, and he reached over to keep the dog in the front seat as he hurried across town to the Do-Nut Barn. She might be there; she had been coming in for an extra hour or two on afternoons and evenings after practice. And this time she'd parked her Beetle out front, so that was good.

Problem was, he couldn't just march up and, well, just *ask* her. But he parked his car and slipped inside the Do-Nut Barn all the same.

"So did you hear what's playing downtown?" he blurted out before he even thought of the words.

Anne looked up from wiping down the counter. A young couple in the corner was finishing up their coffee and sandwich, but otherwise the place seemed late-afternoon quiet. Nothing unusual. Andy's cousin Wanda would be showing up in a half-hour to take over the shift she had traded with Jamie.

"Playing?" She repeated his question a little too loudly, and he blinked his eyes in pain. As Nick would say, *You're killing me!*

"The movie." He lowered his voice to a near whisper to avoid the glance of the guy in the corner. "You know, what they're showing at the Capri?"

"You mean…" Clearly puzzled, she scratched her cheek and scrunched her nose as she leaned in to hear him better. "So…what was the question, exactly?"

He didn't think it was quite *that* odd of a question. So he could still "never mind" and bail out. He took a deep breath.

"I was going to go see the movie. At the theater. Tonight. And I was wondering if you wanted to come along. That's all."

He shrugged his shoulders as casually as he could manage and checked out the window to see how Barkley was managing in the car parked out on the curb. The dog was bouncing from backseat to front.

"Of course," he added a disclaimer. "If you're doing something else, that's no problem. I just—"

Another shrug for good measure.

"Friday night." She kept a straight face. "That's my night to stay home in my caboose and grade papers."

"Oh, okay." He nodded quickly and started to back away, but she grabbed him by the sleeve and surprised him with a grin.

"Just kidding! You don't think schoolteachers really do that every night, do you? I'll go. I mean, assuming it's a decent movie and everything. Did you say you knew what's playing?"

"Sure. I mean, no, I didn't say. But it's an old Jim Carrey movie. *The Majesty,* I think."

Again she smiled, and if someone would tell him what he said to make her do that, he would gladly say it again.

"I think you mean *The Majestic.* Hollywood star with amnesia wakes up in a small town, and everybody thinks he's somebody else."

Oh, wow. Now he knew she was just like her dad, as she had turned on her "I know who you are" look, and he wiped the sweat from his forehead with the back of his hand.

"Is that really what it's about?" he squeaked. Couldn't be. He had no idea someone had already made a movie of his life. And a Jim Carrey movie to boot. It wasn't a comedy, was it? Once more Anne's smile saved his life.

"Yeah, sounds a little far out to me, too. I mean, *Bye Bye Birdie* is crazy enough. But come to think of it, there's your big-star-comes-to-a-small-town thing again, right?"

"Guess you're right." He went along with it. "I've seen some episodes of *Lost in Space* that were easier to believe."

"You've seen that old show too?" She checked her watch. "Tell you what. If you're feeling bored tonight, why don't we just go up to the observatory and catch the Mars program. The telescope's always good, and every visitor has to see it at least once. Then if you still need something to do, I'll give you half my papers to grade."

Nothing wrong with that. He'd heard the popular Simcoe Hills Observatory just above Riverdale housed one of the nicest public telescopes in the region. He'd never been up there before. Besides, sitting quietly through an old movie probably wasn't the most sociable thing he could think of.

"Sure," he replied. "I can pick—"

"Meet you up on the hill in an hour?" she asked, and yeah, that sounded fine with him.

Barkley had pretty well disassembled the flower by the time Jamie hurried back to the car. That, and he'd done an exemplary job of slobber-coating the inside of the windows on all sides, port and starboard. He'd even managed to reach the inside of the windshield, quite a stretch for the little dog.

"You're amazing, Barkley." Jamie wedged himself into the driver's seat and picked up what was left of the rose. "All this in less than ten minutes."

The mutt seemed to grin up at him, obviously pleased with himself.

"So if anybody asks, I just tell them the rose was a nutritional supplement for my dog, is that right?"

Barkley answered with a *thunk-thunk* of his tail and a kiss on Jamie's cheek. Ask the dog if he cared. But Jamie didn't have time. He barely had time to make his way back to the monastery's guest cottage, off-load the dog, change his shirt, and grab an apple to eat.

"Why am I *doing* this?" he asked Barkley, who found his place on the floor next to Jamie's modest bed, waiting intently for the apple core. To him the core looked almost as exciting as the end of a bread crust—and that ranked fairly high. But Barkley tore his gaze away and responded with a sharp bark when someone knocked at the door.

"Father Greg!" Jamie pulled the door open when he saw the caller through the window. "Come to collect the rent?"

"No, no. I saw your light. You're leaving again?"

The tall priest nearly had to duck to step inside, and it occurred again to Jamie that Father Greg might have made a name for himself in the NBA.

"Actually, I've still got a few minutes. They're having a Mars show up on the hill, and I thought I'd check out the telescope thing."

The telescope thing. That sounded like a sophisticated way to describe it.

"Oh yes, the observatory. It's so close, sometimes I forget it's there. But I've always enjoyed watching the stars."

"Anne said every visitor is supposed to see it at least…at least once."

The monk smiled and bent down to scratch Barkley behind the ears.

"No complaints about the dog?" asked Jamie.

"Oh no. The brothers have pretty much adopted him, when he's not out with you. Hope you don't mind."

"Not at all."

"Don't know if you'd say that if you knew what they fed him sometimes. He even seems to have developed a taste for fruitcake, though he does spit out the cherries."

"That explains why he hasn't been eating the dog food I bought him."

"Oh, I'm sorry. I'll tell them to stop."

"That's okay. No complaints about me either, I hope?"

"No, no. Not at all. The brothers are all glad you're here—whatever it is you're looking for."

Jamie looked away. *And when I figure out what that is,* he thought, *you'll be the first to know.*

"We want you to feel free to stay as long as you care to. All winter, if that's the way it works out. No one else is using the cabin this time of year."

All winter? It felt odd to even entertain the thought. It snowed here, right? He imagined what the cabin would look like covered in a blanket of white.

"You like it here?" Father Greg's question almost startled him, but Jamie didn't have to ponder his answer.

"More than I thought I would."

More than a phony like him had a right to. And speaking of phonies, he quietly shoved the empty box of dark hair color for men under the chair with the back of his foot. But Father Greg didn't seem to notice.

"I'm glad. Although it's been awhile since we saw you at morning vigils."

"You mean *early* morning vigils."

"You're right about that." Father Greg laughed. "Early for most people. But honestly, you get used to it."

"I've heard." Jamie checked his watch. "As long as you go to bed at 8:30."

"You stay up later?" Father Greg arched an eyebrow and grinned at his guest. Despite what Jamie had always thought, monks had a sense of humor too. And this one dished it out as well as anyone. "Seriously, don't forget you're always welcome to join us."

"Thanks. I think."

"Oh, by the way." The abbot leaned against the doorjamb as he spoke. "We got an interesting telephone call today."

"Yeah?" Jamie supposed just about any phone call sounded interesting in this kind of place. "Your favorite charity call for a donation?"

"Not quite. A newspaper reporter from the Portland *Oregonian* said he wants to do a feature on the Riverdale Angel, and he'd heard about the gift to the abbey."

Jamie hoped his face didn't look as pale as it suddenly felt. "What did you tell him?"

"Nothing I hadn't already told the gal at the *Sentinel.* And really, there's not much to say, is there?"

Jamie shook his head, and Father Greg once again turned to go. "He said he was going to be here for some photos in the morning."

Great, thought Jamie. *Just great.*

Maybe he would give the early morning routine another try. Only not tomorrow. He glanced at his watch again and nearly bit his tongue.

Yikes. Anne would be waiting.

29

Was that cannon fire? Or was it my heart pounding?

—INGRID BERGMAN, *Casablanca*

What did I just say I'd do? Anne asked herself as she finished her shift and waved to Wanda. *Is this a real date?*

Not if they drove separate cars. And at least she'd managed to smooth away the awkward edge of sitting silently for two hours, watching a film she'd seen before, twice.

Good thinking, girl. She congratulated herself on the strategy. But a date? Or in this case, a semidate? It had been a long time. Not since… never mind. She checked the mirror in her small bathroom once more, wondering if the scar on her forehead showed up a little more when it got cold. There. It did.

"Meridian, medidian, maywidian…" She practiced saying that pernicious word, the one that wouldn't quite slip off her tongue the way she or God intended words to slip off tongues. Goodness, she couldn't even say *pernicious* when she was tired. Not that either word would likely come up in conversation this evening. Even so. She dragged a brush through her hair, trying to tame the windblown look. Why had she suggested this? Too late. She checked her watch once more. Fifteen minutes to seven. She'd better leave.

Only trouble was, the gravel road up the side of the hill seemed a little steeper than she remembered it, and her little Volkswagen convertible seemed reluctant to tackle the incline. Though she had every intention of downshifting, her left leg suddenly refused to obey her wishes.

The nervous twitch in her leg reminded her of the pain of physical therapy she'd left behind. The Beetle shuddered to an unglamorous halt and might have rolled off the embankment if she hadn't yanked on the emergency brake.

"Oh no," she groaned. Not good.

Of course, under normal circumstances she would have simply shifted back into neutral, depressed the clutch, and restarted the engine. Under normal circumstances.

This time her leg simply rebelled when she commanded it to move. More than rebelled. This amounted to full-scale mutiny.

"Come on, you lame hunk of flesh." Sometimes name calling did the trick, since it was all in her head anyway. She never quite understood why hitting her head made her limp, or how it affected her left leg sometimes. But she reached out and squeezed the knee, massaged it until the needle pricks of feeling began to return and she could again flex her toes. Whose idea had it been for her to drive a clutch car? Her own, as she recalled. Something about jumping right back into the saddle after you're bucked off, making sure her head injury didn't change her life.

That sounded very good in theory, but by this time she imagined Joe Bradley was standing up at the top of Simcoe Peak, enjoying the view of the town below but wondering what had happened to the odd schoolteacher who said she would meet him there. He'd last half an hour, maybe, and then either take in the program on his own or head back down the hill. The monastery was actually not far off, down at the base of the hill and just a bit to the west.

"I can't believe this." She whacked her knee and lowered her forehead to the steering wheel. Stupid leg. This was not supposed to happen. She should have just said she'd go to the old movie. And she did not hear anyone pull up behind her, only the sharp rapping on the window.

"Yah!" She might have screamed louder but probably could not have. Her first reaction to the dark shape was automatic—to jam the door-lock button down with her elbow and grip her keys in her fist, ready for an attack. Go for the eyes. If he tried to break the glass, she would—

"Are you all right, Anne?" The voice sounded muffled but familiar. "Anne?"

It took her a moment to realize she'd been holding her breath. And it took her a moment longer to realize Joe Bradley was looking in at her, his words disappearing into mist.

"Sorry." She rolled down her window. "You snuck up on me."

"I flashed my lights. You having car trouble?"

"Something like that." She looked at him and wondered how much to say. She also wondered how good a liar she could be, and the thought didn't sit well. "Actually, my knee gave out, and I'm having a little trouble using the clutch. I thought you'd already be up there."

"Running a little late. But I suppose tonight that's a good thing. You want to ride with me?"

So much for her separate cars idea. At least now he had the unvarnished truth. Sort of.

Let's see what he does with it.

She rolled up the window, and he helped her out of the car. Leave it to a guy to notice how messy it looked, with a crumpled bag from the B&W Drive-In and several empty cans of Diet Coke.

"That's my kind of car," he noted with a smile. She wasn't sure if he meant the mess on the passenger side or the Beetle's classic convertible lines. But when she stumbled on the gravel, he grabbed her arm before she fell.

"Your knee, huh?" he asked.

She nodded but did her best to hobble to the idling Studebaker on her own two feet.

"Just every once in a while," she explained, "it takes me by surprise. Kind of like it just falls asleep. It'll be back good as new in a few minutes. Just have to walk it off."

Or not. She held on for the bumpy ride to the top and noticed the Saint Christopher medal dangling from the rearview mirror. The kind with the saint carrying a young Jesus on his back with the words "Saint Christopher Protect Us" around the outside. The way he drove, they might need it.

At least the car smelled nice. Joe's aftershave and some kind of flower. She saw rose petals littering the backseat, as if someone had literally chewed them up and spit them out. Odd. She said nothing.

"Doing better?" he asked when they made it to the top of the hill.

"Tons." Anne got out and did her best not to limp around the observatory campus. Even so, she was reduced to hanging on to Joe's arm. To help compensate, she would give him the two-cent tour.

"The telescope was put together by four amateur astronomers in the early seventies," she told him, "and it's still one of the biggest public telescopes in the country. These four guys had some connection with a college down in Vancouver, but then they formed a foundation, built the big dome and the buildings, and the foundation has been running it here ever since. It's quite the attraction whenever there's an eclipse or a comet or something like that."

There. She hadn't forgotten. In fact, she'd known all that since the ninth grade, when she'd done a report on the place.

"Cool lighting." He pointed at one of the red light bulbs in the stairway leading up to the main telescope platform. The red lighting had been designed to help visitors adjust to the darkness, of course, much like on a submarine at night. "I've never seen this kind of place before."

Anne had never seen Mars so close, either, and they listened as one of the volunteer astronomers gave a short lecture on the planet. He had gathered their group of about twenty visitors around the platform that straddled the huge telescope, under the dome that had been opened to the stars. And while she listened, she wondered how to bring up the subject…without bringing it up.

"Too bad they don't need a new telescope up here," she finally told him as they waited their turn for a peek.

"This one looks pretty nice to me." He didn't take the bait. She would try again.

"I mean, I can just imagine the Riverdale Angel character coming up here, looking around, and then leaving the cash for a new telescope up here in a plain envelope. Isn't that the kind of thing he does?"

"You're assuming it's a he."

"Don't you think?"

He laughed softly, but by then it was their turn at the big telescope.

"Here, let's take a look."

Well, she *thought* he'd said "you first." Or maybe he thought she'd said the same thing. Either way, she yelped at the static spark that jumped between their noses as they both bent down to the eyepiece.

"Whoa!" He jumped too.

"Sorry." She backed away and stepped on the toe of a little boy behind her, then had to apologize again. She felt her face glowing red, but not from the hall lights. Still, she had to admit it had not been the worst shock she'd ever felt. In fact…

"Are you guys going to look or just make out?" The boy behind them crossed his arms.

Joe stood closest, and he chuckled. So after a little bit of "you first, no you first" back-and-forth, he gave in and leaned over the eyepiece.

"Wow." He stared at the planet in silence for a long minute.

"You can see it?"

"And God said, let there be lights in the firmament of the heaven."

"I didn't know you memorized Scripture."

"Not Scripture. That's from a Charlton Heston movie. Saw it when I was little."

She laughed. "And you didn't forget after all these years?"

"Guess I'm just good at memorizing stuff." He finally straightened to give her a look. "I can't fix cars like your dad, and I'm not a very good doughnut chef, but I do have a pretty good memory."

"I'm glad one of us does."

She hadn't meant to say that, hadn't meant to open the door even that small crack. But he kept his hand on her elbow as they climbed down from the platform. For the moment she forgot about her self-imposed research assignment.

"You're not saying you're forgetful, are you?" he asked as they walked slowly back around the dome, back toward the small parking lot. "I always thought you were Miss Day Planner, with that huge appointment book of yours you're always carting around to play practice and stuff."

"I've got you fooled, then. You really have no idea?"

"Am I supposed to?"

"It's just that, well, you don't want to hear my insipid life story."

"Insipid? I doubt it." He paused. "What's that mean anyway?"

"You know, boring? Bland? Lifeless?"

"Oh. You mean it's not better than the movie we skipped? What about all the former boyfriends you had?"

"I'm sure you don't want to hear about *them*."

She had to laugh once more, but in the back of her mind, she knew this wasn't how she'd planned it. Instead of finding out more about him, she rattled on about herself as they leaned against his car, shivering in the cool night air. But it didn't matter. She told him about San Francisco and her life before (minus the boyfriends). About the crash. About rehabilitation. About returning home to Riverdale. Her family and her church. In between, he would nod and ask little questions, like "How did you like living there?" or "Did that hurt as much as it sounds like it hurt?"

"Now I'm whining and complaining," she told him, and she traced a figure eight on the Studebaker's windshield with her finger in the gathering dew. The wind had finally died down that afternoon, leaving in its place a crisp November chill and the nose-tickling aroma of fallen oak leaves. "That's the last thing I wanted to do."

"You're not whining and complaining. You're just being honest. I never knew many honest people before I came here."

Then what about you? she wanted to ask, but the sharpened words stuck painfully in her throat. She only managed something innocuous about the play, and they bantered on about how rehearsals were going, how the props were coming together...all the small talk she'd wanted to avoid. Finally she managed to change course, offering him a softball question he should have had no trouble fielding.

"So tell me about you." She swallowed hard. "You didn't grow up in Washington, did you?"

They watched Riverdale's lights twinkle below them as he told her about what he called the armpit of Southern California and the traffic and all the things he didn't miss and how Nevada was better, but the cities there weren't as nice as here. He had wanted to be a veterinarian once, he said. Liked animals and kids. Never went to college. Used to like taking long walks. *Used to.* But he talked in the past tense, as if from a long time ago, like a childhood memory, like "when I was a kid in Southern California, we..."

"I never made it to Southern California," she said, hugging her shoulders, when he ended his story. Even with the wind gone, she began to feel chilled. "Always too busy when I lived in San Francisco. But I'll bet you didn't know I'm now the third generation of my family to live right here in Riverdale."

"No kidding?" He brightened up. "My mother…"

But he must have changed his mind, and even in the dark she could make out the way he bit his lip. Instead, he ran his hand over his short hair and walked around to open her door. Still the mystery, but a gentleman anyway.

"Your mother?" She risked another try.

"My mother hated big cities. She always wanted to get back to…the town she came from. Always talked about it."

"Must have been a nice place."

"Yeah, I think so."

Anne looked up at the expanse of stars, took a deep breath of the oak woods, and recognized the wounded tone of his voice. Whatever else he had told her that evening, *this* she understood.

"Did she ever?"

"No. I mean…in a way she did. Eventually."

Well that sounded a little mystical. But he didn't explain further, and she didn't ask him to. He just started up the Studebaker, ran the brittle windshield wipers a few times to clear the dew, and started back down the hill toward her car.

"Sorry if I kept you from grading those papers tonight," he mumbled.

"I'm not."

30

What do you do for noise around here?

—KIRK DOUGLAS, *The Big Carnival*

Saturdays, one to five, was Jamie's shift at the cash register, and that was fine. Even better if Anne showed up to help, which she did sometimes.

"I'll get those tables today," she told him. Was it his imagination or did he see something else behind that smile today? He rocked on his heels at the cash register, wondering, when a stranger strolled in.

Stocky and sandy-haired, the man didn't exactly look like Clark Kent. No glasses either. But he told the world who he was from the way he studied everything around him.

The reporter.

He took a seat by the window and pulled out a pocket notebook. And since Anne was busy with two other tables, Jamie had to bring the man a lunch menu.

"Coffee?"

The visitor nodded, upended his mug, and stared at Jamie when he glanced up.

"Sure. And a turkey sandwich on whole wheat, hold the mayo. And sprouts. You have sprouts?"

"Sorry. Just lettuce."

"Oh. Lettuce is fine." He held out the menu without looking at it, just kept staring at Jamie.

"Anything else?" Sweat rolled down Jamie's forehead now. Worse yet, this guy wasn't letting go of the menu until he got an answer he wanted.

"No, but tell me. You look just like someone I know, only I can't quite place it. Did you ever live in Portland?"

"No. Never have. Common face, maybe."

"Maybe. But..."

Jamie finally retrieved the menu but could tell the visitor wasn't quite satisfied, even after the coffee was served.

"So you know anything about this angel stuff?" He consulted his notebook. "A piano. A roof. A pricey industrial mixer for a bunch of monks. Sounds kind of random—all these big-ticket items just appear out of nowhere, and nobody knows a thing about it."

"Only what we read in the paper." Jamie tried to retreat, but the man wasn't done going down his checklist.

"The lady at the museum says she has no idea. The monks I still have to talk to in person, but this...Father Greg wasn't much help over the phone. And then there's a teacher who's supposed to know about the piano. They tell me she works once in a while here in her family's bakery. Do I have the right place? Anne"—he checked his notes once more—"Anne Stewart?"

She heard her name and looked over her shoulder, while he sort of waved his notebook at her.

"Tom Christy from the *Oregonian*. Mind if I ask you a couple questions? Maybe when you have a free minute..."

The door jingled when a couple more regulars pushed inside, tracking in the autumn rain with them.

"Maybe when it settles down a little, Mr. Christy?" She smiled and nodded before turning back to her table. Obviously the lunch crowd was on its way in.

"You'd think in a small town like this, people would know what's going on," the reporter went on. "But everybody I talk to so far is consistently clueless."

Okay by me. Jamie shrugged and hurried to the back room behind the kitchen, his heart racing. He hadn't been this close to the edge before, and he rested his forehead in his hand, trying to think straight. What now? Go out again and pretend he knew nothing?

"Joe!" Anne bumped backward through the door and nearly dropped her armload of dirty dishes. "Are you all right?"

"Sure!" Of course he tried to straighten out, but too late. "I'm just…"

Just hyperventilating at the thought that if he went out there, the reporter would figure him out, remember the face, yell "*I know who you are!* You're Jamie D. Lane, the famous singer!" He could have used another shot of antiperspirant. Anne set down her load of dishes and looked at him more closely.

"Actually, would you do me a big favor, Anne? That guy at the window table has a turkey sandwich with lettuce coming, hold the mayo. I've got to go home."

"Right now?"

"I'm really sorry." She paused a second, studying his face.

"No, don't be sorry. You don't look so good. I'll take care of it."

Jamie knew she would. Andy's Do-Nut Barn wasn't that big of a place after all. Problem was, Jamie's sudden departure might make the reporter more curious than ever. On the other hand, that could be better than giving him another chance to study Jamie's face.

"Thanks, Anne. You have no idea how much I appreciate this."

Jamie stripped off his apron and started for the alley door.

"Joe!" Anne called after him. "Isn't your car out front?"

Well, yes, though employees were encouraged not to park there.

"I don't want to stumble out there, you know, green in the face." There. That sounded reasonable, sort of. "I'll just slip out here and back around the block. See you at practice Monday?"

Practice, right. He surprised himself that he remembered to mention it. Anne, on the other hand, gave him that haunting "I know who you are" look once more.

"Sure," she replied. "But one more thing, Joe."

He stopped at the back door.

"I'm not going to tell the reporter anything about…" She paused. "Well, I won't tell him anything. I just want you to know that."

What does that *mean?* He was afraid he knew. But right now…

"Thanks," he whispered as he pushed outside without another word.

Anne knew she should not have mentioned that last part to him, about not telling the reporter anything. How did she expect him to deal with that? If he *was* the Riverdale Angel, the way she now thought he might be—well, was she doing the right thing to shelter him? Who was he really? The whole thing was just too weird, and this reporter a little too persistent.

"Good coffee." He raised his mug. His fifth cup. She offered to refill it once again, but this time he waved her off. "No more. Don't want to float away."

She nodded and wished for an excuse to leave for the day, before he could ask a lot of pointed questions. But obviously that's what he'd come for, and the next time she breezed past his table, he held his notebook ready.

"So." He caught her eye. "You're the teacher I've been looking for?"

"I don't know, Mr.…"

"Christy." He tilted his head in a question. "Tom Christy. Remember?"

She nodded but didn't sit down, even if he was the only customer in the bakery by now. He shrugged as if to say "suit yourself" and ran a finger down a page of notes.

"You're the teacher at the school that received the mystery...I mean, the anonymous piano donation?"

She nodded again.

"So honestly, any idea where the piano came from?"

He had to know the answer already, but she went ahead and told him about the music store in The Dalles, about what the store people had told her, all the details she'd already told Barb Miller at the *Sentinel*. Nothing new there. He could have read it all in the paper.

"Just need to hear it for myself," he explained. "You understand."

Okay. But then he wanted to know what people around town were saying about it—oh, and about the laptops, too. So she felt obliged to tell him about the Bill Gates theory, the old-Marylou-Baxter-has-been-keeping-it-in-her-sock-all-these-years theory, and the rich-oil-sheik-who-passed-through-town-and-had-a-flat-tire-so-someone-helped-him theory. He laughed as he scribbled his notes.

"And what about you?" He finally paused, chewing on the end of his pen. "Who do you say this guy is?"

"You're assuming it's a man. But I really don't know for sure."

"Oh, come on. You're probably closer to this thing than most anybody in town. You're the one who got the piano, remember? There had to be a reason for that."

"It wasn't me," she corrected him, edging away from the table. Wasn't he finished yet? "It was no secret that the school badly needed a new piano. He—or she—would have had no problem finding that out."

"Hmm." He frowned, obviously not pleased with her answer. If he was looking for a smoking gun in this mystery, she hadn't done much to point the way. By then he had realized as much and stood to go.

"Next stop..." He consulted his ever-present notebook. "Our Lady of the Hills monastery. We'll see if the monks up there have more to say in person than they did on the phone. Hopefully they're not one of those groups that can't talk, eh?"

For a moment she glanced at the wall phone, wondering if Jamie had retreated to his cottage, wondering what she might say if she called. *Watch out, he's on his way!*

Obviously not, and what a silly idea besides. Not that she cared, but at least Tom Christy left a respectable tip. She frowned at the money. And as soon as he left, she scooped it up and quickly tossed it into the Kiwanis donation cup on the counter.

"You haven't seen that film, either?" Jamie pulled Barkley past another sniff along the gravel trail lined with wild bush roses the brothers had planted. Three or ten miles further, depending on whom you asked, the trail snaked up through the hills to the observatory. Maybe he'd try that hike sometime, maybe on a day when the sun bothered to make more of an appearance. Right now he just wanted to be where the reporter wasn't. Anywhere away, though he had no plans to explain that to anyone. Because if the guy from back in the Do-Nut Barn had already sought out Anne, obviously he would be looking for Father Greg, too. Isn't that what he'd said?

"Nope." Brother Aaron kept his hands in his pockets, too, though his pockets seemed quite a bit deeper. Also his hood, which Jamie sort of envied on a dark afternoon like this. "You notice we don't have a movie player here at the monastery. Or a television for that matter."

"I noticed." Jamie sighed. "Boy, have I noticed."

"You haven't missed it, have you?"

Honestly? Jamie had to think about that one. He'd never had much time to watch daytime televison, between recordings and performances, back in the real world. Even if he'd wanted to. But once in a while, he told

Aaron, he would turn on the television to watch old black-and-white movies until three in the morning. Stuff like John Wayne and Jimmy Stewart, *The Maltese Falcon* and *High Noon*.

Aaron understood that. "But do you miss it?"

"I don't know." Jamie sighed. "But anyway, Harrison Ford plays this police detective, right? Book, that's his name. Book. He finds this little Amish kid who witnesses a murder in a bus station, but it turns out there's a crooked cop involved and so the kid is in danger, too. You following so far?"

"So far. I think."

"Good. So Book has to hide out in Amishland, right? I mean, it's way out in the middle of nowhere, like the Pennsylvania countryside or something."

"I've been there."

"Yeah, kind of like around here, only different scenery. Anyway, that's the great part of this film. This street-smart city cop tries to fit in with these simple, religious country folks."

Aaron nodded, as in "go on."

So Jamie did. "There's this classic scene where he helps with a barn raising—all these Amish people, the guys swinging hammers, and the women serving up tables and tables of food—and for a minute you think, hey, maybe there's a place for him here. Maybe there's a chance. He even falls in love with this Amish girl while he's being chased. Kelly McGillis plays her. And then in the end—"

"Hold it, wait a minute," Aaron interrupted. "Don't tell me the ending."

"What do you mean, don't tell you the ending?" Jamie nearly bit his tongue. "You're not actually going to see this film, are you?"

"No." Aaron shook his head and picked up the pace, back toward the monastery. "No, I'm not. It sounds like a nice story. I just don't want you to spoil it for me."

Jamie stood there in the gathering darkness, watching the monk disappear down the walk with the dog.

"I'll make up the ending myself," Brother Aaron called over his shoulder.

Anne reached for another tissue and hated herself for it. Tomorrow in church someone would probably come up to her and ask if she was all right, on account of her poor puffy eyes. And yes, she was. Fine, thanks. It's just that the ending had been so sad, and that made her cry like a baby, and that's what made her eyes all puffy. Especially since it was past midnight now, and she had to get up by 7:30. They would ask, though, because she never used to cry BC (Before Crash), and most of them still weren't used to the Anne Stewart she'd become. They still thought she had to be the Anne Stewart they knew in high school—the Anne Stewart who ran track or the Anne Stewart who'd been voted "Most Likely to Succeed."

Maybe they should have settled for "Most Likely to Survive." But enough of that. Because Audrey Hepburn—well, she looked so…regal. And that look she gave Gregory Peck from across the room. The way he walked out of the palace with just the memory of their love, and… Goodness. What a film.

Only one thing bothered her, though, and it made her wonder: What was the story behind that name? The name of Gregory Peck's character, and the name of Riverdale's odd visitor.

Joe Bradley.

31

It's par for the course, trying to fool the people, but it's downright dangerous when you start fooling yourself.

—LEE TRACY, *The Best Man*

No, it wasn't like Father Greg to snap at anyone. Even in the short time Jamie had stayed at the monastery, he had gained a pretty good idea of what to expect, and this wasn't it.

"I'm telling you, it has to be here somewhere." The abbot wore a kind of wild look on his face that told them something had clearly gone wrong. This was no restful Sunday afternoon, and a whirlwind of papers fluttered behind him as he stormed out of his office. "It can't just walk off."

But the dog could. The moment Jamie stepped into the monastery's big room, he knew poor old Barkley was going to need a lawyer. A couple of the brothers had already cornered their mascot, who looked up at them with his trusty tail wagging.

"Hey, boy." Jamie wished he'd been here about a minute earlier to run interference, though the dog was obviously innocent of all charges, and the brothers stepped aside to let him by. "What's up?"

"It's *gone,* that's what's up." Father Greg ran a hand through his remaining hair. "It was here, and now it's gone."

Aside from the man's hair, Jamie could have no idea what Father Greg was talking about, and his puzzlement must have shown clearly on his face.

"Have you ever seen your dog walking off with a...a book?"

This was getting better all the time. Jamie did his best to keep a straight face. "Without his library card? Never."

Father Greg didn't laugh, didn't look remotely amused. Instead, he frowned and dropped to his knees to peer under a heavy oak coffee table.

"Seriously, uh-uh." Jamie checked under the table with him. A couple of dust bunnies, a stray penny, a torn scrap of paper. "Burgers and tacos yes, books no. I've never seen him grab anything he couldn't eat. Have you?"

"No." Father Greg patted the floor behind one of the table legs where he couldn't see, just to be sure. "I just don't understand what could have happened to it."

"You looking for any particular title, or just books in general?"

Books in general lined tall oak shelves on either side of the river-rock fireplace in the great room. Thick old books with titles like *The City of God, The Essential Writings of G. K. Chesterton,* and *The Saints' Guide to Happiness.* Father Greg, on the other hand, looked ready to tear his hair out. This had to be some kind of book.

"It's got a reddish leather cover with a brass clasp on it..." The priest put out his hands to show its size, but of course just about any book would be about that big. "And I'm sure I saw it here yesterday morning. In fact, I believe it was right there on my desk before the reporter visited."

"Guy from the *Oregonian?*"

"Tom Christy. He seemed friendly enough." Father Greg finally got up and took a break from his search. "A bit pushy, perhaps, but I suppose that's what makes a good journalist."

"I suppose." Jamie checked under a stack of Catholic magazines, trying to look as cool as possible. "So, ah...what kind of stuff did he want to know?"

"Oh, about the new mixer, of course, who we think paid for it, who might have arranged for it, that kind of thing."

What else? What else? Jamie did his best not to choke the rest of the information out of the priest. He clenched his fist instead.

"I told him we had no way of knowing," Father Greg went on, "as the donation appeared without a name, and the donor obviously valued his anonymity before God. We honor that kind of desire."

"He took that for an answer?"

"Hardly. Mr. Christy was looking for more, but that's all I gave him."

Jamie finally let out his breath. "Good. I mean, that's a good policy. Anonymous. Makes sense to me."

"I thought it would."

What's that *supposed to mean?*

The abbot's face gave nothing away this time, and they continued their search as they talked. But really? Had the reporter asked anything else?

"Maybe a few other questions," Father Greg admitted. "He didn't seem to care for most of my answers though."

"No kidding? What did you say that he didn't like?"

"I told him how we live here."

"You mean all the prayer meetings and stuff?"

"No. I mean by faith. And I told him that as far as we were concerned, this new piece of equipment, coming just in time for the Christmas baking season and right when we needed it, was an answer to prayer, period."

This time Jamie couldn't help a dry chuckle, which he dressed up as a cough. An answer to prayer. That was rich. He might have let it pass if he hadn't known what really happened—who had *really* been responsible. This was no miracle. No angel. Just...

"An answer to prayer?" He couldn't help it. "Would that be like when you ask God for a dog at Christmas, and you get a pair of dumb socks instead, wrapped with a piece of recycled yarn?"

Father Greg didn't answer for a moment, but when he did, his voice had softened. "Sounds as if you may have been confusing God with Santa Claus. Or maybe you still are?"

"Me? Confused?" Jamie laughed. "What gives you that idea?"

"Oh, I don't know. Was this a particular dog? A particular prayer?"

The memory bobbed to the surface, reminding Jamie of the time he'd tried to hold a beach ball underwater at the West Covina community pool. That hadn't worked either. In fact, the stunt had knocked him against the side of the pool, giving him a bloody nose and turning the water around him an impressive shade of pink. Several girls had run from the water screaming that day. And that had been the last time he'd ever been swimming by the way. But not the last time he'd prayed.

Almost the last time, but not quite.

"First, it was a collie," Jamie finally admitted. "I guess because I'd seen all the *Lassie* reruns, and I wanted somebody to play with. My mom worked every day."

"But you never got a collie?"

"Right. So I prayed for a basset hound, which I thought had very cool ears and could hide under the bed with me. But no-go on the basset either, so finally I just told God I'd settle for any old mutt that needed a good home. Wouldn't that have been an easy prayer to answer?"

"You know it doesn't work that way."

"I didn't know anything. I prayed the mutt prayer for three months straight, same as I prayed for my real dad to walk through the door of our apartment. Or even better, how about if my dad would walk in with a puppy on Christmas?"

"Did you ever tell your mother about all this?"

"No." Jamie shook his head. "That'd be like telling what you wished for when you blew out the candles on your birthday cake. And besides, my mom had enough things to worry about."

He stared off in the distance, remembering.

"Sometimes, if I surprised her in the kitchen, she'd be sitting there at the table crying, only she'd tell me her allergies were acting up again. I finally figured out she didn't have allergies, though, the same way I figured out God didn't have any answers to my prayers. No dog. No dad. Just socks. That Christmas I decided God and Santa Claus must have been two different names for the same fairy tale. No offense, but…"

His voice trailed off. And if that sounded like childish reasoning, so be it. Maybe that had been why he'd never told this story to anyone—and maybe why it astonished him as it poured out again after twenty-four years. Of course, Father Greg didn't seem at all surprised.

"Anyway." Jamie came back to the present. "Priests aren't supposed to be surprised at confessions, are they?"

"No, they're not," replied Father Greg. "But I don't think this is a confession. Everybody sins, but that's another matter. Here, you didn't do anything wrong. You were just being a little boy and asking for things that every little boy should have."

"Maybe." Jamie shrugged. "But I really don't know why I told you this whole silly story."

"I disagree. Not a silly story at all."

"Whatever. But it was a long time ago, and what happened to me when I was seven or eight years old has nothing to do with today."

"You really don't think so?" Now Father Greg sounded like a psychiatrist. All he needed was a couch. "Tell me again what you prayed for?"

"Oh, come on. Really, no…"

But the abbot just waited for his answer: All right, then. A dog and a father. And when Jamie finally gave in, Father Greg reached down and called for Barkley.

"Here boy." He scratched Barkley behind the ears until the mutt sat down and started with his leg kick thing. *There, that's the spot.* Did this look like a dog to Jamie?

"Wait a minute. I know what you're trying to say, but this isn't an answer to prayer. This is just a lost mutt I found on a bus ride. I found him, God didn't."

"That's what you think? I think your problem isn't that God isn't answering your prayers. I think your problem is your not being able to see the answers when they bite you on the nose."

No. Jamie wasn't going to admit defeat, yet. Not a chance. But what if Father Greg was right?

"All right, then." He crossed his arms and faced the priest. "Tell you what. Let's just suppose I believed that God answers prayer, which I don't. But suppose I did, just for the sake of argument, okay?"

Father Greg nodded. Okay.

"And just suppose I were to pray something else. How would I know what the answer looked like? And how do I know I won't have to wait another twenty-five years all over again to have my prayer answered? I'd be an old man, in my fifties."

"Watch who you're calling an old man. God's on a different timetable than we are. Maybe he waited until you were ready to settle down before he answered your first prayer."

"Settle down? You're kidding me. I'm a long way from settling down. I'm a long way from…just about everything."

That's exactly what he'd meant to say. But the words seemed to stick to his tongue, oddly false. Father Greg wasn't buying it either.

"All right. You listen, Joe Bradley. You've never told me why you came here, and I've never asked. Some of the brothers think you're a criminal in the FBI witness protection program. Others say you're running from ten kids and alimony payments to three women. I don't think it's either. But whatever it is, you're trying to get away from, God's here ahead of you. And you're a part of his plan whether you know it or not."

"He's here ahead of me?" Jamie looked up at the shelves. "Sounds like a quote from one of your books."

"No, that's just Greg MacCaulay, at your service. Oh, and another thing?"

Jamie closed his eyes. "Go ahead. You're on a roll."

"That second prayer of yours, about wanting a father—"

Jamie groaned. "You're not going to tell me God's finally ready to answer that one, too? I gave up on that a long time ago."

"Ah, I'm way ahead of you on that one." He held up a finger and smiled, but by that time tears had filled his eyes, and he turned away.

"What are you trying to say?" Jamie could not let it go that easily, not now.

"My father died while I was still attending college in California. He had cancer. But he told me something just before he passed away."

Well hooked, Jamie could not help leaning forward to hear the story, now whispered and hoarse.

"He said I wouldn't have a dad much longer, but I would always have a heavenly father. Always." He looked up at Jamie with a question in his eyes. "And maybe that sounds trite. But don't you see it's the same promise for you? God already *has* answered your prayers, if you'd just open up your eyes and take a look."

All right. Father Greg was paid to say this sort of thing. And any other time, Jamie probably would have snickered at the greeting-card sentiment. Laughed and turned away.

Only this time he couldn't. How close was this to true?

And he couldn't help thinking how much it sounded like someone else he knew. A certain schoolteacher, for instance.

"So what if God answered all our prayers, Joe?" asked Father Greg. "What if we had everything we ever wanted? What would we be like? Would we still look for God? Would we be happy?"

"Finally you ask me something I can answer. Do I look happy to you?"

"Happy, no. But searching is good."

"Only if you find, Father Greg. I think searching is okay for a while. But searching without finding sucks."

The priest laughed. "You're on to something there. I still don't know all the answers either, and I've asked the same things you're asking now."

"Is that the best you can tell me? That it's some kind of a mystery and we'll never know the answer? Come on."

"Well, it *is* a mystery. But when it comes down to it, maybe prayer isn't so much about changing *things* as it is about changing *us*. We pray so hard for things we want, and sometimes we see an answer. Sometimes we don't."

"That's for sure."

"But at the end of the day, there's Jesus, waiting for us to see that he's the only one who can fill those deepest empty parts of our lives. See what I mean?"

Jamie felt himself come up short. Close but no cigar. "I don't know, Father Greg. I'm not sure I'm there yet."

At least he could be honest about *that*.

32

I have learned to be content whatever the circumstances.

—PAUL, to the Philippians

I t's Casual Friday here on KRIV, and I'm Dirk Bond." Anne watched
Dirk's hands fly over the radio control board like a concert pianist at his
keyboard, and who wouldn't enjoy watching this artist at work? He leaned
into his microphone with the ease of someone who lived on the airwaves,
who seemed to know more about the sounds and voices in his world than
anyone else she knew. "This afternoon I'm here with the director of the
upcoming Riverdale Christian School annual musical drama, Miss Anne
Stewart. I hope you don't mind me saying how glad we all are that you're
back in town, Anne. We're especially glad to have you here on the KRIV
afternoon show."

He nodded at her, chin-first, which must have been her cue to say
something.

"Thanks for asking me, Dirk." She cleared her throat and glanced
around the tiny studio. It had once been the living and dining rooms for
a nicer Victorian home on Nash Avenue, two blocks from downtown
Riverdale. Someone told her once that it had been the mayor's house during her grandfather's time. And outside it still resembled the home Grandfather must have known. But inside? These days it had been fitted with
extra soundproof window walls and crammed with radio broadcasting

equipment, transmitters, computers—a flood of electronics Anne had never seen before.

Come to think of it, her host had never actually seen it before either. But as manager of Riverdale's small community AM radio station, Dirk had linked in enough Braille printers and voice announcers to help him run the station flawlessly and almost without anyone's help—a technician and two other part-time announcers made up the entire staff. And now, it seemed, Dirk Bond had found his groove. He drummed his hands silently in the air as he spoke.

"As many of us know, Anne is a first-year teacher here in Riverdale." He nearly ate the microphone. "She returned to her hometown after a few years away in the big city. We'll get to that. But first, Anne, tell us about the musical."

She took a deep breath and peeked over at Joe once more. He gave her an encouraging thumbs-up from his comfortable seat on the other side of the glass partition, off in the corner of the room by the coffee-maker. Just above his head the glowing red ON THE AIR sign reminded her what they were doing, and it seemed a concession to the handicapped, sighted, tongue-tied people like her. So why had she agreed to go on the air like this? What if her mind went blank in the middle of a sentence? What if her tongue tripped over a word? What if...

She didn't have time for more worrying, just shot up a silent prayer for words and launched into the sixty-second description of the musical that she had written out the night before, about how hard the kids had been working on the musical, how much fun it was going to be, and when the performances were scheduled. It helped to have all her notes in front of her, and Dirk nodded as she talked. So far, so good.

"That's great, Anne, and we'll repeat that information for our listeners toward the end of the show. In the meantime, tell me about your experience in San Francisco. What made you want to leave Riverdale to go there, and what made you come back home?"

By this time Joe had popped to his feet. While he paced in the waiting room, she wound the end of her short dark hair around a finger, wondering how to make this part of her story sound positive and nonwhiny.

"I, ah, wanted to make a difference in the world, wanted to help kids." She had no desire to hear herself, and wished Dirk hadn't fitted her with a pair of padded headphones. "So when the chance to teach in the inner-city program came up, I guess I jumped at it. I've always liked working with kids."

"Why's that?"

It seemed an innocent question. But she had a hard time getting used to talking with someone who did not look you in the eye, who rocked his head slightly and seemed to stare off to the side as she spoke.

"Most kids accept you for who you are. That's important to me, especially now after…"

There. She knew she had just crossed the bridge. So here goes.

"…after the crash."

For the next several minutes she talked about her experience in rehab, her decision to return to Riverdale, the way many people had supported her. It was a *Reader's Digest* version of what she'd told Joe the other night at their observatory date. She kept track of Joe out of the corner of her eye—sometimes pacing, sometimes standing directly under a studio loudspeaker, tilting his head to hear. She wondered how dull it sounded until Dirk finally wrapped up her segment and hit a green button to run a set of recorded commercials.

"Perfect, Anne." He smiled and held out his hand for her to shake. "And tell your friend we couldn't hear him out there at all."

"Oh. That's Joe Bradley. I'm sorry I didn't get a chance to introduce you. Here—"

She signaled him inside the studio and nodded when he pointed to himself, as in "me?"

"Joe, this is…"

At least her mind hadn't blanked when she'd been on the air, which is what she had rather expected. Joe came to the rescue, though, taking the DJ's outstretched hand and introducing himself.

"Hey, Dirk. Joe Bradley."

"One of my favorite movies," said Dirk, which only brought a question mark to Joe's face. A blind disc jockey who watched movies?

"You know, Joe Bradley in *Roman Holiday*? Nineteen fifty-three, starring Gregory Peck, Audrey Hepburn, and Eddie Albert, directed by William Wyler, written by Dalton Trumbo…"

"Wow." Joe laughed. "Remind me never to play against you in Trivial Pursuit. You really remember all that, or were you just making it up?"

"All true. Movies, actors, sports, entertainers, singers. Ask me anything."

"I believe you." Joe still smiled. Come to think of it, it was one of the first times she'd seen Joe look completely comfortable around someone new.

"In fact, Joe," Dirk went on, "your voice…there's something about it."

Joe's face blanched, and he backed away as if Dirk had a deadly virus.

"Say something else for me, Joe. Better yet, sing something."

"Actually"—Joe managed to spit out the words, though he sounded suddenly hoarse—"I've got to get going. Practice for the show."

That wouldn't be for another hour or so, but Dirk held up his hand, as if trying to slow the hasty exit.

"If you could stick around until just after the news, I'll figure out who you sound like. You might get a kick out of it. Somebody famous. Anyway, I'm sure I've heard the voice before. Just a minute and—"

"Sorry. I'll have to stop by another time." Joe bolted for the door. "My dog's outside. Need to check on him."

"Whatever." Dirk shrugged and returned to his world. "I'll see you around, Anne. And thanks again. Want to be co-host sometime?"

"You don't know what you're asking." Anne squeezed his shoulder and followed Joe outside into a cold November sunshine. What was his problem? He had already almost reached the corner with his little terrier and was about to cross Maryhill Drive before he stopped to wait for her.

"You were real good in there," he told her as she hurried up to join him. "Everybody in town should know about the musical now."

"Yeah." She nodded. "What happened when Dirk started talking about your voice? For a minute I thought you were having a heart attack."

"I just needed to get out." He shrugged, not too convincingly. "Get some fresh air."

"That's a lame excuse and you know it. I mean, honestly. What is going on here? I helped you when you were trying to escape the reporter. And you looked about the same back then. You're not sick, are you?"

He took a deep breath. "I am not sick. But I can't…explain much more than that."

"Can't or won't?"

"All the same. Take your pick. I'm sorry."

"Yeah, so am I." She turned away, headed back toward the radio station.

"Wait a minute, Anne. I want to tell you something."

She stopped, barely looking back over her shoulder.

"I, uh, really admire what you did there today, on the radio."

"What, spilling my guts to the world? Trying to explain why I'm not all here anymore?"

"You can't say that. You're all here."

"Yeah, right." He could say that. The mystery man could say whatever he wanted to. What difference did it make?

"I'm not kidding, Anne."

She almost jerked away when he rested his hand on her shoulder…wasn't sure why she didn't.

"Listen." He gulped. "Maybe everybody else in this town knows what you were like before the accident."

"The *crash,* Joe. How many times do I have to tell you? Not an accident. A *crash.*"

"Crash. Sorry. But what I'm trying to tell you is that I don't know what you used to be like. And to tell you the truth, I don't really care."

That was enough. She whirled and nearly jabbed his eye out with her finger.

"*You* may not care, and heaven knows that makes absolutely no sense to me, but *I* sure do."

"No, I didn't mean that. I was just saying—"

"You're just saying I should be content to be a scatterbrain for the rest of my life, simply shrug my shoulders like it's no big deal?"

"No."

"You're just saying I should stutter my way through the rest of my life? That I should go to sleep every night and never dream?"

"Of course not."

"You're just saying I should forget all my students' names, forget about ever water-skiing again, which, by the way, I used to be pretty good at?"

"Uh-uh. Not at all."

"Let me ask you then: Have you ever given up anything in your entire life? Have you ever lost something you valued a great deal? Like, oh, your mind? Your memories? Your coordination? And then because you look halfway normal, everybody pooh-poohs the hell you're going through?"

"Anne, I didn't mean—"

"What *did* you mean? That I should stop talking about it, smile, and pretend it's all good? Because that's what a woman in church told me the other day. Right to my face, she quoted from…well, it was in Romans, I think: 'Whatever condition I find myself in, I have learned to be content.' There! Well, that's a wonderful verse, but I'm sorry, I guess I *haven't* learned to be content yet."

If it would have done any good, she would have kicked herself for getting so emotional all over again. At least she remembered the verse. She fought to stay composed, though this battle she probably could not win. He looked at her as if she had slapped him in the face.

"And look at you!" She could have punched him, and probably would in the next few minutes if he didn't leave. "Here I am, telling my whole story to the world, on the *radio* even, and…and you! All I can get out of *you* is name, rank, and serial number. Joe Bradley, mystery man. What are you, some kind of prisoner of war? Who are you really?"

In her defense, it happened too quickly to react. And it wasn't much of anything, really—just a quick kiss that stole her words and her breath.

She gasped, which might not have been the most encouraging way to respond. He backed away as if she had slapped him.

"I'm sorry," he whispered, but she could only shake her head, trying to tell him it was okay. She thought of her kids playing kickball at recess, yelling for a do-over.

"No. It's okay." She finally held out her hand. But he had already turned on his heel and hurried off in the direction of downtown.

"Crazy," he repeated as he walked through the Haven of Resurrection Cemetery that night. "Now I've probably scared her off, and I have no idea what I was thinking anyway."

Well, maybe he *did* know what he'd been thinking, and that was the trouble. His heart still raced at the thought of the kiss as he replayed it in his mind, over and over.

Meanwhile Barkley sniffed a bush as a cool November fog swirled in. Never mind the dark. Even if Mr. Young was standing ten feet away, he wouldn't see them. Neither would Sheriff Jim Olivera. So this seemed a perfect time for visiting Mom's place at the columbarium again.

"It's like an impossible situation, right?" He let Barkley sniff all he wanted. "What's she supposed to do after a weird vagrant like me blows into town and volunteers to play the piano? How is she supposed to act? And then to make everything *completely* impossible, I go and kiss her this afternoon. Totally crazy. At least at practice tonight she was good enough not to say anything about it."

Barkley finished sniffing and tugged at the leash. He knew the way back to the place they usually parked the car, behind the row of cotton-woods that edged the cemetery.

"So what do I do, Mom? Just call Nick and tell him to come get me?"

Mom had no answer, which made Jamie wonder if he should try someone else.

33

I don't know who I am anymore. I don't know what
I remember and what I've been told I remember.
What is real?

—INGRID BERGMAN, *Anastasia*

Hey, Anne!"

She heard the friendly voice before she saw Sarah Welsh coming at her in the teacher's room, plate of cookies in hand. And since she knew no way to avoid the other teacher, Anne anchored herself in the middle of the room and smiled.

"Where have you been, girl?" Sarah had the kind of voice that could be heard all the way down the hall, the kind that stopped running students in their tracks. "You must run home faster than the kids after class. *Boom!* The bell rings and you're gone!"

Anne studied her shoes. She hadn't meant it to be like this. She hadn't meant anything to be like this. But since when was *she* in charge?

"It's the musical," she explained, and that seemed a good excuse, or as good as any, though that only accounted for half the reason. Less than half maybe. "We're really busy."

"Ah, *oui-oui*, mademoiselle." Sarah winked. "You and that tall, dark, and handsome mystery man."

"It's not like that." Anne felt the back of her neck heating up and knew she had to correct herself. "I mean, that's not the only reason, that's not really…"

Sarah laughed at Anne's tongue-tied attempt to explain. But Anne refused to start whining and complaining about practices and lesson plans and grading papers and working at the bakery.

"You don't have to explain, Anne. Everybody sees you talking and laughing in the Do-Nut Barn. I think you two make a really nice—"

"Don't say it." Anne didn't know how to stop her.

"Oh! I'm sorry." Sarah raised her eyebrows. Where had Anne heard those words before lately? They didn't sound any better to her this time either. "You know I didn't mean anything by it."

"I know you didn't. Don't worry about it. I'll just be glad when this is all over."

Whose bright idea had it been to schedule the first performances this Friday and Saturday night, separated by an entire week from the last show the following Saturday? What kind of a schedule was that? she asked her friend.

"I thought you told me it was the only thing you could do," Sarah nibbled on one of the cookies herself and picked up the latest PTA news-letter. "With the football schedule and all. You're ready for it, aren't you?"

Anne nodded. Today was…she checked her calendar…Wednesday. They'd been ready two days ago. The kids were outstanding. Only she had hardly said a word to Joe since he'd kissed her last Friday. How could she, after her outburst? Now she couldn't be sure what he was thinking. She couldn't even be sure what *she* was thinking.

Not that she had minded the kiss. Not that she had minded it at all! If things had been different, she might even have—

But things *weren't* different. For one thing, he couldn't know what he was getting into. He couldn't know who she had become. She hardly knew, herself. And what she *did* know, she didn't give high marks. Maybe not even a passing grade.

It hadn't even helped to write down her thoughts, as jumbled as they were, though she'd tried that too. They'd sounded more like the excited ramblings of a giggly twelve-year-old with a crush, but confused and unsure. She'd ripped up the paper into tiny bits before she could embarrass herself by rereading them.

Because she hardly knew who he was either. Or did she? A boy from Southern California who liked dogs and who'd never been to college. Went to Mass when he was a boy, but now, well, she wasn't sure. Dad liked him and he worked so hard, but still she couldn't stop wondering about all the "angel" coincidences. Was this uneasy feeling in the pit of her stomach God's way of warning her, or just emotional butterflies?

"I just thought I'd bring these cookies for you and…the kids." Sarah backtracked artfully. "Thought you might like them at the dress rehearsal tonight."

"Thanks." Anne accepted the plate with a labored smile. "You're sweet."

But that wasn't quite good enough for Sarah, who gave Anne a concerned look as they headed for the door.

"You been taking your iron?" asked Sarah. If a little extra iron could get Anne through this week and next, she'd gladly ingest enough to make her magnetic.

"And magnesium, selenium, riboflavin." Time to lighten the conversation. "I just need to get some sleep when all this is over."

"Okay. But let me know if you ever want to talk about…you know." Sarah wasn't fooled. She backed out of the lunchroom door and into the hall with a smile on her face. "Men?"

"I'll let you know." Anne waved and was about to follow when something in a day-old *Oregonian* on the lunchroom table caught her eye. Tom Christy's familiar round face smiled from the lower left corner of the front page, a teaser headline smudged only slightly by a prominent coffee-cup stain.

The angel, unmasked!

What? Anne riffled to section C, where his column normally held down the first page of that section, alternating between an urban development guy and a gossip columnist. Sure enough, Mr. Christy's latest column took readers right to the quaint small town of Riverdale, Washington, only a two-hour drive up the Columbia River Gorge, but where life seemed much simpler, tucked away in a time warp most people overlooked.

Until now.

From there the column recounted the now-familiar list of big-ticket mystery gifts from the "Riverdale Angel," starting with the school's beautiful new piano and moving through the museum roof, the mixer, the bakery truck, and the bevy of laptop computers for the poor students who needed them so much. Anne could see why Tom Christy was one of the most popular columnists in the Northwest (according to the *Oregonian* ads). He certainly had a way of plucking those heartstrings.

But she'd read it all in the *Sentinel*, or most of it anyway. Christy had a few more quotes in his material though, from people around town who added their theories about who the angel was. Most were pretty amusing, but he'd even mentioned her dad's name and the "Doughnut Barn" with its "rustic" linoleum floors and "well-worn" red-checkered tablecloths. Her dad would laugh at that if he hadn't already seen it. But Christy had saved the best for last—the part that made her catch her breath:

"Coming this Friday," he noted at the bottom of his column, "you'll hardly believe when a confidential source confirms the identity of the Riverdale Angel that everyone's been talking about. I can't tell you until then. But here's a hint: I'll bet a truckload of Andy's doughnuts you'll know the name."

Anne snapped up the paper and stormed out of the room. Dress rehearsal wasn't for another three hours, but before she lost her nerve she had to find Joe. Because if she was wrong about this Riverdale Angel thing, she wanted to know. Had to know. And if she was right, well…

Please, Lord, she prayed. *Let me be wrong.*

He checked his watch to make sure he wasn't late.

"I'm off work in just a minute," he told Anne, though her game face told him he probably wasn't going to like what she had to tell him. Is this how she looked when she was about to assign one of her students to detention?

"I need to talk to you before dress rehearsal," she told him as he finished sweeping the back room of the Barn.

"I know you do." He'd started to get used to the way she wore her emotions so prominently: the storms and the cloudbursts, the sunshine and the doubt. It was kind of nice, actually, seeing what was coming before it arrived, like a good weather map. He would miss it. He would miss a lot of things.

"Have you read this column?" She waved the paper in front of her as he closed the door to the back room. Wanda had taken over on this quiet Wednesday evening. Maybe the fog outside was keeping people inside and home; the tables held just a couple of disgruntled deer hunters taking a break.

"Wait a minute, hold it still." He tried to grip the shaking paper, accidentally found her cold hand. She looked up at him for a long moment, eyes red, before he let go. If not for the fiery expression on her face, he might have kissed her again.

"No," he said. "The brothers don't subscribe to the *Oregonian* up at the abbey. The *Catholic Digest,* yes. Ask me how the pope is doing, or what's happening in the Vatican. Let me tell you about this year's papal coins or the latest decision from the Conference of Catholic Bishops. I could even explain who—"

"Joe." Her voice cut through his vocal filler, and he stopped. He resisted the urge to plug his ears, since she had obviously gathered the courage to tell him something unpleasant.

"Listen, about the other day." Maybe he could deflect some of the tornado before it touched down. "I had no right to be so forward, and I'm really sorry. It's just made things awkward at practice, and as far as I'm concerned, we should just forget it ever happened."

He checked to see how far off-target he'd been, to see how quickly he needed to reload. Instead, her face melted a little. Weird.

"It's not that, Joe. It's not that at all. In fact, I…" She took a ragged breath and visibly changed course as she held up the newspaper once again. What was it about that paper? "No, that's not what this is all about. This is about what's in the column here."

"Okay." He looked at the coffee-stained copy she held out to him.

"I want you to read it and tell me what he's talking about. Read it all the way to the end."

He shrugged. Sure. He'd read the "Riverdale Angel" stuff before in the local paper. So had everybody else, and judging by the crazy range of everyone's theories, he knew he didn't have much to worry about. See? Tom Christy had even listed a few, as crazy as the rest.

"Did Rusty Anderson really say this?" he asked. She didn't answer, just waited for him to finish. *Well. This isn't so bad.*

But his entire body stiffened as he read the conclusion, set off in italics so no one would miss it.

"You think he really knows?" Jamie wondered aloud, but his throat had already tightened so much he could hardly swallow. Tom Christy could guess just like anybody else, and he could tell the world he thought it was the ghost of Elvis if he wanted to. But the last sentence had Jamie hooked—the one about how he would bet a truckload of Andy's doughnuts that readers would know the name.

"I think he knows who it is." Anne finally leveled her accusation, her voice wavering and her eyes glistening. "Do you?"

Jamie's mouth went dry as he looked straight back at her. And though he had a few ideas before, this time he saw exactly what was slipping through his fingers. All because of the lie? Maybe. But now even the truth couldn't save what he had flirted with for these brief weeks. And of course, all the thinking about it didn't take as long as it would take to describe.

"There's this movie," he began, not knowing why he said it or where the thought came from. "Audrey Hepburn and Gregory Peck."

She closed her eyes and nodded as he went on.

"He's a reporter and she's a princess, right? And she sneaks out to spend a day with him, but in the end they both know it can't work, because he's—"

"A reporter and she's a princess," Anne finished. "I saw it just the other night."

"Oh." He gulped, and suddenly he could have kicked himself for ever thinking Joe Bradley had been a clever alias. "So you know the story, then, I guess."

She nodded again but didn't open her eyes.

"Well, then you know… I mean, I was just thinking of that last scene, after they spend the day together, but they figure out they can't…you know, be a couple. And Princess…I guess her name was Anne, too, right?"

"Right."

"Yeah, Princess Anne. She looks across the press conference straight at Gregory Peck."

"You're mixing up character names with actor names. I think you mean Joe Bradley."

"Joe Bradley. How about that. That's really funny, how the names… yeah." He ran out of steam as Anne opened her eyes and looked straight at him once more. He could smell her flowery perfume, the kind that made his head spin, and he leaned closer, not really thinking he might kiss her at first, but…

But she turned away at the last moment.

"I'm sorry, Joe."

"No, no, ah…" What was the proper response at a moment like this? *No, perfectly all right. I was trying to kiss you, but now I don't care. I'm not embarrassed. Not a problem.*

Instead he just stuttered some more until she interrupted him.

"You probably won't understand this, Joe, but I just can't…"

"Don't say it, Anne. You don't need to explain. You don't owe me anything. I just…it was just the perfume. Wasn't my fault."

"No, Joe. You're a good friend and you deserve an explanation." She took a deep breath. "And I'm just not able to get…emotionally involved with someone…I don't even really know yet. I'm sorry."

"So am I. I didn't mean to—"

"It's all right."

Not really. But Jamie had no more answers, especially no classic movie answers. He still owed Anne the truth, though right now the truth seemed just as far out as the Elvis theory. What was the difference? He'd lost her either way. Not that he'd ever had her.

And Tom Christy? Jamie decided the guy had no way of knowing for sure. His gut feeling: The reporter was taking a shot in the dark, hyping the story the way TV newscasters often did. "Alien invaders! Details at eleven!" Only this time Jamie himself was the alien invader.

"See you at dress rehearsal?" he asked. She nodded. So he handed the newspaper back, hung up the whisk broom on a peg, and left through the back door. Maybe he still had a few days before he would have to tell her the truth.

Good thing she didn't subscribe to *Entertainment Insider.*

34

And once more, life louses up the script.

—HUMPHREY BOGART, *The Barefoot Contessa*

Jamie felt the old, familiar backstage adrenaline rush and knew why this had always been his favorite part of any performance—even a performance of *Bye Bye Birdie* by the kids at Riverdale Christian School. The anticipation. Because really, when it all came down to it, this performance equaled any he'd ever done, from Carnegie Hall to the capitals of Europe. Simple, but very good. Even here in the Riverdale Middle School auditorium (the public school across town had a larger venue), the audience still came to be wowed.

And they would be—well, to a point. The kids had worked hard, and they'd all come far. Some even had passable amateur voices, which he hadn't expected. They were just acting a little strange tonight.

"One more time," he told Sean from behind an electronic keyboard in the warmup room. They'd moved the new Kawai out onstage, of course, so everyone could hear it. Sean did his la-la-las and hopped in place.

"You're going to do great," Jamie told him, and he would. More than that, Jamie would enjoy being out of the spotlight, off to the side where three ninth and tenth graders would play the other instruments: a guitar, a bass, and a drum set. The parents would be impressed. They were probably already sitting in the first row, and maybe that would be their only audience, but that would be okay.

Anne, meanwhile, checked on the kids' 1950s costumes, pulling up bobby socks and adjusting ponytails. She made sure the lights were all pointed in the right direction, helped run final sound checks as the audience began to take their seats. He had to admit he had never seen her looking better. She wore a full-length black opera gown and her hair up. When she stepped into the room he had to keep himself from staring.

"You look—" he began to tell her, then changed his mind. She, on the other hand, was all business and probably hadn't heard him.

"Curtain in thirty," she announced, then motioned to Jamie. "And when you're done there, could I see you for a minute?"

Jamie wasn't sure what to expect, especially not this week. Still, he followed her backstage, where the crew was madly placing backdrops for the first act. A few of the girls looked at him and giggled.

"Have you read the *Oregonian* today?" she asked him. He couldn't read her face.

"Haven't had time," he replied, and that was the whole truth. "I've been hiding in here all day, working on lights and stuff. In fact, I haven't seen a soul since before lunch, not since the kids started coming in about an hour ago."

"And you know how much everyone appreciates that, Joe. You've done more than anyone could have asked."

"Forget it."

"I probably will."

He couldn't imagine her joking right now, but she had something else to say, and it obviously wasn't funny.

"Joe, have the kids been acting any differently tonight?"

"Well, yeah. They're nervous. And they keep looking at me kinda weird."

She sighed. "I told them not to."

"Huh?"

"Look out there at the crowd, Joe."

He shook his head. No way.

"Can't do it," he told her. "You know that peeking out through the curtains is major bad luck."

"Not this time. Just look out there. Keep in mind it's still twenty-five minutes until curtain."

He knew what he was talking about with the bad luck. Once, when someone from his crew had peeked out through a curtain, the entire sound system had blown up. They'd had to refund every ticket to twenty-two thousand disappointed fans.

But Anne sounded so determined. Just a peek? He sighed and took just a quick look—and his eyes nearly popped out.

"Whoa! Every seat is taken already. What's going on out there?"

They'd told the kids half-full in the five-hundred-seat auditorium would be incredible but highly unlikely. Proceeds from every ticket sold went to send their mission team to Mexico, so the kids were hopeful. But sold out?

"They've set up an extra row of folding chairs in the back," she told him. "And people are pushing in for standing room only. The fire marshal is going to shut us down if we keep trying to pack everybody inside."

"I don't believe it."

"And if you look outside, there's at least this many again, just standing in the rain, trying to push their way through the main doors."

"You're kidding me, right?"

"I am not kidding you. And do you know why they're all here?"

"Well, that radio interview must've helped. I just didn't know there were so many people in the town of Riverdale who would come out for the school musical."

"That's just it, Joe. There aren't."

Jamie peeked out one more time, just to be sure he wasn't seeing things.

"You still don't get it, do you?" She crossed her arms.

"Am I supposed to?"

"They're not here to see the play, Joe. They're here to see you."

Even above the hubbub of the crowd, he could hear her sigh as she pulled a torn newspaper clipping from beneath her clipboard.

"You'd better read this column," she told him. Tom Christy again.

"I thought he wasn't supposed to write another column until tomorrow. Friday."

"Normally he doesn't. I think the paper got so much publicity, they moved it up a day."

She stood there in the preshow confusion, waiting for him to read the clipping, and so he scanned the opening, in which Mr. Christy said he would name the mysterious Riverdale Angel. Maybe that sold him a few newspapers, but Jamie still believed the whole thing smelled bogus as he scanned the part that explained how he had come to the town at the end of August, staying in a small cabin at…Our Lady of the Hills monastery.

And by now Jamie didn't know if he could keep reading. The day he showed up at the monastery. The dog. His job at the Do-Nut Barn. The '63 Studebaker. The article felt like a well-placed punch in the stomach, and he gasped for air.

"He sure didn't leave out much." Jamie read on; what else could he do? At this point there wasn't much use denying anything, not even the last paragraph, which Anne started to read aloud after he feebly handed it back. Go ahead. The words had already done their damage.

"Sounds like a very normal guy living a very normal life," she read, "except when you consider who he really is. Because this is, as Paul Harvey always says, 'the rest of the story.' This normal guy is Jamie D. Lane, the pop singer, living an unexplained charade in the all-American small town. He's shaved his beard and disguised his appearance. People on the street presumably haven't even recognized him up to now. But we're talking about *the* Jamie D. Lane, the singer who makes grown women cry and millions of dollars every time he gets on stage, but who now makes minimum wage at a mom-and-pop doughnut bakery."

Not quite true, he noted. *Andy's paying me minimum plus thirty-five cents.*

Which made no difference, obviously. Anne hadn't finished reading either.

"And what's even more intriguing," she continued, "I've learned that Jamie D. Lane, aka Joe Bradley, is appearing tonight in the Riverdale Christian School's performance of *Bye Bye Birdie.* When I called, they told me admission is just four bucks and change at the door, and it's some kind of fund-raiser. So I'd guess this is the cheapest ticket you'll ever purchase to see the pop star, maybe hear him play a little. My advice? Skip work early or take the day off. Just get yourself to Riverdale by tonight, and you'll enjoy a rare treat. A little weird, maybe, but when was the last time you attended a good school play?"

Jamie groaned when she finished reading and stuffed the clipping into her pocket. That explained the crowd packing into the auditorium and that explained the crowd outside. He still had no idea how the reporter got his story. But thanks to Mr. Tom Christy, his small town adventure had come to an end.

"Listen, Anne, I'm really sorry. I—"

But she held up her hand and wouldn't hear it this time. "Please don't apologize all over again. It's enough. Just tell me one thing."

"Sure."

"Is it all true what he wrote?"

He paused, and he knew he would answer anything she asked now. "There's no way he could know about all the angel stuff. I'm still thinking it was a lucky guess. Somehow the guy found out about me and put it all together."

But how? The details, the time line, everything. Almost as if Tom Christy had read his diary, if he'd had one.

"But is it all true?" she repeated the question.

"Except for the minimum wage thing." The last thing he wanted was to whimper, but she had to understand. "But you have to believe me that everything I told you about myself was true, too."

"Not counting the minor details, right? Like your name and what you do for a living?"

Her eyes flashed. What else could he say? A couple of the kids needed last-minute help with their costumes, and she bent over to fix a girl's hair-clip. Now he had no choice.

"I need to go," he finally told her. "I don't want this musical turning into a circus."

"It's too late for that." She straightened up and faced him with arms crossed. "The town's been buzzing all afternoon, but we kept the auditorium doors locked so no one would find you."

"You're kidding."

"Are you really that clueless, Jamie Lane?"

Maybe so. He looked at his feet as she continued.

"Well, one thing is sure. I'm not going to let you just walk out on these kids. Not now. They've worked too hard."

"You don't understand," he told her, even as he leaned toward the backstage emergency exit. *Yeah, and this is an emergency, all right.* "If they're really here to see Jamie Lane the pop singer, you have no idea what that crowd is going to do."

"Mr. Bradley!" The drummer, a skinny little guy named Cal, poked his head in from the corner of the curtain. Just like everyone else, his face looked flushed with excitement. At least he had the courtesy to still call Jamie by his fake name. "We're all ready for you out here."

"Just a sec," Jamie nodded. When the drummer disappeared he turned back to Anne. "You still want me to go out there?"

"That's what you do, right?" She pointed out at the stage and checked her watch. "You're a performer, and it's five minutes to curtain."

If that's the way she wanted it, that's what he would do. He took a deep breath and turned toward stage left.

"Joe?" Anne called after him. And when he turned back to face her, her eyes told him everything her words could not.

"I really am sorry," he finally whispered, letting his fingertip brush her cheek. Hadn't he told her that before?

"Me, too." Backstage noise nearly swallowed her reply as she turned to go, then looked back over her shoulder. "Break a leg."

35

When in doubt, tell the truth.

—MARK TWAIN

By the end of the show the kids were beaming at all the applause. With so large an audience, how could they not? Their faces glowed as they held hands and bowed, and they deserved all the praise. Never mind the times Sean forgot his lines, or when Amy missed her cue on "One Boy." It was, after all, a school production, and a pretty good one despite the minor flubs. They'd only been working on it a few short weeks.

The worst part had nothing to do with the kids, but with the turkey in the front row who hollered "We want Jamie!" and "Yeah, Jamie!" in between every few songs. If Jamie had gotten a better look at the guy, he might have slipped back at intermission to strangle him and be done with it.

He might have done it, too, if Anne hadn't appeared onstage and stood shyly in the light of the spotlight. She waited for a moment while the applause died down.

"I want to thank everyone for coming here to…" She paused to study her note. Jamie could have told her she would have a hard time reading it in the considerable glare of the spots. She backed up and launched into it again. "For coming here to support our kids. We know that many of you are visitors to our town, so we wanted to be sure you know what's behind this play."

Jamie could not have wrenched his gaze from her if he'd wanted to.

She held the note up once again, as if her eyesight were failing, then crumpled it in frustration and turned back to her audience. Someone coughed from the back row, and it echoed.

"Sure, it's been fun for the kids, and they've learned a lot just practicing. They've learned even more about music from their volunteer coach and accompanist, Mr. Jamie D. Lane. Come on out here, Jamie."

The applause must have made the auditorium's light fixtures tremble, but for once Jamie looked for ways to escape the spotlight rather than soak it in. Why was Anne doing this? Because this time the light felt more like a laser cannon than what he remembered, and he nearly ducked in pain. But he had no choice, and as the applause continued, he stepped out from behind the curtain and waved at the crowd, then pointed back at Anne. Good. She took the cue.

"We've been honored to have him stay here in Riverdale with us, even for a short time." The clapping gradually died as she continued speaking. "You'll also be glad to know that your support tonight has brought in…"

She dug up her note once again, unfolded its wrinkles, and held it up to the light.

"Has brought in $2,412 to help send students on a special mission trip to Tijuana, Mexico, where they're going to build houses and help put on vacation Bible schools for kids."

That brought more applause, polite and measured this time. Jamie suspected the Portland crowd wasn't overly impressed with a small-town Christian school raising small-town change to send a few kids on a mission trip. But Anne wasn't through; she brought up twenty kids in their '50s costumes and told everyone how much their support meant to them.

She stuttered just a little, but Jamie hardly noticed. And she looked down at her crumpled notes quite a bit, though Jamie knew she didn't need to. In all, he was certain he'd never seen anyone like her, not even at last year's Grammy Awards. The hardest part was convincing himself that he had played any part in this—and that he now had to leave.

Of course, getting out of the building would be another story. With an auditorium full of fans, he'd need some quick footwork after the final curtain call. That's when the auditorium thundered with applause once more as they began stomping and chanting, "Jay-MEE, Jay-MEE, Jay-MEE!"

No, now he knew for certain. Despite the chanting and the clapping, this was not his show. It was Anne and the kids' show, period.

"Sorry, folks," he whispered as made his way around the musicians to the back exit and found the backstage emergency door. This time no one stood in his way. Unfortunately, he'd parked his Studebaker out front, but maybe he could find his way through the parking lot without being seen.

Or not. The lot was double-parked and jammed with Oregon-plated cars, nearly impossible to navigate.

A cold rain hit him in the face, washing away the sweat of the evening, mixing icy sleet with hot tears of relief. Or regret, if he was honest with himself. Regret for what he'd done, or not done. Regret for who he was, and who he was not. Regret for coming, and for not coming sooner.

Most of all, regret for the lie that had poisoned everything he'd discovered here. People who didn't care about getting a piece of him and who didn't care about the size of his bank account. A place where the gift of a new piano made headlines, and where a woman recovering from a car crash could still teach school.

Yikes! He lost his footing on the slick surface and grabbed for the nearest car, hanging on to the rearview mirror of a dirty SUV. Just as easy, he thought, to slip back into the comfort of his blame game. Why had God let him come here to see what might have been his—only to snatch it away in a single day? What kind of a God would do something like that?

Only he knew it wasn't God. For a moment his mind cleared as he raised his face to meet the rain, and he knew exactly who to blame.

It's my fault, he prayed for the first time in a long time. *I'm really sorry.* Only who was he apologizing to this time? It felt good and clean and cold and bone chilling all at once, and he gulped in the air as if he could breathe for the first time. Maybe he could—even if it was too little and too late. He smiled, even if the dark parking lot behind the middle school was a strange place for a prayer meeting.

By now the crowd had already started spilling out of the front doors and down the steps of the auditorium, looking for their prey. The girls in front splashed out into the pool of yellow light under a streetlamp with the look of sharks who had caught the scent of blood in the water.

And then he heard the familiar rise and fall of the "It's him!" squeal, and he was just not ready for this yet. He could hide in the bathroom, back inside. Except the door had slammed shut behind him and a car with one of its headlights gone headed straight at him, threading its way through the lot.

His car.

He would have run the opposite way, except that would take him straight toward the crowd. And he had to find out who had stolen the Studebaker anyway. So he stood there, staring, as the car swerved uncertainly and the brakes squealed. Two men in dark robes sat in front, and one reached back to open the rear door as they slowed.

"Get in!" hissed Brother Aaron, and the car didn't even come to a full stop as Jamie dove inside, and the door slammed behind him. He hardly had a chance to see who his rescuers were before they sped out of the parking lot and away, right past the startled crowd. As Barkley licked his face, Jamie had to laugh at the bizarre rescue.

"Father Greg?" He wasn't sure he was seeing straight. "How did you—"

"Don't even ask." Father Greg smiled as he took them around town and up the back road to the abbey. As usual, Barkley bounded from side to side, taking it all in.

"I have a feeling you two could have been successful car thieves," Jamie told them, "if you hadn't decided to become priests, that is."

Brother Aaron started to laugh, then apparently thought better of it and explained: "We heard about the column and thought maybe you could use a ride home."

"I'll bet everyone in town has heard." Jamie held on as they rocketed around the corner, spraying gravel.

"By now, maybe," said Father Greg. "But not very likely. You know how the morning *Oregonian* doesn't get here until midafternoon."

None of that mattered anymore. Everyone knew who he was, and he couldn't just strut around town, eating at Juno's and bumming quarters off Velma Cartwright to do his laundry, pretending to be the average Joe he had never really been.

"Thanks for the rescue," he said when they reached the abbey. He slammed the door and headed for his cabin to pack his suitcase. "I never thought I would get out of that place alive."

And then the thought occurred to him.

"Wait a minute." He turned back. "How did you know I would need a ride anyway?"

Brother Aaron pointed at their driver. "He said you would."

"Oh." That didn't exactly explain it, but Jamie would leave it at that. And with that he hurried off to stuff his things back into his bag and find a way back to California, which in the past few weeks had turned into no-longer-home. But if not there, then where? Half-packed, he leaned against the wall in the cabin, trying to stop his head from spinning.

"Knock-knock." Father Greg peeked in the door as Jamie tossed another pair of socks into his bag.

"I'm here."

Father Greg didn't come in, just stood under the feeble yellow porch light. As he did, the rain massaged the cabin's little roof with a steady thrumming sound, a sound Jamie normally loved to fall asleep to. But tonight was a long way from normal, and Jamie couldn't leave the abbot standing on the porch.

"I need to tell you something." Father Greg finally broke the silence. "And I need to apologize."

"You're the last one who needs to do any apologizing. Now, me— that's another story. In fact—"

"It's my fault about the newspaper column today," Father Greg interrupted.

36

You get nothing! You lose! Good day, sir!

—GENE WILDER, *Willy Wonka
and the Chocolate Factory*

Jamie could have imagined dozens of scenarios before he'd ever dream of this one: Father Greg, responsible for Tom Christy's column? But in a perverse sort of way, it all started to make sense. The details Christy had provided about him—all were details Father Greg would have known.

"I want you to know that I am so sorry it turned out this way," Father Greg began. "I feel responsible. And if I could have done anything to prevent it, I would have."

Jamie lowered himself to his bed and reached out to scratch Barkley, but the dog must have slipped outside. None of this made any sense.

"Wait a minute." His forehead throbbed now. "Back up. What did you tell him? Why did you tell him?"

"Okay." Father Greg nodded and looked at the floor. "I wasn't sure before; I only suspected it. But when I read the newspaper column today, I'm nearly certain I know exactly what happened. Tom Christy stole my journal."

"Your *what?* You mean that book you were missing awhile back?"

"That's right. He came to ask me questions about the new mixer, and he must have walked away with my journal, thinking he could get some more details. It was there before he visited—right out on my desk—and gone after he left. The brothers and I looked everywhere."

"I see what you're saying, but I'm still not sure what that has to do with me."

"Well, I didn't tell Mr. Christy much of anything that day he visited. I did explain to him about God's provision, which I notice he didn't quote me on, but I can assure you I didn't tell him about you."

"That's great, but sounds to me like you're saying two different things here. You say you're responsible, but you didn't tell him anything. Besides, what could your journal tell him that he couldn't find out someplace else?"

Jamie peered out his window as a set of headlights came bouncing up the gravel road. Wonder who that would be.

"There's nothing outstanding about my journal, at least not to anyone else. It had my thoughts and impressions, prayers. I remember several days when I wrote, when I wondered what a singing star like you was looking for in a place like this."

Oh no. Jamie finally saw it coming. He got to his feet as Father Greg went on.

"Jamie, I've known who you were from the first day you came to us."

What? Now Jamie knew how it felt to be a flat tire. Deflated. After all the air leaks out, what's left?

"So I turned out to be a good source for that fellow after all." The smile turned meager, since it came at Jamie's expense.

"But he can't *do* that!" Jamie paced in front of the window for another couple of minutes. A second set of headlights drew closer, behind the first. "He can't just walk into the abbey and steal your private stuff."

"Obviously not. I still don't have any proof though."

"Yeah, except for what he wrote in his column, right?"

"He actually lifted some of the phrases I used to describe you word for word."

Jamie shook his head. "I can't believe it."

"I am so sorry."

"Look, it's not your fault, okay? But tell me this: How did you recognize me in the first place, especially when nobody else did?"

"The eyes." He reached into an inside pocket and pulled out a shrink-wrapped CD. "A well-meaning visitor from Cincinnati sent me this last Christmas. The year before, it was one of those Chia Pets. You know, the kind with grass seed and—"

"I know what you mean." Jamie had to smile, even now. He took the Jamie D. Lane *Something Special* CD and turned it over in his hands. The cover featured a black-and-white closeup of a bearded Jamie—very different from how he looked now, yet still much the same. Of course, the black-and-white photo wouldn't show the different eye color from the contacts he was wearing. "Hey, you didn't even open it up."

"We don't have a CD player here, or I might have. To tell you the truth, though, I'd planned to give it to one of my nieces and never did. I wish now that I had."

"Are you serious?" Jamie handed it back. "Then you would never have figured out who I really was."

"Exactly." Father Greg sighed, held up the CD one more time to compare faces, and turned to go. He stopped at the door. "We were hoping you'd stay at least through next week, through the last performance."

"I've caused enough trouble already."

"I don't think so. And I thought you had a commitment to those kids."

"Maybe Joe Bradley did. Jamie Lane is packing up."

"That doesn't sound like you."

"You have no idea how I sound. I—"

A car outside skidded to a stop as the driver laid on his horn briefly. Jamie looked out just in time to see a second car nearly rear-ending the first. It wasn't the cars that caught his attention, though, but the flash of brown fur just under the front bumper of the lead car.

"What in the world?" Father Greg hurried outside, with Jamie on his heels. They both reached the crumpled, bleeding dog at the same time.

"We're proud of you, Anne." Andy slipped an arm around his daughter and gave her a squeeze. Even Anne's mom had made it to opening night, and she smiled at them both. Mom would fade back into the woodwork, as she always did, but the smile looked heartfelt.

"It was the kids." Anne looked out over the nearly empty auditorium, mostly local families now. Grandpas taking pictures. Parents giving hugs. The out-of-towners had cleared out the minute they realized Joe—or rather, Jamie—had slipped out before the encore bow.

Just as well. He would have been mobbed. She wasn't sure if he would be coming back now. Or what it would be like if he did.

It could not have amounted to anything anyway. She knew right from the start they were too different. Unequally yoked and all that. But…

"Did you hear what I said, Anne?" Her dad came into focus when he leaned in a little closer and raised his voice.

"Oh." She shook her head and did her best to smile instead of breaking out in tears. "Sorry, Dad. What did you say?"

"I *said*, don't worry about coming to work tomorrow afternoon. Wanda will put in a few extra hours until we can find someone else. I'm assuming Joe isn't coming back?"

"I don't know. He didn't say."

"Did he say if he was leaving town? Or when?"

She shook her head, and the not knowing weighed heavier and heavier.

"Did he say anything?"

"I'm so tired, Dad." She had to leave. So tired. And she could no longer hold back the tears.

Neither could Jamie, but for a wholly different reason. He knelt in the mud, sheltering Barkley as best he could from the rain and gently holding up the little dog's head. Barkley shivered, and the headlights from the second car glimmered behind them, throwing windshield-wiper shadows all around the scene of the accident.

"Do you want to bring him inside?" Father Greg wanted to know, but Jamie just shook his head because it was too late for that. They would only have a few short minutes. And it didn't matter how hard the rain pelted him, he would not let Barkley die alone.

"It's going to be okay, little guy." He scratched Barkley softly behind the ear, and the dog responded with a single thump of his tail. But that was enough to get the message across, enough to remind him that what Father Greg had told him was true. In the mud and sleet, could he still doubt that this little dog had been the answer to a young boy's prayer? As much as he didn't understand about a wild and unpredictable God, this part finally made sense.

Sort of. He did know he would not beg God for the life of the dog, only that it was enough to have seen the prayer answered this way, this once. It *had* been answered, hadn't it? And having seen it and touched it, even the senseless made a little more sense.

"Look, I'm sorry, but it wasn't my fault." The driver stepped out of his rental car just long enough to confirm the blame. He didn't look as if he wanted to get his two-hundred-dollar brown leather shoes muddy. Jamie didn't even look up to see who it was—one of the reporters, one of the paparazzi who had descended on Riverdale for the show. "He ran out right in front of me. I couldn't help it, see?"

The guy turned to the other driver for help. "You saw what happened, didn't you, Alan?"

Alan apparently had too, or said he had. He also said their newspaper would pay a vet, if that would help, and he offered Jamie an umbrella. As if that would help keep him dry now. Jamie shook his head; he could only keep watch over the dog God had given him, watch the life slowly ebb as the muddy rainwater puddled around their bodies. They could call the veterinarian, but anyone could see they only had a few moments now, at best. Barkley couldn't open his eyes, and now he couldn't wag his little tail. And finally he couldn't move the air into his lungs.

"It's okay, little guy." Jamie buried his face in his dog's matted fur and cried in a way he never had before. Cried for the person he used to be and maybe no longer was. Cried until he had nothing left, and then he quietly thanked God again for the little dog, and he didn't care who saw or watched. But finally he cradled the cold, limp rag doll and stood to see the fool who had run him over. As the rain continued pouring down, he stared through the rental car window at a face he wished he did not recognize. But the man looked just like the photo by his column, and Jamie had to ask.

"So does this give you something else to write about, Mr. Christy?"

37

Everybody! Everybody wants a piece of me!

—PAUL NEWMAN, in *The Hustler*

Tom Christy wasn't the only one writing about the Riverdale Angel and the discovery of Jamie D. Lane in the little town of Riverdale. Once the word got out, the media circus quickly grew into a media feeding frenzy, as America rediscovered its best-loved pop singer in the most unlikely of hiding places.

"All the network morning shows," Andy counted on one hand, "plus all the news, the late-night stuff, the radio talk programs. Dr. Jim's doing a major story during prime time… Good publicity for Riverdale, I guess."

They all stared out the windows of the Do-Nut Barn that next morning as the TV vans paraded past, each one splashed with bright network graphics and crowned by a satellite uplink dish. Across the street at the American Legion hall, an NBC van from Seattle found a parking space next to the CNN and NBC outfits and disgorged its team of photographers and technicians. The on-camera personality seemed the most worried about his hair in the wind.

"Maybe we should invite them inside," suggested Anne, pouring coffee refills for everyone at the counter.

Instead, the door blew open, and Belinda Carter from the Chamber of Commerce tumbled inside with a load of soggy leaves at her heels.

"Little breezy out there this morning, Belinda?" Andy wanted to know.

Belinda looked more flustered than windblown. "We have never had this type of opportunity presented to us before." Belinda tended to speak in more multisyllable words than everybody else. She sent memorandums and scenarios instead of memos and plans. That sort of thing. And now her round face looked strawberry red from the excitement. "We're anticipating a special *Prime Time* report tonight. They're even requesting permission to present the musical live on national television. Can you believe it?"

"Uh, wait a minute." Anne stopped pouring decaf in the middle of Cy Morrison's cup. "Who's giving that kind of permission? I'm not so sure how the kids are going to react."

"I provided them your principal's name, Anne." Belinda dismissed the question with a sweep of her hand. "And listen. This is consequential. I'm ensuring that every downtown merchant receives one of these."

"What's that?" asked Andy, as she passed out a one-page, hot-pink flier. He read the first paragraph and started to laugh.

"What's so amusing?" Belinda crossed her arms in defense. "I thought it was unambiguous."

"Oh, it's clear, all right." He couldn't stop chuckling. "But seriously, you want us to say this *every* time we mention the word *Riverdale* to the media? Every time they poke a camera in our faces from now on?"

Anne read it, too, and couldn't help joining her dad's giggles.

"Repetition is the key to brand identification," explained Belinda, putting on her college-professor tone.

"Hi, I'm from Riverdale," he snorted and looked down at his paper, " 'sportsman's paradise, gateway to the Simcoe Mountain Recreational Area, and home of the NWTF record wild turkey.' "

The only turkey Anne knew of was the one who had lied to her—to the whole town. Even so, she couldn't help remembering the stricken look on Joe's face when she confronted him with the Tom Christy tell-all column. And truthfully, she couldn't help feeling some of that pain herself, with what was left of her heart.

"The key is to capitalize on our geographical advantages," Belinda went on, "as well as our appeal to a demographic that…"

Anne missed the rest of their conversation as she watched the NBC crew set up. The anchorman paced around his group, holding his hair and practicing his lines from a clipboard. They would probably lead with the story of how they had discovered Jamie D. Lane hiding out in the little town, then throw in a few details about how cute his little game had been, how he played some piano for a school musical, and about how he bought Riverdale.

"Well, we're not for sale," she mumbled to no one in particular.

"What's that, Anne?" asked Walt Rutgers. Walt didn't hear so well.

"I said we're not for sale." She set her jaw. "Riverdale is not for sale."

That only confused Walt even more than usual, and for the rest of the day he would be asking people who was buying their town. Anne didn't have time to get into it. She would have to find another piano player for tonight's performance—assuming their resident pop star wasn't going to make another appearance.

"Here come the brothers." Her dad pointed at the rusty Toyota pickup that belonged to the abbey, threading its way through the media traffic. "Don't usually see them so often."

Even more unusual, Father Greg himself was driving. They watched as the truck pulled up close to the curb, but a CNN van had blocked the way. So he looked both ways and backed tailgate-first right up onto the sidewalk and to the glass front door.

"Must be some pretty important fruitcakes," Walt observed over his coffee, and in the bustle of the street, it seemed no more out of place than all the rest. The half-dozen media crews hardly gave them a second glance.

But no sooner had the truck backed up to the door than the covered bundle in the back began to wiggle, and Jamie Lane slipped out and through the door. He waved at the driver as the Toyota pulled away.

"Well. Look what the wind blew in." Walt had a comment for everything. Question was, had anyone outside noticed? Jamie locked the front door behind him, and no one else one said a word.

"I don't know if this is the best place to say it." He looked from face to face—a half-dozen regulars, Andy, and Anne. "But I want you all to know that I apologize for what's happening here. I didn't mean for it to be this way, honest. But I know it's all my fault."

"That may be so," said Belinda. "But the way I see it, this is the best thing to happen to Riverdale in a decade. The economic impact is going to be considerable, and we're hoping to see a spike in the retail and services sectors."

Andy looked up from his cash register with an amused grin. "She means to say we're making hay while the sun shines. But after last night, Joe, we assumed you were done working here. Am I right?"

Jamie nodded, and the serious expression never left his face. "I was just afraid everyone would be mad at me for…you know, the big lie."

Andy smiled and put out his hand. "I'm honored to have been your boss, even for just a short time. You come back anytime you want."

Easy for him to forgive. Everybody else except Anne joined in the backslapping too. She held back behind the counter, busying herself making a new round of coffee. By that time a couple of the camera crews had caught on to what was happening, and when her dad refused to open the door, they pressed camera lenses to the glass anyway. *Welcome to life in a fishbowl,* Anne thought.

"Just ignore 'em," Andy told everybody. Obviously he'd become the overnight media strategy expert, just like Belinda and everybody else in town. "But I'll bet you're used to this kind of thing, eh, Jamie? Man, I'm still getting used to calling you that. You still seem like a Joe."

"I'm really sorry about that." Jamie apologized yet one more time, but Andy blew it off.

"By the way," added Andy, "where's Barkley this morning? I was saving him a couple doughnut holes. You leave him back at the abbey?"

"Barkley was…" Jamie started to answer, then seemed to stumble on his words. "No, I didn't bring him today."

"Hard enough getting yourself through the media, I'll bet. Aren't they all camped out up at the abbey, too?"

Jamie nodded, and for the first time all morning, Anne felt sorry for him. He looked the way Anne felt when a sudden headache took her breath away and wound her forehead into a knot. But he had brought something else, which he pulled from a small backpack.

"I just wanted to show you that I wasn't a total phony." Again he faced the Do-Nut Barn crowd, but his eyes were on Anne. "This belonged to my mom, who's buried over in the cemetery."

"Your mom?" Anne whispered, and despite herself, she crowded around with everyone else to see the old photos, pasted carefully into yellowed pages with those old-fashioned corner stickers that people once used to secure photo collections.

"Hey, who knows?" Jamie tried to smile, though she'd seen him do much better. "Maybe I'm actually related to some of you folks."

He explained what he knew about his mother and her family, how his mother had lived here until she became pregnant with him, and that she'd left alone for L.A. before he was born. He'd never heard anything about his father, and didn't expect to, but most of the photos showed Penny Lane during happier days: as a teenager on a horse, or opening Christmas presents, or building a snowman in front of a small house somewhere.

They all agreed the house looked like that small rental at the end of North Grant Street, a nice older home that Bernie Swift the barber had built in the forties. He'd planted a couple of nice pink hawthorn trees in front that still bloomed every spring, but the house itself had burned down about ten years ago.

Oh. What about this photo, with Jamie's mother standing with an older man in front of a mid-'60s Mustang?

That would be Delay Lane. Walt thought he remembered Jamie's grandfather—vaguely—while Andy seemed to recall something about a Lane who worked the counter at the S&H Car Parts place. But that had been thirty-five years ago.

"Oh no." Anne slapped her cheek. "I just remembered something I was supposed to tell you."

She was actually surprised it had occurred to her even now.

"The gal from the museum, I forget her name…"

"Aggie Myers," her father added.

"Right, Aggie. She called here one afternoon and said she'd found a little information on your distant aunt in the museum archives. Nothing real big, I don't think, but you might have been interested. I said I'd tell you, but… I'm sorry. I should have written it down. I forgot."

"It's not important." Jamie shook his head. "I know she was here now. My mom. I mean, I knew it before, but it's real for me now. I know what kind of place she came from. My roots, too. Maybe that's all I needed to find out."

He never seemed to look at the battery of cameras in the window, just turned the pages of his family album as if handling a valuable antique. And it struck Anne as funny that Jamie had actually been in Riverdale before she had, though only for a few short months, and not where anyone could see him.

"I did beat you here, didn't I?" When he laughed again, Anne almost forgot his name wasn't Joe Bradley anymore. Almost forgot everything that had happened over the past couple of days. Almost, but not quite.

"Listen, there's one other thing I need to ask you." Jamie looked straight at her with a hint of the old smile, and she nodded. "I know you have good reason to be upset, and I wouldn't be surprised if you didn't want to have anything to do with me. But I was still wondering if we could have a cast party for the kids after tonight's show."

She hesitated, not sure what to say.

"I've already asked the brothers," he added, "and they're okay with our having it in their living room, lounge, whatever they call it. As long as the kids don't get too wild and crazy."

"I'm sure that wouldn't be a problem, but…"

"Great. So could you make sure everybody comes? Tell 'em I'm buying pizza."

"That should do it."

"And I'll see you at the auditorium an hour before show time."

Which meant she wouldn't have to find a stand-in accompanist after all. At the moment, that seemed like a mixed blessing to Anne.

38

You'd better beat it. You can leave in a taxi. If you
can't get a taxi, you can leave in a huff. If that's too
soon, you can leave in a minute and a huff.

—GROUCHO MARX

Jamie peeked out his window once more as the afternoon darkened. A quick bite to eat, and he'd try to make his way back over to the middle-school auditorium. This time he counted just three vans parked down the road a bit, past the spot where Tom Christy had killed Barkley. Jamie still wondered how the reporter had the nerve to come back to the abbey after stealing Father Greg's journal, and then never say a word about it. Amazing how he could claim it wasn't his fault he had bowled over Barkley in the dark. The dog just jumped in front of the moving wheels, was that it? Jamie was even more amazed the abbot had insisted they "let the Lord deal with him." That would have been fine with Jamie, as long as that meant God would strike the reporter with leprosy, or worse, and the sooner the better. He shook his head, trying his best to avoid the memory, trying to pretend that maybe the perky little mutt would be waiting for him next time he returned to the abbey.

Jamie knew he wouldn't. The good news was that Father Greg had chased the reporters off the hill the other night, and then arranged a long clothesline across the field where the road came up the hill, sort of like crime-scene tape. Several new signs warned news media to keep a distance.

The bad news was that with their long-lens cameras, they could probably take a closeup of his latest pimple. He resisted glaring in the direction of the vans and opened up the door for Brother Aaron.

"I brought you something before you leave." Brother Aaron set a small mug down on Jamie's bed. "Split pea soup. It's not mealtime, but I thought you might be hungry."

Jamie nodded. "Good man. Now you're sure you don't mind doing this other favor for me?"

"Ten large take-and-bake—four with pepperoni, four with sausage, and two veggie supreme."

"The veggie's for the grownups." Jamie winked as he handed Aaron his debit card. "Maybe we can have 'em warmed up by the time the show's over. You're sure you know how to work one of these things?"

"Not a problem." Brother Aaron slipped the card into the folds of his robe. "The PIN is S-I-N-G, just the way you told me. But…" He paused at the door, as if trying to remember his instructions.

In less than an hour he returned—without the pizza.

"What happened?" asked Jamie.

Brother Aaron handed the card back to Jamie and turned aside, lowering his voice. "I tried, but your card didn't work."

"What are you talking about?"

"Well, when I tried to pay for the pizzas, I just gave Pete Juno the card, right? Just the way you told me to. He knew who it belonged to, and he had no problem with that, just the way we thought. But after I ordered the pizzas, he put the card through his little scanner thing there on the counter, and it wouldn't work."

"Oh, come on. The card works, Aaron. I've been using it for months. It works fine."

But Brother Aaron could only shrug his shoulders. "I'm sure you're right, and it's just one of those glitches. That's why we always use cash. But

Juno tried it three times. And each time he said it told him there were insufficient funds."

"Maybe his reader machine wasn't working."

"That's what we thought at first. But another customer came up with a debit card, and it worked just fine. Actually, Jamie, it was a good thing you didn't go there. The place was packed with reporters and all those people. They were cleaning Juno out. But he said nobody else had a problem with their cards."

Jamie scratched his head.

"This is crazy, but maybe it's a computer thing and they have the problem worked out by now. Too bad you don't have an ATM here at Our Lady of the Hills."

For a moment brother Aaron looked at him as if he was serious, then forced a relieved smile.

"You're probably right."

"There's a cash machine down at Halcombe's Market. If you drive me down there right now, we can make it back in plenty of time. Hopefully we won't run into any media types on the way."

The overcast sky helped, and so did the off-and-on drizzle. All the TV reporters seemed to have taken a break.

"Any colder, and it's snow," observed Aaron, peering past the squeaks of the windshield wipers of the little pickup. Actually, a little snow would have been fine unless it kept all the reporters in town. Jamie slouched down low as they passed a van with a public-radio logo on the side. He thought he got a few stares from a FOX News rig. But the good news was that Halcombe's was still open, and no one noticed as Jamie hurried up to the cash machine.

"Do your thing," he whispered as he punched in the amount and the personal ID number. The machine rumbled and thought about his request for a long minute before spitting his card back out and displaying an apologetic message on its little green screen: "We're sorry, but we are unable to process your request due to insufficient funds. Please contact your Klickitat Valley Bank representative during regular banking hours if you need further assistance."

"There's gotta be some mistake," he mumbled, but not loud enough for a woman passing by to hear. *I've got at least a hundred thousand in this account.*

Or he had the other day. Just to be sure, he asked the machine for a quick account balance. Thirty-one cents.

Hadn't Nick said something once about Jamie draining his account down to where he wouldn't even be able to afford a stamp? Weird. Thirty-one cents. Obviously, he could pull funds from any one of a dozen other accounts—assuming they weren't cleaned out as well—but that wasn't the point. No one was supposed to know about this one. No one else was supposed to have access, not even Nick. He punched the ATM's buttons so hard it set up a beeping that wouldn't stop.

"Mommy," said a little girl in her mother's shopping cart. She couldn't have been more than five or six. "That man is trying to break the piggy-bank machine."

Jamie glared at them, snatched the receipt as it spit it out, and turned to leave. The beeping would stop eventually. But he still had no idea what had happened to his money, and the party was off. After all that had happened, maybe it was time to finally call Nick again.

"The number you have dialed has been disconnected or is no longer in service. Please check the number and try again."

And again and again. Jamie punched the number from the grocery store pay phone, but the result was no better than with the cash machine.

Nick's home number had been disconnected, and his cell number sounded just as useless.

"This is Nick." His voice sounded far away and underground. "Page me or leave a message, and I'll get back to you."

Which is what everyone and their dog said on answering machines. Nick, however, didn't call back, not even when Jamie paged him three times. Maybe he wasn't wearing his pager. And maybe it was time to call his office. Of course, this being Saturday, all he could probably do was leave a message. But when he dialed Nick's Nashville office, a real voice actually picked up.

"Patterson Agency."

Jamie cleared his throat in surprise. "Alice, what are you doing in the office on a Saturday afternoon? Or actually, what time is it there, three hours later?"

He heard a gasp, then a thinly muffled cry, as if she held her hand over the phone.

"Mr. Patterson! Line one! It's Jamie!"

"Uh, actually, Alice, I was just hoping to talk to Nick, but his home number has been disconnected and—"

"Jamie!" C. J. Patterson broke into the conversation the way he always did. As founder and owner of one of Nashville's leading talent agencies, he could afford to. "We've been reading the papers, Jamie, worried sick about you. Trying to get ahold of you all day. Are you all right?"

"Nothing to worry about, C. J. I was just on a little bit of a retreat here, and I wanted to ask Nick a couple of things before I headed back."

"Nick! You know where he is?"

"Not exactly. I haven't talked with him in weeks."

"Then you haven't heard."

"Heard what? What's to hear? What's going on?"

"All right, son. I know you've been under a lot of stress, and I don't want you to do anything else right now. We're going to make it right. Just stay where you are. Soon as I can break away here, I'll be flying out to…Alice?" He raised his voice to yell across his office. "Alice, are you going to get me those directions to that hole in the wall where Jamie—"

"You still haven't told me what's going on with Nick."

"I'll fill you in. You just have to promise me you won't talk to anybody, especially not the press. Just stay low, and stay where you are, hear?"

Jamie tried to ask another question, but C. J. had already hung up, leaving Alice to fill in the details.

"She says he came by her house last Tuesday night," said Alice.

"Who says?" Jamie didn't follow. "Whose house?"

"Oh, sorry. Tammi's." That would be Tammi, Nick's ex-wife. She had custody of the couple's young daughter.

Alice went on, "He told her he had a conference in Philadelphia to go to and couldn't take Emily this weekend. But C. J. doesn't know anything about a conference. In fact, they had a meeting Thursday morning that Nick missed. No explanations, no notes, no nothing. He's *gone*, Jamie."

"What about that girl in L.A. he always tried to hook me up with? Erin something? He always seemed more interested in her than I ever was. Maybe she knows where he is."

"Should I look in the Los Angeles phone book under 'S' for 'Something'?"

She waited for him to remember, but…

"I didn't keep her number, sorry. But did anybody think to go check out his apartment? Maybe he's…"

Jamie shivered at the thought.

"We did that, Jamie. When his landlord let us in Thursday night, Nick's apartment looked totally cleaned out. Clothes, papers, his laptop, all gone."

Not a good sign.

"Speaking of cleaned out, that's what I needed to talk to him about. One of my checking accounts has been emptied, and I needed to find out if he knew anything about it."

The silence at the other end of the line told all.

"We've called the police, Jamie," she finally told him, her voice low. Anyone could tell it looked bad, very bad. "And we're having our accountants look into everything. Whatever's happened, we're going to take care of it, just the way C. J. said. I'm sure there's some good explanation."

"Yeah, and maybe he'll send me a postcard from Acapulco."

39

You may waste your whole life claiming you are
seeking truth, and never come to the knowledge of
the One who is Truth.

—ATHENAGORAS

About halfway through his walk, Jamie decided hiking from the grocery store to the middle school had been a stupid idea. *Yeah, I'll handle it, Brother Aaron.* Right. The umbrella kept his head dry, but his pants were quickly soaked below the knee from the driving rain mixed with snow. His running shoes felt as if they had turned into a couple of cold, wet sponges, and he made squeaky squishy noises with each step. Was it supposed to get this cold in November?

It gave him a chance to think. And the reporters probably didn't expect to see him hoofing it around town. It gave him a chance to be alone for a few minutes, at least until he made his entrance again at the auditorium. He wondered how crowded it would be tonight, now that the news had been out for more than a day.

But yes, he'd taken the long way around. As the rain pelted down, he started to jog down the gentle slope toward the small town of Riverdale, population 2,138, according to an old sign that looked like target-practice Swiss cheese. He suspected the city limits had been moved outward long ago.

He couldn't see much in the distance with the rain and the mist, but he could make out some of the rain-slicked roofs of the city, the grain elevators, and four church steeples. The tower by city hall where the volunteer fire siren wailed every Tuesday and Thursday at noon, fire or no fire, just to be sure the old thing still worked. And as he neared an old one-lane bridge over the Little Klickitat River, he stepped carefully before grabbing the bridge railing for balance. Gravel and sleet made it plenty slippery here.

A light flickered on in the distance, probably in a home on the outskirts of town, and he could imagine Andy setting up in the bakery just about now. Or Father Greg and the brothers finishing up their day of work in the hills above him. Both would look at their clocks and hang up their aprons, secure in their faith and in the rhythm of work. Four thirty. The brothers would head for their evening prayers and their simple dinner. Andy would head on home for an early Saturday supper with his wife, waving at the people who knew him on the street, people he had grown up with, wheat farmers and small-town bankers, the optometrist and the mayor.

And Jamie envied them both, more than he ever thought it possible to envy someone. He envied Anne, too, for having a place to come home to. He stood quietly in the gathering dusk, lost halfway between two worlds, with a foot in both but unsteady on his feet, unable to know either. And he wondered if it was wrong to envy so much.

"Funny," he told God as the river gurgled and stewed beneath his feet. "I thought I was pretending to be someone else here in Riverdale. Turns out I *used* to be pretend. And I wasn't ever really me until I came back to this little nothing town."

Now, of course, it was too late to do anything about it, and he knew that as well as anyone. Still, he didn't mind mentioning it to God for once.

"And there you have it, God. Is that a prayer?"

It didn't even seem like a prayer—mainly since he hadn't really asked God for anything, just told him something honest. And if it took another thirty-five years for God to answer something honest in return, well, that would have to be okay. He would wait. So he stood there in the gathering dusk, soaking up the still beauty of the little river valley. He could have stood there for hours if not for the cold that crept into his damp shoes and up his legs. As he stood there, watching the lights of the town come on, a car rumbled up behind him and slowed to a stop on the bridge, its headlights stabbing the dusk with two feeble beams. He could recognize the rumble-buzz of Anne's Volkswagen convertible anywhere. He wasn't exactly sure what she was doing on this road, the one that led up into the hills, but he was afraid to ask.

She didn't ask what he was doing out here in the drizzle either, just rolled down the passenger-side window.

"I can think of better times to be out on a walk," she told him.

"To be honest, I am getting a little wet." He looked at his feet. "Okay, I'm soaked."

She reached over and pushed open the door for him to climb in. "We still have plenty of time before the show. I was going to get there a little early. Thought I'd run up to the monastery to see if you needed a ride."

Oh.

He collapsed his soggy umbrella and climbed inside the little car, grateful for the lift but unsure what he would say to the person he had lied to for so long. He didn't have to worry about it right away, though, since neither of them seemed overly talkative. In fact, neither said another word for the half-mile drive to town. But when Anne pulled into the empty middle-school parking lot and turned off the engine, his stomach growled loud enough to be heard even over the sound of the rain.

They both had to laugh.

"Was that you," she giggled, "or were we followed by a bear?"

"Sorry. Cup of soup doesn't go a long way." He didn't mention the canceled pizza party. "I kind of forgot to eat much lunch."

"Forgot? I thought I was the only one who did that kind of thing."

"You think you're forgetful, girl, but you don't have nothin' on me."

"You're just saying that."

"I don't think so. You ever see that TV commercial where the singer is up in front of an audience, and he says, 'Hello, Detroit!!' and the whole audience goes 'huh?' and somebody whispers to him, 'Uh, this is Pittsburgh'?"

"I think it might have been an ad for getting more sleep. Mattresses or sleeping pills."

"Right. Well, that was me. I really did that, only we were in Madison, and I thought we were still in Minneapolis."

It felt good to laugh. A little strange, but very good, as if a crack in the logjam had opened once more.

Anne looked at her watch. "Well, I do remember we still have more than three hours until the show, here in…*Riverdale,* and I think if we don't find something quick to eat, you're either going to collapse or your stomach is going to be rumbling during the performance. Either way…"

"So we should get something to eat."

"And I know just the place."

Just the place turned out to be the back room of the Do-Nut Barn, where they balanced on stools and ate cream-cheese bagels and drank steaming mugs of coffee.

"Can't stay away from the place, huh?" Andy stuck his head in to check on them. Anne held a finger to her lips and pointed at Jamie.

"Oh, right." He looked over his shoulder and must have understood; he backed out without another word and let the swinging door hide them from anybody out front.

"See?" Jamie nodded at the door and took another bite. "This was my life before I came here. Always hiding, always worried about people chasing me. And if I wasn't, I'd get tackled by people asking me to autograph their bellies with a Sharpie or hitting me up for all kinds of weird stuff."

"And you thought it would be different here."

"It was, wasn't it?"

"Maybe until the Riverdale Angel arrived."

He groaned. "I'm thinking that was my big mistake."

"Maybe so. But people sure had fun trying to guess who it was."

"Thank you." Jamie did his best Elvis impersonation. "Thank you very much."

Again, Anne laughed, the nicest sound Jamie knew. If he had come here just for that, the time might have been worth it. But obviously he couldn't hide here in the back room of the Do-Nut Barn forever.

"They had fun until they found out," he went on, "and then it was kind of like, 'Whoopsie, we didn't really want to know.'"

"You almost pulled it off, didn't you?"

"Except Father Greg knew right from the start. I didn't count on that. You knew too, right?"

"I thought I did. But…I'm just curious. What were you *thinking* when you came here?"

He shrugged. "At first I thought it was all about me. You know, bringing my mom home the way I promised, searching for my roots, that sort of thing."

"Nothing wrong with that."

"Yeah, but the longer I stayed, the more it turned into sort of an experiment to see if people would like me without all the…money and the spotlight and stuff."

"You mean, if you were just the average Joe? Are you sure that's all it was?"

"Of course I'm sure. I mean…" He sighed. "No. I don't know what I mean. Maybe I just liked the feeling of making people happy but not having them turn around and shake me down for more. It just didn't end up quite the way I wanted."

"I'm sorry." She took his empty mug and placed it with hers in the dishwasher. "But there's one thing I need to thank you for."

"No, you're confused. I'm the con artist, remember? You're supposed to be angry with me and throw me out of town."

"I already was, and I almost did. But you're also the only person I know who doesn't compare me to who I used to be."

"Who *were* you?"

"That's what I mean. You don't seem to care that I forget things and stutter."

"Having a good memory is overrated."

"That I get all emotional and angry at things that don't matter so much."

"They matter to you."

"That I still have trouble walking and chewing gum at the same time. Literally."

"So we all have issues."

"That I still see red every time I think of the guy who almost ended my life."

"I would, too. But God's working on you, right?"

"God?" She looked at him sideways. "That doesn't sound like you."

"Well." He smiled. "At least that's what Father Greg would say. Me, I'm still figuring it out."

"So am I." She laughed again, then turned serious. "But you have no idea what it means to me, that you don't care what I was like before."

He closed his eyes and silently repeated her words: *...that you don't care what I was like before.*

"I should be telling you the exact same thing, Anne."

When his hand rested on hers, she didn't move, just thought about it for a few moments.

"Maybe we do have something in common after all," she finally told him.

"Maybe. Does it matter now? I guess my experiment didn't work."

"No, I think it did. You proved to yourself that you didn't need to be rich and famous for people to like you. My dad liked you. The kids liked you, even before they knew who you really were. And I—"

He caught his breath to listen as she went on.

"And you proved that you don't have to buy an entire town for God to love you. I'd say that's a pretty good thing to find out. A pretty good start."

"Wait a minute. You slipped in that last part. How do you know I proved that...about God?"

She shrugged as she took her hand back and finished the last of her bagel. "Sometimes things work out in ways you don't expect, don't they, Mr. Lane? Now—do you leave after tonight, or are you going to come back for the last performance?"

He didn't even think about it this time. "I told the kids I would help, right? And the cast pizza party is still on—just postponed until next week."

"I'll take that as a yes. Oh, and Joe—I mean Jamie—"

He raised his eyebrows at her.

"When I drove up to see if you needed a ride, the brothers told me what happened last night. I'm so sorry to hear about Barkley."

For a few hours he had almost convinced himself it hadn't happened, almost forgotten about wanting to strangle Tom Christy. And now he wished she hadn't heard, especially not right before the second performance.

"Thanks," he mumbled. "So am I."

40

Your statues are dead.

—JUSTIN MARTYR

"M iss Stewart!" He caught her off guard in the school hallway between the auditorium and the warmup room, and her first reaction was to brush off another reporter. She'd learned to cope during the past week's media feeding frenzy, leading up to their finale performance of *Bye Bye Birdie*. But this fellow would not be brushed off.

"Remember me? Tom Christy with the *Oregonian*. We spoke in your bakery. You used to be Jamie Lane's friend here in Riverdale, is that right?"

Used to be? This reporter couldn't know how much time they'd spent together the past week, sipping coffee in her caboose, talking. But she had to give him credit. Anne couldn't walk away from *that* question. And at least he only had a notebook, which was slightly better than answering questions in front of an obnoxious camera.

So, all right, a couple of questions only. She paused to face him.

"He had a lot of friends here," Anne finally answered.

"Had?"

"Has. I meant *has*."

"Sure." He scribbled in his reporter's notebook as if she had just told him something highly articulate. "But can you tell me how people feel about being deceived all this time? You never really knew who he was, right?"

She had to think about that one to make sure the words came out the way she wanted them to.

"I can't speak for everyone else in town. But from what I can tell, most people understand why he did what he did, and they're excited about having him here for the last show."

"So why *did* he do what he did?"

"You would have to ask him that yourself."

"You sound angry."

If she wasn't before, these questions might do it. She bit her tongue to keep from saying what she really wanted to say.

"I used to be angry."

She winced at the confession, which she should have kept to herself—but he was quick enough to grab it.

"So you used to be angry, which we can all understand. What changed?"

Which was actually a good question. What *had* changed? She closed her eyes and crossed her arms, looking for the answer, wondering now how much to tell Tom Christy. Because anything she said—and probably a lot she didn't say—would be sure to find its way into print.

"Now I know how he feels," she mumbled, mostly to herself.

"Excuse me?" Tom Christy looked up from his notebook. That obviously didn't sound like the answer to his question.

"I'm sorry, Mr. Christy. You asked what changed. I guess I just got tired of being an angry person all the time. And take my word for it: I still have a lot I could be angry about. God's still working on me."

He looked up as he wrote, and the pen kept moving as she dabbed at the corner of her eye.

Don't get emotional! she ordered herself, as if her emotions followed orders anymore. Maybe they did once, but *not now!*

"I appreciate your honesty, Miss Stewart." He swallowed and rested his pen. "What about tonight's performance? Anything different about tonight?"

"Not really." She shook her head no, and it gave her a chance to recover. "The kids are just thrilled so many people have shown up for the show. As a result, they're going to be able to do a whole lot more ministry when they get down to Mexico, and—"

"Oh, speaking of Mexico." He speared the air with his pen to make a point. "Has Jamie told you anything about Nick Anderson?"

She looked at him; no bells rang.

"Nick Anderson, his manager?" Tom Christy explained. "I hear he got into a couple of Jamie's bank accounts. He's under investigation for felony embezzlement. Reports just came through this afternoon, thought you might know."

"I don't. I don't know anything about that."

"Word is the guy siphoned three million and hightailed it to Mexico with a girl."

"Joe—I mean Jamie—didn't say anything about that to me."

"No, I guess he wouldn't. So I take it he usually didn't discuss his finances with you."

"Not at all."

"How about religion?"

"Excuse me?"

Another jab out of nowhere. This reporter seemed to specialize in those kinds of questions. Three or four easy setups, relax a little bit, and *bam!*

"I hear he's found some kind of religion here. Are you the one who's talked to him about that?"

Anne wondered where he'd heard such a thing. "That's another one you'll have to ask Jamie about."

"Just thought I'd try." Tom Christy shrugged. "So are you going to miss Jamie Lane?"

Would she miss Jamie Lane? Anne still had to translate the name from Jamie to Joe before she could see his face in her head, almost like translating Spanish to English when she heard it spoken. And somehow the thought of his face woke up a memory, a vivid memory of a dream she'd had last night: flying with outstretched arms over the hills surrounding Riverdale, she and Jamie, with news reporters chasing them on the ground. Barkley flew along with them, and the view from the air was beautiful, so beautiful.

"Miss Stewart?"

"Oh, sorry." She couldn't help smiling at the memory, as if she had recovered something lost. And she had! "I was just remembering a dream."

He looked at her blankly.

"No, no," she told him. "You don't understand. I haven't been able to dream for more than two years, ever since I was in an automobile crash. I think this is the first time I've dreamed since then!"

Obviously, this was cause for celebration, though Tom Christy probably didn't see it that way. And she wasn't going to describe it to him either. But thankfully one of her kids rescued her just then with a shout from the far end of the hall.

"Miss Stewart!" a girl hollered. "Molly's sick and throwing up in the restroom!" Anne smiled at the reporter. The joys of a schoolteacher were never ending.

"Excuse me, Mr. Christy. Another actress with butterflies in her stomach. I need to run."

What could he say? She skipped down the hall, wondering about what Tom Christy had told her, about the stolen three million dollars and the rumor that Jamie had "found religion," but still clinging to the memory of her very Peter-Pannish dream. And when she turned the corner, where no one could see her...

She held out her arms and ran.

Andy Stewart held up his hands to get the small crowd's attention, while Anne made a quick count. Twenty-two in the cast, along with their parents, grandparents, and friends. They had probably crowded sixty or seventy people into the living room of the main lodge at Our Lady of the Hills monastery. Not to mention Joe...er...Jamie Lane and his monk friends, who had volunteered to serve the refreshments. And though Jamie had at first suggested a cast party last week, after the second showing, this had actually worked out better. Now they were done, all done, hallelujah, and the relief showed through on all their faces and in their excited chatter.

"If no one minds," her father's voice boomed out over the crowd as he stood on a chair to be seen, "I'd just like to offer a word of thanks for this food, and then we can dig in."

Everyone could smell the take-and-bake pizza Father Greg and his crew had warmed up just in time for their arrival after the musical.

"A little late for you guys, isn't it, Brother Aaron?" Jamie said it low enough so only one of the monks (and Anne) could hear him. The monk smiled as he brought in another steaming pizza on his shoulder. And everyone bowed their heads where they stood as Anne's father started into his prayer.

"Thank you so much, Lord, for bringing us together, for bringing so many people to this play, for answering prayer. We thank you for this food and for the brothers who have helped prepare it. And most of all, we thank you that we don't have to be stuck in the past, but that you give us a future and a hope. In the name of Jesus, amen."

No one else seemed to notice, but Anne was sure Jamie nodded his head. And as she looked up, she noticed Brother Aaron make the sign of the cross, then set the pizza down on a folding table with the rest of the food. It was odd, she knew, for all these different people to be meeting here. A couple of the kids came from unchurched homes, but by now she knew the others. Several were from Community Baptist and the rest divided between the Riverdale UMC, Shepherd of the Hills, and Immaculate Heart.

"I've always seen the monks around town," Amy's mom whispered as she took a plate of pizza. "But this is the first time I've ever been up here."

"A-*hem!*" Father Greg took his turn to speak, and they all paused from their pizza when he pinged a glass with his knife. "It's time to make a few presentations to our guest of honor."

That would be Jamie, obviously, and a couple of the kids pulled him to the front. Strange time to turn shy.

"We wanted to make sure Joe remembered his friends here at the monastery, so Brother Aaron and his crew prepared a special treat for you."

He extended a wrapped package about the size of a large brick, and Jamie quickly tore off the string and the aluminum foil wrapping paper before holding it up with a smile for all to see.

"Fruitcake!" He grinned as everyone clapped. "I would never have guessed."

But they had yet another package, which Sean Merchant presented with a flourish.

"You guys didn't need to do this." Jamie hesitated. "I really don't deserve…"

But Sean didn't give him a chance to finish, just pointed at the book-size package once more, telling him to open it.

"A Bible." Jamie held the leather-covered volume the way a new father would hold his newborn, looking uncertain whether it would break in his grip.

"You don't have one," Father Greg asked quietly. "Am I right?"

"Now I do."

Anne could see the tears, though at first he hid them pretty well with his hand.

"Read the inscription," insisted Amy, pointing to the inside front page. By that time Jamie could no longer shield the tears, and he passed the Bible to her to read.

"To Joe: 'He who finds his life will lose it, and he who loses his life for my sake will find it.' Matthew 10:39. And it's signed from Anne and the *Bye Bye Birdie* kids."

Everyone clapped all over again while Jamie cleared his throat and thanked them all in a husky voice, well-marinated in emotion. No one said anything about how they'd written "To Joe" instead of "To Jamie," but he didn't seem to notice as he sliced his fruitcake and passed it around to everyone in the room. He was the last to notice the camera crew that had quietly slipped in the side door.

"I'm sorry, this is a private gathering." Anne wasted no time striding over to the cameraman and holding her hand in front of the lens. No way would she let one of those media types crash this party, not if she could help it.

"Don't mind us." The reporter sidestepped in front of his camera crew while they continued filming. "Nobody will know we're even here."

"That's not the point." Anne could feel her cheeks heating up; pretty soon she would be stumbling over her words without even trying. "You weren't invited, and you have a lot of nerve just pushing in here."

The reporter ignored her when he noticed Jamie approaching. All he wanted was a good clip for the evening news. That's all, and he'd be out of their hair. That wasn't too much to ask, was it?

"Jamie!" He pointed his microphone, and the portable camera lights came to life. "Can you tell us when you're returning to L.A.?"

Anne would have grabbed the camera if the reporter hadn't stepped up just then. But Jamie stood staring at the lights as if he had just turned into a moth.

For a moment Jamie's camera instinct kicked in, just when he didn't want it to. See that little red light? That's where you look. That's the direction you give your best smile.

The rest of the party went quiet at the reporter's question, and the camera rolled on before Jamie quite recovered his senses. By that time the reporter had repeated himself.

What about the new tour, and how soon was he returning to L.A.? When would he be leaving this dead-end little town? (Not the exact words used, but the clear intent everyone understood.) The reporter could not know the same question had dogged Jamie for weeks, the question he had run from until he could run no more. And by this time he felt like that marathon runner at the Olympics several years back—the guy who came dragging into the stadium hours after everyone else had finished, barely moving his legs, surely ready to collapse. Old footage of the poor guy made the sports highlight tapes every once in a while.

Don't stop now. Jamie looked around the room at the *Bye Bye Birdie* kids. Weeks of extra effort and practice showed up as dark lines under their eyes. Their parents had put up with plenty as well. And no one had volunteered more hours than Anne, who deserved every bouquet of flowers she had received at the last curtain call—and more.

So…how soon was he returning to L.A.? They all stared at him, waiting for the answer he knew he had to give.

41

Faith is taking the first step even when you don't
see the whole staircase.

—MARTIN LUTHER KING JR.

Anne slowed but did not stop, and her breath came out in foggy puffs
as she made her way across Haynie Ridge Road, past a couple of the
horse ranches that flanked Riverdale's heights, and looked across the
plateau. She knew why people paid to live up here—halfway up Observatory Hill, high enough for a commanding view over Riverdale's rooftops.
But she ran on, not stopping to admire the morning sun glimmering on
late November frost, the kind that never quite melted before the shortening day slipped back to shadows. She ran on, never mind the gathering
cold that numbed her face and turned her hands red.

And no matter hard she tried to forget, the words she'd written in the
front of Jamie's Bible danced in her memory.

He who finds his life will lose it…

So did you find your life here, Jamie D. Lane? Or did you lose it?

She would have asked him out loud if she'd thought it would do any
good. As it was, a little righteous indignation might have come in handy
with that question too. But no matter how hard she tried, she couldn't
locate the outrage that had stained her life since the crash. Oh, but she
should have resented that man for what he'd done! Slipping into town like
a traveling salesman, lying about his identity, and stealing her heart—a

heart he had no right to take and she had no right to offer. Yes, she had every right to some good old-fashioned fury.

Except he'd had the nerve to apologize once again.

"I know I've said it before, Anne." He'd looked straight into her eyes before leaving this morning with his record-agent executive whatever, the boss of the fellow who had embezzled so much money. "But I didn't mean for it to turn out this way."

Maybe not, but this is how it turned out. With all the excitement, they'd hardly had a moment to talk again. And she could hardly choke out a good-bye as she gave him a bag of doughnuts for the trip. She positively detested good-byes—and none more than this one—but the C. J. fellow seemed in a great hurry this morning, and they were gone. They had to catch a plane in Portland.

And that was it.

"...and he who loses his life for my sake will find it."

Well, she had certainly lost hers, all over again—though for whose sake, she could not be sure. She could only tell herself it had been for the best. Hadn't it? He'd been searching, she now knew, but she had not been the one to lead him to the Cross. Or she would not be. She left that up to God; her heart always got in the way.

And so she kept running, faster and faster, trying to outpace the tears. She'd be late for class again if she didn't.

"We'll get you back to L.A., boy," C. J. Anderson steered his Lincoln rental car south out of town on their way back to the airport. Two or three hours down the Columbia Gorge Highway to Portland, depending on whether the ice got slick along the way. "And we'll get all this mess straightened out. Your concert schedule, your financials, everything. And then when you come back, you're gonna be bigger than ever. Believe me: You don't need Nick."

Right. Jamie couldn't help glancing back over his shoulder.

"You forget something, kid?"

Never mind how Andy Stewart had once warned him against looking at life in the rearview mirror. He swallowed hard and turned back in his seat.

"I don't know."

C. J. might not have heard; he went on about how shocked and hurt he was to hear about Nick's disappearance, how Nick had worked for him all these years, how Nick had been like a son to him and all that. All the papers had said Mexican authorities were looking for the fugitive, but so far they hadn't picked up much of a trail.

"And speaking of papers, they found a bunch of them in Nick's apartment." C. J. sounded as if he was explaining the plot of a crime-scene TV show. "Some of them had a guy's name on them, scribbled out. Not much to go on though."

"A guy's name?"

"'Spencer.' Nobody has any idea what it means."

Uh-oh. As C. J. went on, Jamie wondered what good it would do to explain about Spencer the ID man, who would be as long gone as Nick and the girlfriend. And now did it matter? As far as he was concerned, well, maybe it was better this way.

"We're going to catch him, Jamie. That much I can tell you. In fact…"

But Jamie didn't hear the rest, only stared out the front window at a grain barge headed downriver, the same way he was headed, and it was wrong, all wrong. Up ahead and just across the bridge, Biggs Junction looked busy, full of truckers stopping for a late breakfast.

"You don't worry about a thing from now on," C. J. assured him as he lit a cigarette, "and we'll put this weird little vacation behind you, right?"

C. J.'s cigarette smoke had never bothered Jamie all that much; this time he rolled down his window and gasped for air.

"Is that what you think it was?" Jamie asked between deep breaths. The chilled air blew his hair back and made his eyes water. "A weird little vacation?"

"Hey, no offense." C. J. held up his cigarette with a "who, me?" expression on his face.

"Can you stop here, please?" Jamie pointed at the truck stop parking lot, and C. J. raised his eyebrows.

"Already? We've only been on the road twenty minutes."

But they stopped anyway, just in front of the Junction Diner, the bus stop where Jamie had once found a skinny little dog begging for a handout. Jamie sat chewing his lip, drumming his fingers on the armrest, before he punched open the door with his elbow and hopped out.

"I'll wait right here." C. J. slipped the car into park and doused his smoke in the ashtray. "We can get something to eat if you want. But I thought you already had enough breakfast."

For a moment Jamie didn't answer, just paced next to the car, his hands on his hips.

"Are you okay?" C. J. wanted to know.

No, not exactly. And yeah, this was more than just an early potty stop. But now he knew what he had to do. Finally Jamie slipped back into the car and slammed the door.

"We have to go back, C. J."

"What?" C. J. looked at him as if he'd just brought in a deadly virus.

"We just do. Please."

"Did you forget we have to catch a plane back to L.A. in"—he checked his watch—"four hours?"

"We'll catch your plane. But I'm sorry; this is important. I have to do this."

"Do what, exactly? If you forgot something, we can have it shipped."

"This isn't something we can ship."

And that was all he said. C. J. sighed and seemed to give up.

"Okay, then look, kid. I know this whole deal with Nick would be enough to spook anybody. I don't blame you for a minute. But you've just gotta work with me, okay? Let's not do anything stupid."

"Stupid?" Jamie had to chuckle as he buckled his seat belt. He pointed north at the hills rising from the river. "This is the first smart thing I've done in a long time."

C. J. groaned and shook his head. But he put the car in gear and followed the signs back over the bridge toward Riverdale.

"This job would be great," he mumbled, "if it weren't for the clients."

"I'm really sorry, C. J." Jamie reached out and snapped on the radio, tuning it to a country station before C. J. could object.

"Didn't know the girl got to you that bad." C. J. popped a stick of gum into his mouth and glanced at his client out of the corner of his eye. The man wasn't as oblivious as Jamie thought.

But Jamie didn't answer as they headed back up Highway 97 the way they'd just come, the same route he and Barkley had traveled nearly three months before. Only three months? Only this time his duffel bag in the backseat looked a bit heavier, maybe on account of the Bible from Anne and the kids. The Bible he'd already started reading.

Oh, and the doughnuts. The half-dozen glazed were slightly squished but tasted no worse for the wear, and when he had opened the white paper sack, it filled the car with a powerful aroma of bakery.

"Not bad." C. J. inhaled his first one, and that had to be better than nicotine. "You make these yourself?"

"Matter of fact." Jamie offered him another, taking in the view of the

Simcoes as their snow-dusted peaks began to peek over the horizon and the men swept north on Highway 97. Just like glaze on the doughnuts, the plateau had taken on a cold cloak of patchy snow, and the glazed fields lay quiet and fallow, waiting patiently for a distant spring. Riverdale, on the other hand, lay warm and secure as it always had, nestled against the foot-hills, tucked in against the chill, steaming here and there from roof vents and smokestacks. Pretty soon he'd be able to make out the steeples and grain elevators, just to the west of the highway. And if he knew where to look…

"There, see?" Five minutes later he pointed at the tiny hillside clear-ing in the distance, off to the left of the highway, just above town. C. J. might not be able to make out the cross set up behind Our Lady of the Hills monastery, but that was okay.

This time he could.

"Take the next left," he told C. J.

Anne checked her lesson planner on the desk to make sure she remem-bered. Okay. She closed her eyes and prayed as the morning buzzer ush-ered in her second-period class.

Lord, help me get through this day. Or maybe just this next class.

She could feel the tears, ready to bubble up for the slightest reason. And after the past couple of days, Anne had plenty of reasons. But instead of the usual elephant herd of seventh and eighth graders, she opened her eyes to an empty classroom.

What?

Maybe their first period went long, but that hadn't happened before, that she recalled. She squinted at the clock again, just to be sure. Nine thirty. Then down at her day planner. English Comp started at nine thirty. They should have been here by now. They couldn't all be tardy, could they?

She picked up the phone on the wall next to her desk and quickly dialed the front office, trying to keep the edge of panic from her voice. But where was everybody?

"I have no idea, Anne." But the secretary started coughing, almost giggling. Who said something funny? "I'll check with—cough—Mr. Howell."

Click. If this wasn't the oddest thing. She slowly hung up the receiver, looked around the classroom once more, and stepped over to the door to peek through the little eye-level window.

"Oh!" she shrieked to see him looking in, a shy grin on his face. A moment later Jamie pushed open the door and stepped inside.

"I'm sorry." He held his hands behind his back like a little boy who'd been caught with his hands in the cookie jar. "I didn't mean to scare you."

"Too late for that." She did her best to recover from the shock. "But I thought you had to catch a plane."

"I do." He nodded. "But I couldn't leave without, um…"

He fidgeted and looked at his shoes before holding out a delicate pearl ring in the palm of his hand. *Oh!* Anne caught her breath.

"This belonged to my mother," he whispered, then cleared his throat. "And to my great-grandmother. I want you to have it."

Anne felt her mouth go dry, and she narrowed her eyes at the gift as he held it out closer. So beautiful! But what did he mean by it, exactly?

"Don't worry." He smiled. "It's not a marriage proposal. Not yet. But see, here's the thing: I want you in my life, Anne. And I couldn't just drive away without telling you that. I had to make sure, one way or the other. Nothing else really matters. Not singing, and for sure not being famous."

She heard a giggle and looked at the crowd of kids peering in at them from the hallway. So *there* they were!

"He told us to wait in the hall, Miss Stewart." Amy Phillips grinned at her from the front of the crowd. "Said he had to talk to you alone and that he'd send us all backstage passes to his next show if we waited. But if you don't want the ring…"

"Don't you worry, Amy." Anne looked back at their celebrity, took the ring from his outstretched hand, and slipped it on the ring finger of her right hand before holding it up for everyone to see. "There, see? It fits me just fine."

She hadn't heard the kids cheer so loudly since the last performance of the show, but it didn't matter. Hadn't they ever seen a kiss before? At least they couldn't hear her as she whispered into his ear.

"You haven't seen the last of me, Jamie D. Lane."

Acknowledgments

Years ago my wife and I were greeted with open arms by the wonderful people of Goldendale, Washington—a small county seat in the wheat fields of south-central Washington State. It was an experience our family, including our young kids, would never forget. And as the rookie newspaper editor there, I had the opportunity to talk with many people in the community—farmers and sheriff's deputies, pastors and eye doctors—people who would leave a lifelong impression on me.

The work was both satisfying and demanding. And every week I would carefully set aside the newspaper my staff and I produced, complete with stories of record-breaking pumpkins, school board meetings, or the demo derby at the fair. I knew then that I would need the papers again someday, not just for old time's sake, but also for the book I would write about a special place like Goldendale.

The Celebrity is that book, though I can readily offer this disclaimer: Clearly it's not meant to represent actual people or events in any way. It does not hold strictly to the town's actual layout, though many will recognize the inspiration for the setting. It's simply a tribute to the kind of folks whose values and faith represent the strength of our country. The kind of people who live in Goldendale and in countless other small towns across North America.

Along the way I have been grateful for the help and support of many in this ministry of writing, especially to my wife, Ronda. Her insight and instincts helped me craft the story. Thanks, also, to Julie B. for helping me understand the challenges of drunk-driving crash victims. And, finally, I always appreciate the enthusiasm and dedication of everyone on the WaterBrook team, as well as sharp-eyed editors like Dudley Delffs, Jamie Cain, and Jennifer Lonas.